Emily,

I hope wherever you are, you find a copy of this book, and see this note. It is the only way I could think of to express my sincerest gratitude for allowing me the privilege of writing your story.

I just hope I have done it justice.

Warmest regards

James

THE
COLDEST GAME

JAMES THORNTON

DON'T POKE THE BEAR

June 2022, somewhere in the US.

E mily was knitting. Emily was always knitting or it certainly seemed that way to George. The strange thing was nothing ever got completed. Emily's interest was flaky at best. As soon as she was halfway through one thing another would take her fancy and she was off. There were never and had never been any Christmas presents of jumpers that itched like mad, gloves with a finger missing or scarves that could suffocate you. Just non-stop knitting. Emily did do other things than just knit but those things did not irritate George. It was the irritation that made it seem like the knitting was never-ending. Perhaps if anything ever came of it, perhaps if he ever got a nice winter jumper then he might feel differently, but instead, all he got was a constant, repetitive clacking sound poking him. Clack, clack, clack, clack, clack. From the corner of the room, clack, clack, clack, just out of his eye-line, clack, clack, clack. The moment's respite when Emily went to the bathroom or made some tea was George's greatest pleasure in life.

George sat slumped in his familiar armchair engrossed in the TV. Well not engrossed, more hypnotised. He was not watching something interesting, or enjoyable, or anything that offered escapism. In truth, he didn't really know what he was watching and that was the problem. He was not being offered anything to challenge him, surprise him or simply teach him. Just a bland soulless monotonous drone resonating around the room. It didn't matter what channel, it didn't matter what show, it was all just a drone to George. A drone from in front of him, incessant clacking from the other side of the room and George was stuck in the middle. Is this really all there is to life in your eighties? he thought. Are we in God's waiting room? That was the real source of George's frustration. He was bored.

George was drawn from his hypnotic state by something crossing his peripherals. Through the window, he witnessed a brown-red leaf float over the fence and land right in the middle of his perfectly manicured, perfectly emerald, perfectly edged lawn. A trespasser. An invader. A problem that needed to be fixed. Though George hated anything disrupting his perfectly maintained garden, it was also a blessing in disguise. Finally, he had a purpose. It was actually worth getting out of bed today.

George appeared at his front door like a cowboy entering a saloon. He was armed to the teeth with his secateurs, pruning shears, trash bag and grabber stick. He would deal with the intruder first and then remove any dead foliage with dignity. George looked down at the brown-red leaf bathing in the sun. He had nothing against the brown-red leaf so long as it would stay where it belonged. Not in the middle of his emerald lawn. George picked up the leaf with his grabber stick, gently so as not to break it. Though this leaf was dead, it did not give George any right to destroy it. Those were Mother Nature's decisions and not his. He raised the grabber slowly and placed the leaf elegantly in his bag. He then sat the bag down and delicately removed the late petals and stems from his plants, laying them to rest with the leaf. George ruled his domain with kindness.

George's newfound calm was short-lived as loud screeching stole it. A car recklessly cornered into the street. The engine rumbled as the car swerved from side to side. Inside the vehicle, a sweaty down-on-his-luck, architect hurriedly tried to prepare documents for a pitch he so desperately needed to succeed. For most of his journey the architect had kept one eye on the road and one on his documents as he frantically sifted through trying to compose order but, with little success from this method, he had resorted to periods of full focus on his documents and no eyes on the road. This was one of those moments. George could sense a danger manifesting. Scouring the street his gaze landed on a small boy on the opposite sidewalk. Headphones on and staring at his feet, he ambled along giving no due attention to his surroundings. This was quiet suburbia and he was used to its peaceful safety. He was not old enough to consider this could change as he had never experienced anything else.

"Boy, boy, watch the road," George called out with no response.

He moved to his gate and closer to the child.

"Boy, boy," he yelled out but still nothing.

George glanced down the street as the runaway car edged closer to the kerb and looked across at the boy, still in a world of his own. George started to move towards the boy. He could not amble, this was no time for ambling, George had to move. George had to move fast. Screaming to get the boy's attention as the engine got louder and closer. George picked up the pace. A man in his eighties was now sprinting like an athlete. It must have been at least fifty metres of top-speed sprinting before George reached the boy. The driver finally looked up and realised the perilous situation he had stupidly put them all in. He slammed his brake, desperate for an emergency stop. George flew across the last bit of road and shoved the child across the sidewalk towards the garden fences. The driver locked eyes with George and cried out as the tension took control of him. Almost in slow-motion, he was witnessing the consequence of his own disorganised and anxious nature. The octogenarian, who had come from nowhere, was rapidly getting closer to the bumper and the car was still moving. Nearly ripping off the steering wheel, nearly pushing his feet through the footwell, nearly wetting himself, the car skidded and jolted to a halt mere inches away from George. The sweat-drenched face of the shameful driver looked up apologetically at the old man. His hands gripped the wheel so tight it had drawn blood, and the rest of his body shook. George was calm. An outstretched finger would have been able to touch the metal of the car but George was calm. He looked at the man, disapproving but unaffected.

***

Martin snatched the remote from George and switched off the TV. Though George would normally lecture Martin for such an impolite and disrespectful action, he knew it was best to let Martin get this rant out of his system. It had been going on though and George had gradually regained focus after drifting off as Martin went on and on and on.

"…and some little boy apparently. Nobody saw a little boy. There isn't even a little boy on this block let alone this street."

"There was a little boy, Martin. I have not imagined it. I am not doolally."

"I don't think you are doolally Gramps; I just think you may have been mistaken. The mind can play tricks on you if you overexert yourself. Sprinting at your age is dangerous."

There it was again, those words, 'your age'. Martin had been brought up by his grandparents since his parents were tragically killed on 9/11. He had recently moved upstate to college and suddenly saw his grandparents in a different light. Though they had never shown him any reason to think they may be losing their marbles or physical control, he had it in his mind that their age was a risky time of life. George put it down to the arrogance of youth. Emily knew Martin's stubborn streak that always fought for what he believed was inherited from George. To her, they were one and the same, though neither could see it or willingly admit to it.

"I just think that now I am away, it might be time for someone to help. Just to pop in and help you and Gran around the house."

George ignored this impertinent suggestion. He had considered challenging Martin to a race but he doubted it would go down well.

"Perhaps we could arrange a gardener once a week?"

"Right, that is too far, Martin. How dare you. Does my garden look a mess? Does it look like I cannot manage it? Does it look like we can't manage anything? Do you know how disrespectful you are being? A gardener once a week. This kind of horticultural perfection is not a once-a-week thing. God damn."

"I was just—"

"Being an ass is what you were just. I know what it is like at your age, I know what it is like at college. You think you know it all. You think you have it all sussed out but do you know what you find out more and more in life? You never know it all. Nowhere near it. Not at twenty, not at forty, not at sixty and not at eighty."

"Gran, can you help me here?"

"Don't poke the bear," whispered Emily to herself, "both of you."

"Don't turn to her. You are being just as disrespectful to her as you are to me. Here is what is going to happen. You are going to leave now. You are going back up to college and you are going to explain to all your peers how you know nothing about anything yet and you will never know it all. They are going to thank you and, you never know, you may become their false prophet."

"Very funny Gramps—"

"I am not joking. I want you to leave now. We will see you next weekend for lunch and hopefully, by then you will have remembered your manners."

Martin stared at his Gramps with steely determination but his resolve was soon dismantled by the stern look in George's eyes. Now was probably the time to do as he was told and retreat. He had planted a seed and perhaps he could nurture its growth but in a more delicate and manipulative way. His young brain was obviously sharper than their old grey matter.

George waited until the car pulled away before slamming the front door.

"How dare he," shouted George.

He marched back into the living room awaiting agreement of Martin's wrongdoing from Emily. Emily, who was so used to the two stubborn men in her life arguing about this and that, had completely zoned out for most of Martin's visit. She preferred the fun moments as was her nature. She had no intention of remembering arguments as her life flashed before her eyes. She had offered him a drink and something to eat, so to her, Gran's duties were done. She looked up at George who stood waiting for acknowledgement that he was right and smiled. She knew this would appease him and isn't actually her agreeing or disagreeing with anything. When it came to those two, it was nice on the fence.

George was appeased. Emily agreed that Martin was in the wrong and George was right to react as he did. Martin would return next week with his tail between his legs and George would know he had bestowed more education on his Grandson. Gramps' duties were done. He sat back down in his armchair and flicked the TV on. The room was soon awash with the familiar monotonous drone and repetitive clacking. George's fingers grew tighter on the arm of the chair.

His eye and the corner of his mouth were twitching. His foot tapped.

"Oh, what is it?" asked Emily, herself now irritated.

"Him," said George, "well not him really."

"Then what?"

"This, all this. We are in our eighties but we aren't dead. He just reminded me that is how we are seen and I can't understand why."

"Well, this is life for people our age. You just have to accept it."

"So now you are saying 'Our Age.' Just accept it. Jesus. Do you remember Henry and Lily?"

"Of course, I do George."

"Well, what would Henry and Lily do?"

Emily looked back down and returned to her knitting. George stood awaiting a response but none was forthcoming. He slowly and despondently returned to his chair and flicked through the channels. The monotonous drone and the clacking filled the room once more until abruptly the clacking stopped. Emily put down her knitting for the first time in what felt like years.

"So, what do you suggest dear?"

THE MUSTANG, THE PONTIAC AND THE KENWORTH W990

In the corner of the cheesy Diamond's Wonderland, the theme park on the pier, there was an adult-only area. Cornered off with a tatty red rope to prevent children from entering. An eighteen only sign lay on the floor obscured by the muddy footprints that had walked over it. In charge at Diamond's was a supervisor known as Stony Ste and even if children attempted to pass the rope, he wouldn't do much as he was always out back with his stoner friends. Not that he cared either way. Moving was too much effort. The machines beyond the rope didn't attract children anyway. They were for adults. Desperate adults. Designed to suggest a grand jackpot was about to pay out whilst taking every last coin from anyone who had fantasies of paying the rent this week. The locals called Diamond's Wonderland Little Vegas. The locals loved irony.

The main room was awash with glaring neon hitting you from every angle. Lights flashed, bells rang and children squealed. It was a non-stop performance of tinny symphonies from one machine to the next. Beeps, buzzers and electric melodies altered just enough to avoid any copyright lawsuits. The machines in the adult section beeped and buzzed as loud as they could, desperate for attention. Lights flashed brighter than ever but George and Emily walked straight by, barely noting their existence. They had not come to throw money away.

George's eyes lit up when he saw it. He had never seen a game quite like it. He had of course been in arcades before but not very often. He had taken Martin here about ten years ago and Martin's father about thirty years earlier. Though the décor was still as drab as it had been in the 1980s, the machines had advanced with technology. With Martin, the racing games had a wheel and a two-speed gear stick attached to an upright unit and a large screen. With Martin's father, the machines were Pac-Man, Donkey Kong and Frogger. This was different, this was space-age to George. An actual race car that moves as you control it. The windscreen projected the game world. A race track. Daytona.

George paid his dollar and hit the ignition. Audio of roaring engines blasted from the speakers in the seat. The volume made George's ear hairs shake, sending tingles down his spine. Emily stood beside the fake car, leaning in to watch the show. Two red lights appeared on the screen and the countdown began. The final beep occurred, the lights turned green and George floored the accelerator. He spun the car around the first turn and the vibrations knocked Emily back. This was not a game; this was a ride. The car shook, jumped and span vigorously throughout the race until it came to an abrupt halt and rested down like a lioness whose hunt was over. A shaky George emerged from the cockpit. His face was white and he looked ten years older. Concerned, Emily rushed towards him. George winked at her.

"Oh, I see, I'm going to have to watch you, aren't I?" teased Emily.

George sat in his armchair with the TV drone tiring his soul. Emily sat in her chair knitting away. The clacking was not its usual rhythm. It sounded forced. Every few minutes she would stop and sigh. George's fingers tapped the arm of his chair in rhythm with the clacking. When the clacking stopped, the tapping stopped and when the sigh came it was contagious. Emily put away her needles, her current temporary project and her balls of wool in her knitting bag. Normally this would be set beside her so she could retrieve it at ease. Emily went to the sideboard and exchanged the bag for the Monopoly set. A local version which had Diamond's Wonderland in the first brown square. Yet, the parts were long gone. George had given Martin a lesson in capitalism which resulted in the board being thrust down the waste disposal unit. Though Martin was reprimanded, George was quite happy to see the end of it.

Laying in the box, where the board should be, was a laptop. Kept in there because, as George often said, who would ever steal a Monopoly set should they break in? Emily searched 'activities for seniors' and page after page of excursions, watercolour classes and tearooms came up. As though they had a safe search filter on. George grabbed the computer, highlighted the word 'seniors' and replaced it with adults. Their eyes scoured the many varied and high-octane opportunities that came flooding their way. Emily grabbed hold of George's hand, moved the mouse and clicked.

***

There was applause from the gallery at the track as a new lap record had been set by the car in pole. The owner had grabbed the mocked-up laurel, trophy, champagne which was actually sparkling wine and his digital camera. There had been a lot of recent articles about a group of retired Nascar drivers visiting karting tracks. Wearing disguises, they would only reveal themselves if they broke any records. It was an in-bet for the drivers, but to the owners of the track, it was invaluable advertising. Race fans in the gallery expected to see one of their idols behind the helmet but instead, a red-faced and sweaty OAP revealed herself. Jaws dropped. She had just broken their records. The other competitors shuffled off in embarrassment. Emily had lapped them all.

***

The sun was out and the factor fifty coated the couple from head to toe leaving them looking like ghosts. Though they were seeking thrills and life-affirming action, they had no desire for more wrinkles. Risking their bones was fine as there was the reward of excitement. Anyway, most of the lotion would wash off in the ocean should they end up in it. But this was not their intention. This was an opportunity for something a little more fun. They could push things here.

The beach bum who ran the rental shack for all water toys and vessels was another of the lazy generation. Like Stoney Ste, his heart was not in the job. His only interest was catching the sun whilst making minimum wage and extra tips for turning a blind eye. It only took a few bucks for George to rent the specialist equipment usually reserved for licence holders. Powerful Kawasaki Ultra machines capable of speeds up to sixty-seven MPH. The jet skis sped off and within ten minutes arrived at the beach of Isla Duerta. Twelve miles offshore, renowned for its natural beauty and variety of animal life. George whipped out the hidden basket he had pre-arranged with the beach bum for a few dollars more.

"Oh George, how lovely," said Emily as she took the blanket and laid it down.

The couple sat on the golden sand watching nature and enjoying the simple pleasure of shared tranquillity. They drank champagne and fed each other strawberries. George set the radio to play their song and they danced. Then, as the sun set, they reminisced about their youth and that evening in Monaco. They ended this night the same way.

"Oh, George."

***

A northwest wind was blowing in at twelve mph. Though the sun was shining and it didn't feel too powerful to people on the ground, for anyone in the air it would be rather precarious. Especially to students or newbies to the sport.

"Hey guys, we will see what we can do shortly but for now we need to let this wind speed subside a little before we can… prepare for take-off." Rupert was every bit the upper-middle-class rebel who had stuck it to his parents and their country club friends by choosing a career in extreme sports. He had a tendency to overuse and overenunciate the word 'guys' and always waited for validation of his wordplay.

"Prepare for take-off, I like it," Emily faked amusement but it was enough to encourage Rupert to continue the briefing. Once completed he headed back in to wait for the weather to change. George and Emily stood there, weighed down by the backpack, jumpsuit,

AAD, helmet and goggles. Looking more out of place than a cat amongst pigeons. Rupert soon returned with further information on the weather and it wasn't good.

"Sorry guys, the wind is actually getting stronger and is now at thirteen mph. At fourteen mph, we are not permitted to take students and beginners up. It's the law. We are going to have to take a rain check today. Sorry guys."

"What if we sign some kind of waiver?" asked George.

"Afraid not guys. It's an insurance thing more than anything. You won't be able to get any, so if something should happen, the risk is too much for us all. Sorry guys."

"Surely, we can choose whether we take that risk? At our age we have earned that right, haven't we?" argued George.

"You said our age," jibed Emily but George was not amused. He understood health and safety and its legalities but it frustrated him when he felt it was a stick used to prevent him from doing something.

"We should be able to sign a waiver. We should be able to say we take responsibility for anything that happens to us. Too much red tape in everything these days," grumbled George.

"Guys, I am as frustrated as you are but the law is the law and mother nature is mother nature. You can't change either of them. You could land on someone and without insurance where would we be? Sorry guys." With this final statement, Rupert collected up his gear and headed back in. An entire day wasted, thought George. He hated when plans went astray.

"Rupert," called George and jogged up beside him, "perhaps I can make it worth your while?"

George pulled out his wallet and started to rummage through his notes trying to gauge what denomination would get Rupert's attention. No matter what amount George would withdraw it was met with a look of disapproval. Though he tended to be a stickler for thorough risk assessment, he could still have brain-dead moments when anybody told him no. George had always had a stubborn side and Emily knew when this side of his nature was clouding his judgement. She had been on board with all their recent activities and keen to try as much as possible.

Though she would never mention it to George, she often thought it was good they were being active and trying new things as it wouldn't be too long before it was no longer possible. A harsh reality that George would not consider or want to hear. So, for the quiet life, she would keep this thought to herself. But she was not going to bite her tongue on this stupid idea and was quick to let George know. She marched up to him, grabbed his arm away from his wallet and pulled him to the side. She whispered in his ear and his demeanour sank. With his tail firmly between his legs. He apologised to Rupert and sulked all the way to the car.

"What happened to the daredevil girl I first met?"

"She grew up a long time ago."

***

Emily's knitting needles were clacking away. They were back to acting their age. There was probably good reason that people of certain ages were expected to act in certain ways. Being plain dumb was for your childhood and teens, exploration and seeing the world was for your twenties. Mortgages, careers and children were for your thirties, forties, fifties, sixties, and quite often until you breathed your last. If you had children or anyone you were once responsible for, like Martin, you were kind of expected to leave something behind to help them. Emily didn't worry about this. She knew Martin may need a home-cooked meal now and then, and a heart-to-heart or some boy-talk with George but he would find his way and he would do fine. She was sure of it. Perhaps he could be a little less of a worrier himself and gain some confidence but this would come in time. Maybe he would meet a girl at college who would bring this side out of him. Love makes us brave.

Emily's moments alone with her thoughts were soon interrupted. An engine roared like a racetrack was directly outside their house. George had gone out earlier to collect the Honda Civic from the shop. It had been having minor repair work as fifteen-year-old cars often do. Still having only done forty-five thousand miles it only needed a new fanbelt. Martin gave George a new phone for Christmas and he wanted so much to play his music in the car but the Honda only had a CD player. He had enquired with Emily whether they could upgrade but she was adamant she wanted to keep the CD player. It had character, she would say. Emily's heart skipped a beat when she realised, she may have misunderstood exactly what George was asking when he spoke about upgrading. The revving of the car became less a fleeting annoyance and more a message of foreboding.

A deep breath and eye roll were all Emily could muster as she gazed upon the black 1970 Ford Mustang Boss resting by the kerb. It certainly wasn't an upgrade on the music system George was after. If anything, this was a downgrade in that department. She doubted it would even have a tape player. Emily stood at the window staring at George as he revved the engine and smiled at her. This was a standoff. A pointless one as both knew exactly which way it would go. The daredevil side of Emily had never really left her and eventually, this mix of chrome, power and nostalgia, would lure her out for a closer inspection. She arrived at the window of the car trying hard as she might to maintain her scowl but the corners of her mouth betrayed her. They always did. She would never make a Poker player.

"And what do you call this? Where is the Honda?"

George revved the engine.

"George. I'm serious. How much did this cost?"

George smiled and revved again.

"George—"

The engine roared as George opened the door and allowed the beast to settle into a content purr. Emily slid into the inviting leather passenger seat and gently caressed the walnut dash in front of her. The façade was over and the final remains of her poor attempt at a mask withered revealing her wide excited eyes.

"So, where to Starsky?" asked Emily with a smirk.

"Starsky and Hutch drove a Gran Torino," said George.

With a thunderous roar, and vibrations that made the car feel like a rocket, they pulled out down the road at a sensible speed due to limits.

"Damn laws," said George.

"Damn laws," agreed Emily.

People stared as they drove past. At first, they would admire the car and then retreat in shock when seeing the little old couple in the front. It was the reaction they wanted and the effect they enjoyed. New thinking was something everyone should be open to. Much like a lot of their generation, a new perspective was a lesson they had learned the hard way. So, if they could make a young person rethink just by putting square pegs in round holes then all the better for society they thought.

They pulled up to a red light and were soon joined by a modern red Pontiac driven by a pair of shades. The shades lowered as the young man behind them studied the Mustang up and down like judging prize cattle. Emily greeted him with a polite smile disguising her first impression of this arrogant ass. She did not care for her snap judgement as she knew he was just young and dumb. He would mature, he would realise what mattered in life and he would become humble. But not in his early twenties, driving this red Pontiac and living off his family's wealth.

The shades looked across Emily and revved his engine a couple of times. George did not flinch. The shades revved again. A smile grew at the corner of George's mouth.

"No," said Emily.

The shades smiled across at George. Like two mischievous boys in cahoots for some ill behaviour they were about to indulge in. A man in his twenties and a man in his eighties who, in this moment, were both just boys.

"George, don't be braindead."

"What would Henry and Lily do?"

The lights hit green and both muscle cars roared into action. This was as much a race as it was a display of mechanical skill and advancement. This was boys and toys. The Pontiac pulled ahead and swerved in front of the Mustang. It stole the driving line and held the older car at bay. The modern Pontiac could easily beat the 1970 Mustang in a drag race but this was not that simple. This road led towards the outskirts of town and the hills that surrounded them. The road was snake-like with hazards everywhere. Non-stop bends, curves and turns, the possibility of oncoming traffic, fallen trees or foliage, roaming wildlife and missing barriers. This was about skill. Skill and guts. This might be a little too reckless, considered Emily, but she pushed these doubts aside. She knew George had this. He still had the skill, the reactions and the speed of thought.

George yanked the stick down hard and floored his accelerator. Feigning to the left and then sliding to the right he had soon drawn level with the shades. The younger man, surprised by the manoeuvre, hit the gas and the faster car bombed ahead. The lead was short-lived as he approached a right bend and had to slow right down. The Mustang was back on him. Weaving and sliding behind. Confusing him. Outside or inside. He could not shut off both routes and could not control the car well enough at speed. Condensation covered the shades. His grip on the wheel was unstable as his whole body perspired. He focused on his mirrors, watching for telling movements from the Mustang. The image that met him was a gentle old couple looking like they were on a Sunday leisure cruise. Another bend fast approached. A blind turn to the right with the edge of the forest lining the outside left. George had eased into the right-hand lane forcing the shades into the risk of oncoming traffic.

"Drop back kid," George whispered to himself.

"Perhaps we should now, George," suggested Emily tentatively.

Both men took the turn in unison. George on the inside and the young man on the outside. The sun was high that day and for a moment both drivers were blinded. The older man should have known better but instinct had kicked in. The two cars rumbled on, neither getting ahead, neither falling back, both handicapped by the sun and landscape. The sweat-drenched young man was realising he had bitten off more than he should but was motivated by the idea that once around this corner it was all straights. He had the faster car. George was aware of the increasing danger but kept going. Motivated by his natural instincts and inability to back down from confrontation. He wanted the kid to accept defeat and George could give him some encouraging words as he bestowed a life lesson. The cars roared on.

"Drop back kid," yelled George.

"George. Stop it now," cried Emily.

Out of the blinding light of the sun came the unmistakable shadow of a haulage truck. The Kenworth W990 was not a light piece of machinery. It was heavy plant and not something you wanted to argue with. Both cars could outrun and out-manoeuvre this monolith of the road but the surroundings did not afford either of them this luxury. The Pontiac was running into a head-on collision with a tank and the only way he could avoid it would be if the Mustang were out of the way.

The safe time had passed. To move the Mustang now was going to be of great risk of life to its passengers. George began to shake. He realised he had taken it too far. He realised he should act his age. He knew a young man's life was going to needlessly end. Like his own son had on 9/11. George froze as the gravity of the situation hit him. All he could think of was how helpless he felt when he took that call in 2001 and how some other father was about to feel the same. Emily grabbed the wheel and threw it hard to the right. The car span towards the cliff side to the right, allowing the Pontiac to move in front and avoid the nose of the oncoming truck. The rear end of the Mustang protruded across the centre of the road as the truck smashed into it sending it spinning. It skidded across the tarmac into the forest edge until it careered into a thick trunk and came to a sudden stop. The car lay still and silent as smoke towered up, turning the blue sky grey.

D-DAY

June 1944, Normandy, France.

This had been no pleasure cruise. Troops arrived by flat-bottomed Higgins boats launched ten miles from the Normandy coastline. The notoriously rough English Channel dispensing sea sickness with every wave. Men vomited into their crafts. Water smashed against the sides, each punch breaching the gunwales and filling the vessels. Green-faced soldiers were forced to bail the vile vomit sludge with their helmets. Though it was cold, the men were sweating and their stomachs were in knots.

The crafts arrived on the shore, the bow ramps lowered and, at once they were engulfed in rapid artillery fire. The front row stood little chance of disembarking and their brothers behind them were forced to use their lifeless bodies as shields. Men with no cover had to clamber the side and drop into the marshy, rough coastal waters still too deep to stand up in. Weighed down by heavy gear, many sunk to the bottom and, before they could remove the weight, panic hit and they breathed their last. For the ones that made it onto the beach, the first thing that hit was the stench. Emanating from the soon-to-be rotting bodies and separated limbs strewn across the beaches. Men released their bowels on round impact, through fear of the charge or the horror of the situation they could never have imagined. The whole beach smelled like a sewer. Then there was the blood. A small cut doesn't give off much odour but tens of thousands of people losing limbs or having vital organs punctured with bullets, can be debilitating. It was a combination of smells no man would ever forget and so few would speak of again. The necessary horror locked up somewhere so as not to haunt the ones who survived it. Though the smell of blood, faeces and urine was overpowering it could not get the better of the men. This was for the greater good.

Bullets sped through the air leaving a trail of earie screams behind. As if each one cried out death as it flew until finding its home in the shoulder, leg or throat of boys of eighteen, nineteen, twenty. Machine guns flanked the beach from higher ground positions on the cliffs at the easterly point. These were the primary target. Disabling these guns would leave the beaches in the hands of the Allies. What lay on the other side of the highest points was not something to think about. Keeping faith in the intel and commanding officers was all these men could do. This was war and they were young. Believing the Generals had their best interests at heart was motivating if not misplaced.

Before the troops had any hope of reaching the gun bunkers, there were other hurdles to overcome. The enemy had spent months constructing defences and treacherous obstacles along the coastline known as the Atlantic Wall. A two thousand four hundred mile long line stretching from the north of Norway down through Belgium and France and ending at the Spanish border. A barricade formed of seven million land mines, thousands of concrete artillery bunkers, tens of thousands of tank ditches and razor-sharp barbwire spread throughout. Get through all that and there was a chance. Only a chance.

Cpt Miller, who would have been Milyukov, had his family name not changed when his father entered the US through Ellis Island, had made it onto the beach and crouched behind a wooden post. He was a captain by age only. He had never been a military man or even a people person but being in his early forties meant the younger men looked to him for guidance. For that reason, he had been put in command. He may not have had the tactical mind of a seasoned veteran, or the desire to end enemy life on the say-so of his commanding officers, but he was a father himself. Back home in Red Hill, Nebraska, on the Kansas border, he had a young son. On this beach in France in June 1944, he had thousands of them.

Miller pushed back against the wooden post, trying to squeeze his shoulders out of view of the gunners on the cliffs or any stray bullets. His focus was the mission at hand and his personal agenda to get these boys home. Which was more important to him was irrelevant as they went hand in hand. They must take out the gunners if the men had any hope of ever returning to their loved ones or a chance of adult life.

Chain after chain of razor-sharp barbed wire straggled from the ends of the wooden posts cluttering the beach. Every now and then the sun broke through the smoke and reflected off the wire making it look like it was grinning. The grin of a serial killer luring you in with a charming offer of dinner before slitting your throat for dessert. Due to air strikes, weather and warfare some of the wire had fallen. Buried under the sand, protruding from posts, twisted forward, twisted backwards and even broken off as tiny daggers lying in wait. Designed to delay, designed to frustrate, designed to injure enough that if it caught you then you would be facing the enemy disadvantaged. Miller cut the end of the tangled wire from his cross-post forcing it to the floor. It was safer underfoot for his boys as this was all about advancing and advancing fast.

The depleted numbers of the 1st Infantry looked at Miller with pleading eyes. The situation was desperate as they crouched two metres back from Miller behind a sand barricade formed from a tank ditch. Nine young men were now all sons of Miller and he was determined to not lose a single one. Miller signalled to Sergeant Russo, a man in his thirties from New York with the ballsy attitude of having grown up in Hell's Kitchen, also ranked due to age. He would never be promoted through intelligence or the patience needed for preventing death of men under your command. Russo's eyes were unlike the others. He didn't show fear, he showed excitement.

Miller's rigid fingers pointed to Russo, instructing him to lead a party past the posts and up to the next cover. A destroyed Sherman Crab tank whose chain mail had failed in its only purpose. It had been a mighty explosion. A deathly boom accompanied by deathly screams. The bloodied body of the gunner hung from the top hatch as he had tried in vain to escape the burning inferno below him. His only exit route led straight into the line of German fire. Bone protruded from his arm where high-speed metal had ploughed through muscle, cartilage and flesh. Blood had cascaded down his arm like Hell's own waterfall and congealed with sand below. Less than two hours earlier Miller had shared a cigarette with this lifeless corpse. He was already losing sons.

Russo's legs were shaking. Eager to advance but having to await the order. Russo had to resist his natural devil-may-care attitude and listen to his superior officer. Listen to Miller. It was a big ask of him as he had never been good with authority. They heard the main gun that covered their position firing round after round far off to the right. This could only mean the gunners were unaware of Miller and his remaining small group of men holed up by the sandbank. They had been stealthy; they had been careful and they had listened. All with great speed.

Miller's hand stayed upright in its lower position. Russo could see it and Miller maintained eye contact with him to make sure he didn't jump the gun. He was chomping at the bit. Russo's hand was lowered to the left, with one fingered raised and the boys knew to wait. Miller's finger was rigid and Russo's shook. Russo made the boys nervous. Russo made everyone nervous but at the same time, he was the first to volunteer for anything. All balls and no brains. Maybe he did care for the well-being of the squad but more than likely he just wanted to go home a hero and garner adulation in his neighbourhood. The gunfire stopped and this was the moment.

"Reloading. Move out. Go, Go, Go."

"Let's move," cried Russo, echoing Miller's command.

Four boys flanked left and five right as they rushed this opportunity to make the cover of the Sherman Crab before the machine gun attacked. If the machine gun attacked. The Germans would be busy reloading and their eyes not focused on the beach. Miller's boys may reach the cliff without anyone even knowing they exist. The boys flanking right had an advantage as the gunner's attention had been to the group's left. They were out of sight completely and could have made the journey with a casual walk. The boys on the left had to sprint. If anything grabbed the German's attention it would be their activity. The German guns moved fast and spread far.

Without looking at the terrain, the four on the left sprinted from their cover on command. They had one goal. To make the tank without getting shot. The first boy only made about thirty metres; the dreaded click heard by those following him. The boy at the rear had time to escape the blast of the murderous landmine erupting under the front soldier but the other three were mercilessly caught. The front soldier took the brunt of the explosion, tearing him to shreds. Both legs blown from his torso and one arm severed. His remaining limb used to assess the damage in his horrendous last moments before he passed.

The other two men in the vicinity were thrown across the sand. One had shrapnel embedded deep within his stomach. Blood gushed up through his throat, drowning him. The other crashed against a cross-post and barbed wire wrapped him like a ribbon on a Christmas present. Each attempt to wriggle free from his metal captor resulted in a tighter grip and further injury before machine gun fire put him out of his misery. The land mine had caught the attention of the gunners and their now reloaded cliff-top machine gun. The fourth soldier didn't stand a chance. Though their losses were another bitter pill for the fatherly Miller to swallow he took comfort in the fact they were not in vain. Even with nearly fifty percent of his small group slaughtered he still had over fifty percent of his boys alive. On that day, at that place and at that moment, this was nothing short of a miracle.

Tank ditches did two things. Trap tanks, before heavy artillery could disable them, and offer cover. If a tank occupied one it became the cover but if the ditch was empty soldiers could hide against the inner sand walls and be invisible to the enemy. An empty one up ahead was the next position. Heavy gunfire had rained down on the Sherman Crab they were using for cover but had since ceased. Whether this was to save ammo, reloading or their focus was elsewhere it was another opportunity to advance. Miller commanded immediate movement forward and Russo lead the charge. Miller brought up the rear as the most likely target for a gunner returning to a target area. They had more time to aim for the rear. He gripped his gun in ready position with his finger trembling on the trigger. His boys held their guns by their sides so as not to slow them down. Miller was ready to engage if needs be and draw attention. He would make that sacrifice if he must. Russo would have to lead them from there. Though he was a hot head, leadership took balls and Russo had more than two.

As the boys ran to the tank ditch, they did not encounter any opposition. Not Russo at the front, Miller at the back or anyone in between. They all dived behind the tank ditch wall; thankful they were invisible to the German guns. If only for a moment.

Miller looked at his men with an incredulous smile across his face. He had no idea what was happening at this moment or how they had managed to get there, but they had. They crouched behind the sand wall, all injury free and could see the cliff base less than thirty metres away. Miller was not going to get complacent though. Why hadn't the guns fired on them when they advanced? The gunners had pelted them with rounds whilst they took cover behind the tank. They knew their position, so why let them advance?

The squealing of a banshee grew ever louder and ever closer before passing overhead. The deafening sound of the explosion that followed answered Miller's questions. Allied warships had moved perilously close to the shore and fired on the German positions. Whether the German gunners were killed or abandoned their positions was unclear, so the threat still existed. Miller would expect his boys to abandon in such a futile situation but also to return if possible. He looked out on the shadowy outlines of Destroyers from different allied navies. It sickened Miller to think they could take out these gun bunkers from the safety of seaborne positions but instead chose to send so many young men to the slaughter. He gazed along the sandy wasteland they had crossed and saw slain body after slain body lying in some ghoulishly contorted position. A scene only bearable by the dead. Rapid machine gun fire recommenced above and Miller knew they must take the bunkers themselves. This is why so many had been sent to storm those beaches.

"Captain, you and your men will join our assault."

Miller looked over to see who the command was coming from and the anonymous uniform bore more stripes than his so he respectfully acknowledged this. Anyway, it was safer for his boys to have the support of a platoon and not be picked off one by one.

"Yes Sir. What are our orders?"

"We scale this cliff. Your men take that route on the right. We must take out that gunner."

The five remaining boys of the 1st Infantry under Miller were primed and ready. They were a brave group but they had to be. There was no turning back, there was no backing out. The world and the future of it depended on these boys on this beach on this day. Inside they feared. Fear was good though. Fear kept them alert. Even Russo was afraid, though he would never admit it.

Miller led the boys up the cliff. Using only hooks and ropes without the luxury of safety nets or metal pegs. Climbing in unison meant there was nobody to help you if you fell. Bullets were fired down from the top of the cliff but the overhanging edges and rocky terrain made it difficult for anyone to get any clear shots. Screams rang out as one of the new members of the united platoon plummeted seventy-five feet to the pebbled sand below. Bones shattering on impact. His rope hacked from its hook. Opportunity to cut the ropes had been there as soon as the hooks flew up but the Germans had waited for allied soldiers to climb before cutting them. As horrific as it was, it made sense to Miller, this was war, why not kill two birds with one stone?

Time was more precious than it had ever been and the sadistic killing motivated the boys to get up that cliff and fast. The longer they lingered the more likely to die. Miller could see fear swallowing his boys. He needed to get them to the top, find the nearest cover, and let them take a moment. Let him reassure them. They had to stay organised and composed. The Germans were waiting at the top for them.

Private Rygarth, who looked no older than fifteen and was unlikely to have even shaved yet, panicked. He began to rush. The thought of his rope being cut was too much for him to take and he was scrambling up that cliff for dear life. Miller reached over trying to grab Rygarth's leg. He needed to hold it together a little longer and fight that fear. Miller would get them up together. He promised it but his grip slipped and Rygarth continued up. Miller screamed at Rygarth to stop but the young soldier was past listening. He was past anything. He wasn't even there anymore. It was a shell of a soldier scaling that cliff. The moment Rygarth's head breached the cliff top, the world stopped still for Miller. The sound seemed to go on forever and Rygarth seemed to stay standing tall for an eternity. This was another moment of longing for Miller. It felt that way as he had lost another of his sons. Rygarth's body crashed past his platoon, nearly taking others with him, until it hung from his rope halfway up the cliff with a hole the size of a penny streaming blood from his forehead.

Russo's mind was ahead of Miller's as he reached for his grenades. Miller soon followed suit as did his four remaining boys. On a count of three Miller gave the command to throw and five grenades, already primed, soared over the cliff top and exploded. The men then moved like Rygarth before them but they had cleared the path. They finally clambered over the edge to find the grenades had done more than just clear the path. One had breached the gun bunker through the small gaps. Finally, something had been easier than expected.

Miller investigated the smoky remains of what was their principal target. The gun barrel now faced upwards as gravity helped the soldiers avoid the deathly gaze of its tip. Four German corpses covered the floor with body parts detached. Swastikas on the arm were barely visible as blood had turned the black bits red and the red bits redder. Miller gazed at the faces of the corpses and they all looked young to him, like someone else's sons. They were the enemy though and whilst they wore that uniform and carried weapons intended to kill him and his sons, they were not human. He had to think that way as his normal humanitarian nature would never get any of his boys through this.

As Miller was leaving the bunker, pleading whispered from beneath the bodies. The strength of whisper that is all someone can muster though they try to scream. The body preventing them. Miller edged back in with his gun aimed in the direction of the sound. The pleading began to sound like praying and the language was not German. Of European descent, Miller was sure, Eastern European but exactly where he had no idea. Miller inched forward and, as the smoke cleared, he could see the trembling lips of a desperate man. His face covered in mud, blood and debris. Miller laid his gun down and began to dig the man from the debris. He took his canteen from his belt and lifted the man's head. He poured the water into the man's mouth and for a moment, the man looked at Miller. Gratitude in his eyes.

The man spluttered bloody spit from his mouth. In agony, he reached to his left arm and only then did Miller see the man's left arm was not where it should be. Not below the elbow. Mushy shreds of uniform entangled in his torn flesh. So many of the 1st Infantry lay injured down on the beach and needed any medical supplies available. But Miller acted on instinct. He couldn't get back down to the beach and they could not get up here. Here was a soul that needed medical attention and needed it now. Using his morphine, Miller calmed the man, using his water, he cleaned the man's wounds, using some debris he fashioned a splint and using his bandages he wrapped the man's arm. The man's breathing began to regulate. The man had calmed. Laying there with his head on a pillow of what was his platoon's uniforms, he looked up at Miller and smiled. A pained smile was all he could manage but it said it all. Thank you.

"What is your name?" the man whispered.

"Captain Miller of the 1st Infantry Division."

"No, your name. I need to know the name of the man I will always be grateful to."

"William Miller of Red Hill, Nebraska."

"Karl Petrov thanks you William Miller."

Karl Petrov survived D-Day but was one of two hundred thousand prisoners of war captured by the Allies that day.

Miller joined up with Russo and the four sons he managed to save who had dutifully waited for him outside the bunker. There was stony silence and nobody would meet his gaze. What had he missed? What had happened whilst he was in the bunker? What was going on? Russo finally raised his eyes to Miller's and with absolute contempt uttered one word.

"Traitor."

THE TRAGIC DEMISE OF
MARY MILLER

July 1944, Nebraska, US.

I t was a peaceful July afternoon and the children played soldiers in the fields surrounding the Nebraska farm. Red Hill was a small town with just over three thousand inhabitants. It was the sort of place you could spend a day lazing by the river or grafting on your plough and, either way, you would spend your evening on your porch listening to the sounds of nothing but the crickets and enjoying the validation of a productive day. Lazing and grafting could go hand in hand in these towns and nobody would judge anyone on which one they were doing on any given day so long as they did both in balance.

Mary was having one of her grafting days. She was slaving in the kitchen, preparing lunch for the children and farmhands. The children were a mixed group of offspring of locals but they may as well have been the offspring of whoever was supervising them that day. They knew to listen when told what to do and this obedience was well placed as every adult in Red Hill wanted what was best for every child. They were a team. They were a huge family. Many of the farmhands were in their teens and early twenties and Mary had known them since they were born. They used to be the children playing in the fields whom she would make towers of sandwiches for. Red Hill was not Xanadu, but only in name.

The land had been generous this harvest and the corn crops had grown high and plentiful. News had come from overseas that the Führer was on the backfoot and all the brave men and boys of Red Hill would soon be coming home. The community was planning a huge celebration and this bountiful harvest was going to fill their stomachs well. The peaceful afternoon was soon disturbed by a confusing and ominous atmosphere. Word had spread through the farm hands about commotions back at their homes and one by one they were dropping tools and rushing off. Mary came from the kitchen to find out what was happening but nobody knew anything for sure. It was just something. Something awful at home. As the final few farmhands had left the fields, Mary rounded up the children and brought them to play closer to the farmhouse so she could keep an eye on all of them by herself. On the horizon, the country road leading to the farm had a user. One lone young man on a bicycle carrying a messenger bag. He could only be coming here. Mary understood the commotion now. It wasn't panic that caused the people to go home but excitement. An excitement to be shared with loved ones. It was the news they had all been waiting for. Their men were coming home. The war must have been over for the US troops. It had gone on long enough. From December 1941 to July 1944. Nearly three years but finally it was done.

Upon seeing the name Mrs M Miller as the addressee, Mary tore open the Western Union telegram, expecting confirmation that William would soon be back, but her heart sank to the pit of her stomach when she saw those fateful first words 'I regret to inform you.' There must be some mistake, she thought, she scoured every corner of the telegram desperately seeking some abnormality which could mean an administration error had occurred. Sergeant William Miller has been lost in action. There was little more information. Telegrams seldom contained much. The name was correct but it only said lost in action and not killed in action. So, it was just a matter of time before William would return. Hope had returned to Mary Miller of Red Hill, Nebraska as so many of the other townspeople grieved the deaths of loved ones. Seventeen telegrams were received in that small town on that fateful day. All but Mary's said killed in action and Mary was going to cling to this as though her life depended on it.

***

October 1944, Nebraska, US.

A few months had passed since the people of the town learned of the tragic deaths of so many of their brave men. The loved ones left behind had spent the time grieving. Going about their daily business with dignity, whilst releasing the agony within once they were behind closed doors. They were not through it yet and wouldn't be for a long time. If they ever got through it at all. They were good people who would support each other but sometimes it was a struggle to offer empathy when people's emotions were so polarly placed.

Mary Miller had not grieved at all, as she had been offered hope. She would go about her business quietly carrying this with her and appearing empathetic. However, she couldn't really relate to the general feeling of the town. Bubbling just beneath her surface was an air of indifference to the other townspeople. She wasn't like them as her William would be returning. She had felt sadness in the aftermath of the event but she had grown to pity those forever imprisoned by loss. She was just keeping up appearances now. Every day she would show concern for the wellbeing of whomever she was talking to and they would appreciate her concerns. This was how she saw it anyway.

The people of Red Hill would explain it differently. Mary Miller had not shown empathy. She had been cruelly smug. The daily façade with whomever she was dealing with was passive-aggressive. She would float down the street and, in the stores as if she was above all others. She would feign concern and they would feign appreciation. Mary Miller believed she would soon have her husband back and her life would go back to normal. It had been three months and she had heard nothing more. She was deluded.

It was a Tuesday like any other and Winnie Shaw was waiting in line for her groceries. Winnie had taken the death of her husband Hal with relative ease. This was not much of a surprise to anyone in town as Hal was not nice to know. She only married him as she fell pregnant when young and was forced to. He was forced also and this may be what had led him to become such an odorous ogre of a man or maybe he was always destined to become one. Winnie had barely known him before she was his wife, and since he had left for war, she rarely wore her trademark scarves and sunglasses that hid the effects of Hal's trademark abuse.

Mary Miller stood behind Winnie Shaw in line for groceries. This was an uncomfortable position for either lady to be in and time seemed to stand still. Mary thought Winnie was heartless for showing such a lack of care for the death of her husband and Winnie had no time for Mary's misplaced sense of superiority. The usual forced smiles had been offered and Winnie had turned back to the front. Though she tried to ignore Mary Miller she could not help but overhear, or eavesdrop, the conversation occurring behind her. As the conversation grew, Winnie got more agitated. Her fingers were twitching, her toes were tapping and she was running her tongue along the bottom of her top teeth. Unaware of her body's subliminal behaviour. Mary Miller was offering her usual council to a young lady who had lost her great love and was destined to carry this trauma with her for the rest of her life. Mary Miller's council was not what this young lady wanted or needed and Winnie Shaw could listen no longer.

"He isn't coming back," Winnie erupted, "You need to stop lying to yourself and stop masquerading around town as if you are a guiding beacon of hope to all these poor people who have suffered."

Mary froze, speechless from this abrupt interruption.

"Look, Mary, I am not saying this to be malicious, I am trying to help you. You need to know this so you can start to accept it and begin your grieving process. You have that boy to think of. He needs you and he needs you thinking straight."

"Thinking straight? How dare you. Who do you think you are Winnie Shaw? I will thank you to keep your nose out of my affairs."

"Mary darling, I am just—"

"Just nothing. Just because you don't have a husband no more."

"Oh, for God's sake girl. Neither do you. He ain't coming back ever. The sooner you accept this, the better."

Mary, looking like she was going to attack Winnie, dropped the bag she was holding and stood motionless. She stared deep into Winnie's eyes as her own slowly glazed over. As though she was no longer present. Her lips trembled and with no warning, she screamed. She screamed in Winnie's face. There were no words to this scream. There were no commands or arguments. It was vocalised turmoil; it was loud and it was long. A primal release. She needed this and Winnie had elicited it from her. It could have been the idea of William coming home leaving her, it could have been the last thread of hope leaving her or it may have simply been the lie she was living. Whatever it was that truly caused it, two things happened that day. People said Mary was mad and Mary never left the farm again.

***

June 1949, Nebraska, US

Henry had been playing with his friends in the woods. The woods were not too far from the farm but far enough to be out of sight. It was a place he could just be an eight-year-old, which is something he rarely got the chance to do these days. The war had ended four years ago and many of the surviving men had returned home to Red Hill. Henry's father, William, had not returned but that was okay. He had stayed on to help develop the new world. He was doing very important work with governments. Or so Mary would tell Henry. She had originally concocted this story to protect Henry from any truth or grieving that could be avoided. Mary believed that if she held off long enough for Henry to grow up, he would be able to process it easier and deal with it in a more becoming way. She didn't want him to necessarily forget his father, just to be unaffected when he did discover the truth.

Henry played quietly with his friends. He needed to be discreet as he was meant to be working in the fields. A lot seemed to change around the farm after the war. The local farmhands never came and most of the work was done by him and his mom. Mary would tell him this was normal and the farm hands were only here during the war as the crop was needed for the effort. Mary was very quick-witted when she needed to be and, if it was to protect Henry, she would use anything she thought could be of benefit. When Mary had her off days, Henry would cover the lion's share of the work and this was one of those off days. If she found he was shirking off in the woods then there would be hell to pay. Sometimes Mary's love would be shown in screams and kicks. She would tell him she just loved him too much. Mary wanted Henry to know he had done wrong and she believed a kick from her was better than ending up dead.

Mary stood up in her room and popped down more of the pills she was adamant were making her better. There was nothing here but dependency and addiction. Mary chose not to look on the brighter side of life. She chose not to look to a better future. She felt darkness. It surrounded her. Her future was nothing and her present was limbo she currently resided in. Her future was going to be with William. It looked so colourful when they were younger. Before he went to fight, they had spoken of plans for later life. The fact William was a bit older than Mary was what made her feel so secure. It felt like a blanket. Warming and safe. Now there was nothing but a bleak wait for the inevitable end.

Henry had been her pride and joy. He was born in 1941, just before William had shipped off. The only joyful memory that ever managed to fight its way into her head was a beaming William holding Henry in his arms. So proud, so strong, so happy. The memory weakened with each passing year and the time it lingered in her mind decreased. It no longer had the strength to block out the misery for long. She looked out the window and scoured the farm. The plough sat lazily on his haunches and Henry was nowhere to be seen. Sudden rage seized Mary. If the ploughing wasn't done, the crop wouldn't be ready for harvest, they would have nothing to sell and nothing to eat come winter. No money would also mean no medicine and she would have to go through cold turkey. Something she was not prepared to do.

Mary threw her blanket around her shoulders and stormed down the stairs. Intentionally making as much noise as possible. If Henry heard, he would rush back to the plough and she would not have to go further than the porch. No good could come to her being outdoors. This was now how she thought. She had become a recluse and feared the world beyond the farm. In reality, she feared the world inside the farm as well. It was so easy for any person to pay an uninvited visit. They were the real problem. People. People never had good intentions. They were all against her. Mary's tactic worked. When she arrived at the porch, Henry was back at the plough. Mary stood on the decaying wood of the porch and lit a cigarette. She picked up a glass from the table, the dregs of last night's liquor, and her off day routine began. Her off days would often be longer than a day. There was no guessing as to how long she would be of no use around the farm.

Henry had learned to fend for himself for a long time. He could make simple meals. He could collect food and build fires. He could even wash clothes, though not very well. He knew his mother was ill but he did not understand the complexities of the disease and had no idea of the pills she took to balance her mood. He knew the best thing to do was simply work hard to maintain the farm whilst keeping up with his education. He felt terribly guilty for leaving his work to play with the children in the woods, but he kept doing it. It seemed so natural to him to have friends even though his mother would tell him it was wrong and people were bad. He was a confused and conflicted eight-year-old but something inside made him often choose to follow his gut instinct. Even if it did get him in trouble with his mom. He knew the belt was coming later.

Mary stood on the porch staring at Henry as he pushed that plough up and down the field. This was an archaic way of working the land but with no money to improve anything it was all it was ever going to be. Liquor in one hand, a cigarette in the other, mood pills pumping through her bloodstream and venom in her eyes. She could feel the hate rising. The lines of decency and clarity were starting to blur and Mary's brain was about to be fuelled entirely by hatred as it often was. The problem was that he reminded her of him. As Henry was ageing, he was really taking on his father's looks. On the good days, this would be a blessing to Mary as it would warm and comfort her. She would see the good growing from the good. She knew he would make something of himself. On the bad days though it took a much darker turn. He would make her blood boil. He would make her skin crawl. She would only find her sweet relief with the aid of the belt.

Henry lay in bed that evening listening intently to every creak he heard. Was that the floorboard in the hallway? Was it the door? Was it the walls? He was restless. He was often restless and could rarely relax. He never knew exactly when he would be in trouble or punished but he knew to expect it at some point. He was always on edge. He knew he was meant to keep his distance from others but it just felt wrong. He was always fighting his own demons. His desire to socialise with other children. To play and be a child. He wanted to play games and have adventures but he knew these thoughts must be pushed deep down and never come out. Nothing good would ever come of any games or adventures. He was even told to keep himself to himself at school which was making the other children think he was peculiar.

The handle shook and the door opened with an uneasy clatter. It swung back against the wall and an unstable Mary stumbled in. She leaned against the door frame until she had composed herself to make the crossing to where she would find her next support. It was less composed and more a desperate dive but the depressing form of Mary Miller had found her way to the end of Henry's bed. Henry had not moved and barely breathed. He had stayed laying in the foetal position, facing away and scrunched his eyes. Maybe this would make her go away. Maybe he would get through this evening without getting the belt. On her good days, she would tuck him in, wish him sweet dreams, kiss his forehead and even tell him she loved him. He would sacrifice that all if it meant she would never come into his room at all. The off days were unbearable.

"Henry, look at me."

Though he wished he could be invisible at that moment, he knew he wasn't. It was a strange instruction as she would normally aim for his legs and buttocks with the belt. This command felt coated with greater danger. Henry placed his hands against his face, spreading his fingers just enough to see through, and slowly turned to face his mother. Something was different this time. Very different. The belt was nowhere to be seen and Henry strangely wished it were. This felt worse. He sensed something bigger than the belt. There was an ominous and unnerving atmosphere that had taken hold of his bedroom. He looked at his mother through the gaps between his fingers and saw a broken soul looking back. There was no rage in her eyes and the redness of her face was anger. She was tearful. In her hands, she gripped a photo of the day of Henry's birth.

"I'm so, so sorry Henry," cried Mary before letting out a wounded yelp. Sounding like a small animal caught in a trap.

This was a new situation for Henry to comprehend, let alone deal with. He was eight years old and had his manic-depressive mother sitting at the end of his bed, fuelled by drugs and alcohol, breaking down. He shortened the gap between his fingers. Maybe he could shut it all out.

"You just look like him. So much. The more you grow the more I see him. Oh William," she wailed, "why did you leave us?" Mary placed her palm on Henry's cheek and gently swept away his hands. Their tear-filled eyes met and Mary lowered herself to embrace her son. She was overcome with all-encompassing love and knew she would need to hold on to him tightly. Though it was normally nice to be held by one's mother, this strange situation was making Henry extremely uncomfortable. The cocktail of drugs and liquor that Mary lived on made Henry wary of her and her sudden mood swings. The trust was not there and never fully would be.

"You are just going to leave me too. Everyone leaves me. Why don't anyone want me?"

"He is coming back Mom?' Just doing some work for the greater good?"

Mary's mood switched in an instant. She wiped her eyes, sat up and glared at Henry.

"Course he is coming back. What a stupid question. Don't be a dummy. You need to be smart and keep this farm going so he returns to a good farm and a smart son. He won't like you if you are a dummy." With that Mary struggled upright and stumbled back to the door. She switched the light off and closed the bedroom door. It was silent, but only for a heartbeat. The handle turned and the door reopened just enough for Mary to peer around. Henry could see one eye, brimming once again with venom.

"Never ask me that again." The door slammed shut.

Henry had not long returned from school and, fuelled up on bread, he was already out in the fields. Henry was not in a happy place. They had been taught about the possibility of a country forming in Germany, allied with the Soviet Union and opposed to all things American. They were apparently the enemy. The children in the school had used this new ammunition as a way to bully the peculiar Henry. A couple of children had called Henry a son of a commie before, but he had no idea what it meant or why. It was just something they had learned from their parents and had no idea what it meant either. It still hurt Henry though. He had no friends at school and out of school was expected to have no friends either. He was expected to go through life with no relationships at all. Everyone is bad. His mother would remind him often. They all want something from you. The world is full of cruel intentions.

"Henry," a voice came from beyond the trees. It didn't matter whether the voice came from Elizabeth, Ben, Lolly or any of the group of children that played in the woods. It was drawing him in. He was torn. He was always torn between his natural instinct and his mother's instructions. Maybe something was wrong with him. He was built wrong. His mother must have his interests at heart. She had told him no and he needed to listen. He had only been shown contempt by other children that day and he was starting to understand his mother. Who needs friends?

"No," he whispered to himself.

ENEMY AT THE SCHOOL GATES

October 1949, Nebraska, US.

Days and nights had become a very repetitive affair. Much had life for Henry. He would get up early to clean and prepare the tools he would need later. Go to school, do his homework and then tend to the farm. This cycle had become Henry's life for the last six months and six months to an eight-year-old can feel like a lifetime. Henry wanted to do the right thing and listening to his mother was the right thing as proven when she rewarded him for all his efforts. Tonight, was one of those nights. There was to be a radio play performed and Henry was allowed to stay up a little later to enjoy it. These radio plays were often very realistic but it had been eleven years since Orson Welles had scared the heck out of the nation with his adaption of War of the Worlds, so people were very clued up that it was just a drama. Tonight, was something special, a cop show called Dragnet had only been on for a few months. Henry was going to be a gumshoe when he grew up.

Henry and Mary sat on the porch as the crickets chirped. The radio crackled away as Henry played with the antenna trying to find the reception sweet spot. It had been working so well for the George Burns and Gracie Allen show but something had interfered with it. After a while of twiddling and twisting and audio spitting parts of what appeared to be words, the sound became clearer and with a final adjustment to the knob, the station was tuned in. It was worth the effort.

"Ladies and Gentlemen, the story you are about to hear is true. The names have been changed to protect the innocent—" The program had got no further than the famous introduction when interference rendered it inaudible again. Henry was quick to twiddle with the antenna again and get the sound back but only managed to retune to the news.

"Due to rising tensions in Allied-occupied Germany, the Soviet Union has announced the formation of the German Democratic Republic, in East Germany, which is governed under Soviet control and Marxist ideals. The Soviet Union continually failed in fulfilling its obligations under the Potsdam Agreements causing friction and division between the former four zones which resulted in the formation of the Trizone in the West. Known as the Federal Republic of Germany since May this year. An iron curtain is more prominent than ever across Europe as the communist influence expands." A solemn-sounding newsreader signs off as Mary switches the radio. She sinks back into her chair as her focus drifts away. Sadness takes over her face.

"I want to listen," argues Henry, ignorant to the suffering of others like most eight-year-olds.

"Go to bed, Henry."

"No. This is my reward. I want my reward."

"Go to bed," screamed Mary. Henry was used to his mother telling him what to do and, more often, what not to do but he had never heard her voice raise so loud. The shock of this blast had kicked in his fight or flight instinct and he did not hang around. Mary reached down for her bottle and poured a large glass of relief. This was not enough. It could never be enough for what she forbode. She had been dealing with it for years now but soon she would no longer be able to protect Henry from it. She pulled out her pills, popped a couple and washed them down with a large swig of whisky.

The next day at school it all began. All anyone was talking about was the division between the Allies and the difference in ideals. Nobody had ever spoken highly of the Russians but at least they were on our side before. Now people were speaking of them as the enemy. The curriculum had all changed that day and, instead of the usual maths lesson in the afternoon, the class were learning about the DDR and the Soviet Union. The words that kept being delivered with an undertone of evil were Marxism and communism. It seemed too much for children to understand but they were constantly told it was very important to follow current affairs and very important they knew that communism was bad and should tell an adult if they see any communism anywhere. Henry couldn't imagine exactly what a communist was but the picture he had in his head was of a monster. It was how it had been described to him. Someone who takes the souls of children and makes them evil in their own image. Someone dark and sinister in long cloaks, hiding in the shadows, waiting for the unsuspecting to meander passed and then pouncing. Icy chills would rip through his body just thinking about it.

The days went by and political education was very much a part of the children's life. The education board felt it imperative that America's young were to know everything that was happening overseas and how it could affect them back here. The children were to be given the full facts as to the danger of communism and the commies that may have snuck into the country. They were the deadliest plague on the planet. It was early years indoctrination, but it was important for this generation to hate their enemy as they will be needed to pick up the fight when their parents no longer could. How long this fight would go on nobody knew but they could not let these political ideals devour America and the preventative measures would come from educating the future defences. Well, educating them as much as they needed to know to suit the task at hand and decrease the risk of independent thought.

The classroom had a new feeling for Henry. It was a sudden change in atmosphere like when the wind changes in spring. He could feel eyes on him from behind and when his teacher faced the blackboard the whole class would turn to stare. All his classmates whom he had known for a long time were seeing something different in him and something they did not like. Henry had no idea what they were looking at or why. He had never had much to do with them due to his upbringing but once again they were showing Henry his mother was right to think people are generally bad.

"Eye's front," shouted the teacher and all children quickly span back into order. As the class went on, the children would take turns staring at Henry. As soon as the teacher turned to the board, the girls on the right would glare at Henry, and the next opportunity those on the left would turn to Henry. There was no kindness in their eyes. There was something malevolent about them. The children behind Henry just stared the whole time. He could feel it.

The class were silent as they were dismissed for lunch. They collected their belongings and made their way out. Henry stood by his desk a little longer, as he had no desire to leave the teacher's side. Each child had either purposely barged into him as they passed or hissed. Like they wanted to say something but not in possible earshot of the teacher. No, this was something that they could not be heard to be saying. They had to be able to deny anything. Once in the playground, Henry felt vulnerable. There was only one teacher on yard duty that day and he was rarely around as he often disappeared for a smoke. Eyes seemed to eerily glare at Henry from all corners of the playground. Children started to inch towards where Henry stood. To onlookers, this would appear a simple child's game but this felt much more sinister.

The first children that went past Henry would hiss again. Soon adding shoulder barges into Henry's side. A barge and a hiss were becoming the go-to. Henry was scared and wanted to run but where to? There were no teachers around and the children were soon aware they had free reign on the playground. The group of children hounding Henry soon became a mob and he was being pushed and pulled as they circled him. They hissed and grabbed and barged and kicked and pulled and hissed and slapped and hissed and spat and called him a commie and jabbed and poked and called him a commie and needled and as Henry collapsed to a ball on the floor with a mob of children towering over him proclaiming him the enemy all he could hear were the repeated hissed words above him.

"Commie, Commie, Commie."

That evening Henry was not himself and even Mary, in her usual distorted perspective on life, could see this. He had barely said a word since coming home. He had looked forlorn out in the field and he was a million miles away when Mary asked what was wrong. With no reaction, she gently pushed his arm to grab his attention and he jumped and cowered behind the chair. This was something big thought Mary. She tried to find some semblance of sobriety so as to allow her brain to function properly and plan her next move.

"Who was it? What did they do? I told you to avoid people," Mary snapped, "look, you can either stay behind that chair or tell me what happened." Mary reasoned that her usual brutish approach would tend to get Henry to respond and so why change tact here? Henry could take no more today and ran to his room.

A gentle knock on Henry's door as he lay curled in a ball on his bed. A voice softly floated into the room as the door slowly opened. Perhaps a moment of sobriety had broken through and Mary was going to be a mother here. If the cause of Henry feeling upset in any way was down to her, then it was character building, but if it was down to anyone else then she was as protective as any mother ever.

"Henry, hon, tell me what's up," she whispered as she deftly sat down on the bed and stroked Henry's hair.

"What's a commie? I know we hate them, but what are they?" Henry asked without moving from the security of the curled-up ball he had become.

"Well, you know what they are Henry. They have been teaching you at school."

"Why did all the children call me one?"

Henry told his mother what had happened that day and she was not surprised. She was not shocked. She kind of expected this day to come. She had received word of the rumours that had circulated the town for the last few years and had tried to protect Henry from them. She thought if he avoided other people then they would not be able to say anything to him and would leave it alone. Now it had got to the children there was no escaping the situation. Children only said what their parents said and Mary knew she needed to show the parents they were wrong. She needed to get them all back onside like before the war. A supportive community.

"Come on, let's go," said Mary grabbing Henry gently by the arm and directing him towards the door.

"Where?"

"To educate them."

Henry's eyes were darting all over as he walked down the street into town. It was the first time in years that Mary Miller had left the farm and Henry couldn't remember the last time she held his hand, but right now they both gripped each other like vices. Mary was scared to be out in public again and Henry had a newfound fear of the town. As they entered the main stores, the atmosphere could be cut with a knife. The people of Red Hill were not expecting to see the mad farm women in town anytime soon and yet here she was with her offspring. Surely cut from the same cloth. Eyes were burning at them before they had even got properly through the door.

"What do you want, Miller?" said one person.

"The very nerve." Said another.

"We don't want you here."

"Why do you hate us, Miller?"

"Commie scum."

Mary had prepared her responses in her head since the moment she had decided to return to town earlier. She knew exactly what the people would say and was ready to deflect every attack with reasoned diplomacy and delicate reproach. The townspeople would accept her explanations and reasoning and welcome her back into the fold. It would be a new beginning for her and Henry and she would sort herself out. There was still life to live and a wonderful existence could be had. She just needed to accept William was never coming back and grieve him. Something she had actually done a long time ago. She was ready for this.

"William Miller is a commie." Mary Miller froze. The panic set in, and the overwhelming hatred and disgust of the people cut to the core. She was quaking as she desperately searched for the words she had so carefully planned earlier. Her mind was blank and nothing came to her lips but dryness. Her eyes were dampening and her legs softening. She was afraid and her instinct was simply to run. Run whilst the legs would still carry you and that is what she did, leaving Henry behind.

Henry arrived home a mess. His jumper was torn and his nose bleeding. A pathetic-looking Mary came to apologise but Henry refused eye contact. The first time in years his mother had shown any maternal nature resulted in him being beaten by local children. Why had she made them go out? What was she trying to prove? She always said that people were no good and she was right.

"You mustn't think that way, Henry."

It is the only way he could think as it was how he had been programmed by Mary and now all he saw around him was constant confirmation that she was right. Commie scum echoed in his mind as he grinded his teeth.

"They said Pop was a commie. They said he helped commies and then defected after D-Day."

"Don't believe them, you never believe them." Mary held Henry tightly by his shoulders. "Look at me. Look at me. He is not a communist... he is nothing."

Henry looked at her bewildered.

"I'm sorry Henry, I should have told you long ago. I received another telegram a few years back. He died during D-Day. They made a mistake saying he was lost in action."

"So, he was a hero?"

"Yes, he was. I should have told you but I wanted you to keep working hard at school and at the farm."

"I don't understand."

"I never intended to have this conversation with an eight-year-old. Just remember he loved you and make him proud. When you are a little older, I promise I will explain it all to you."

Henry shook his mother's hands from his shoulder and pushed past her as he escaped to his room.

He moved his bookcase in front of his door, something he had not done since he was little. Though Mary could have moved the bookcase, she never did. Even when her mind was not fully there, she knew it was a line she must never cross, and she didn't.

Over the next few months, Henry's life became very reclusive. He was ostracised at school and would hide in his room when home. Henry had completely neglected the farm work and his mother didn't seem to care. She had tried to rebuild their relationship at first but soon the drink and drugs had taken control once more and she was lost to her dangerous escapism. The farm was falling into disarray. Henry was working. Just on his own things. His own education. He had decided that the answer to his life was in books. Whether it was knowledge or escape it lay in books and he could enjoy this without any need of any other humans.

He had started reading the anti-communist pamphlets that were being distributed all over the US. He had wanted to understand the word commie and why it was bad, more than just being told they were the enemy. Why were they the enemy, he had considered and decided to find out for himself. The many pamphlets he read had the author's and government's desired effect and had installed a greater understanding of communism and a stronger hatred towards it. He was an incredibly bright kid and he could see the future implications for the US if the commies did take control and it all sounded bleak.

However, the many pamphlets also had another effect on Henry. There was a section in one entitled 'Signs They are Commies' which showed certain things to look out for in strangers including certain words. Just occasional Russian words that the commie would slip up with and give themselves away. 'Proletarsky,' which meant Proletarian which in turn meant workers which was also 'rabochiye.' Henry would memorise these to help avoid any future uncomfortable situations with the townspeople. Once they had forgotten about his dad, he could look out for other commies and they would welcome him and his mom back in. They would be seen as one of them again as soon as the townspeople forgot.

Though he had specific reasons for learning these Russian words it soon became something else. He found he had a knack for remembering new words. Foreign words and their meaning. The bookshelves at his local library, like many in the US, did not include much literature on learning Russian as a second language and, even if it did, anyone who borrowed it would have been met with a lot of suspicion. So, Henry borrowed books on French, Spanish and other safer choices. Lapping it all up, he was thoroughly engrossed and found he learned a lot quicker without the distraction of hatred he tolerated at school.

A MOTHER'S PRIDE

March 1953, Nebraska, US

Joseph Vissarionovich Stalin, The General Secretary of the Communist Party of the Soviet Union has died," a newsreader br almost with joy in his tone. It was very strange to hear as there was always the expected solemn respect in a death announcement. Not this time. He had been suffering from a short-term illness and had ultimately succumbed to a stroke.

"Good riddance," said Henry as he turned off the wireless that sat in the pantry. Within moments eggs splattered against the windows and cries of 'commie' surrounded the farmhouse. It was never-ending. As the cries and insults increased, and the eggs barraged the Miller home, Mary's nerves could take no more and she collapsed to the floor.

The doctor had given instructions to Henry, he was to look after his mother. It was clear she would never be able to operate as she once did. She wouldn't be able to tend to any farm work, she wouldn't be able to cook or clean, she wouldn't be able to leave her bed. Henry was suddenly the caregiver in their relationship and he was only thirteen. Whatever idea of childhood he had ever known was certainly over now. His daily routine had taken on an even stricter regime of work. He would go to school, he would do his homework, he would do his farm work and then he would make dinner for him and his mother and tend to any needs she may have. Mary was lucky to have Henry and she knew it. When she had left him in town, all those years prior, their dynamic had changed. He had looked at her differently. It was pity in his eyes every time he looked upon her. But now that pity was what made him so caring.

***

April 1953, Nebraska, US

Henry approached his mother with a warm bowl of porridge. It wasn't much but it was all she could manage and all he could muster. The farm was falling apart and the annual harvest decreased yearly. There was only so much a thirteen-year-old boy could do and the local community would never offer any support. Not to the Millers. Since she had become bedridden Henry had been doing all he could to make her more comfortable and had brought the wireless up to her room to keep her company when he wasn't around. They would spend each evening listening together after dinner to whichever programming was on. Henry still enjoyed the exciting cop shows and also spy thrillers. Mary preferred the comedies like Andy and Amos. The strange consequence of her situation was that she had found the ability to laugh again. Such a torrid lifestyle she suddenly found herself living had actually brought her some joy. Or perhaps she just accepted there was nothing else.

Tonight, the main broadcast was an address from President Dwight D Eisenhower. It would be known in history as the 'Chance for Peace Speech' or alternatively the 'Cross of Iron Speech.' Finally, he was going to address the nation on how the death of Stalin was going to affect the American people. It was an exciting evening in the Miller house as they knew the end of the Cold War was imminent and they would no longer be treated as outcasts. Life could go back to normal. They could get some farmhands. The farm would prosper and Henry could rebuild. Red Hill would be the same home to him that it had been to Mary in her youth.

The excitement was short-lived. The people had been expecting some sort of declaration agreements had been made or new foreign policy put in place that would ensure a peaceful future around the world. All that had been said was a question to the new leadership of the Soviet Union as to whether they would try to aid peace in Korea and Asia, work in concert with other governments in disarmament and whether they would allow other Eastern European nations free choice to form their own governments. The Millers were cynical. Henry switched off the wireless and tidied his mom's blankets. He collected up her bowl as she reached out and grabbed his hand. She squeezed and stroked it whilst looking at Henry.

"I'm sorry Henry." It was all she said. There was no elaboration on it but there didn't need to be. Henry knew exactly what she was saying and it was fine. It offered him the closure he had needed for so long.

A new positivity had entered Henry's young life and he was finally being influenced by a positive role model. A young teacher called Mr Reynolds had started at his school and he seemed so different from the rest. He was originally from New York and had said he wanted to move down here for a slower pace of life. Henry could somewhat relate to this. The idea of a city as big as New York scared Henry whilst also exciting him a little. It was a fine balance. Reynolds had of course been told of the mad Miller woman who lived at the farm by the men in the local bar but he was not making any judgement from their reports. He had no need to ever meet her and so no need to form any opinion but he was sure that her son shouldn't suffer for whatever sins of the parents. It's hardly fair he thought.

As chance would have it, Reynolds was also a language scholar fluent in many tongues and he and Henry would often enjoy conversing in French or Spanish. It was so helpful to Henry to have someone to practise his skills on as he was fluent in the words but sometimes, he would slip on accent, tense or pronunciation. Reynolds would pick him up on this and Henry would correct it at once. He never made the same mistake twice. Whether this was something he had wisely learned in his childhood or he simply had one of those brains was unclear, but it certainly was not a disadvantage.

Reynolds loved to show off his language skills to Henry and Henry lapped it up. Whether it was a French play on words or a naughty double entendre in Spanish, Henry would giggle away. Sometimes there would be splashes of Italian, German, Portuguese and occasional curses in Russian. It was these curses that had really got Henry's attention. Not because they were swear words, that made any boy red with mirth at that age, but the language they were in. Henry had long wanted to start learning a new language. He had wanted to learn one that could benefit his future opportunities.

His love of radio cop shows had formed his ambition to be a police officer and, since he spoke three languages already, he aimed to do this by working with the CIA in some way. Henry figured that if he could speak Russian then he would be a huge benefit to them as he could translate and decode. He could never ask the librarian for any books on the Russian language, not with his family's reputation but perhaps he now had an alternative avenue. He knew Reynolds wouldn't judge him like that and so he took the chance and asked if he had a book Henry could borrow to begin learning Russian.

The response he got was unexpected. Reynolds' voice took a sudden serious tone and he looked around as if he was being watched.

"No. Of course not. I don't have any books on Russian and nor would want any." Reynolds was behaving strangely. Biting his lip as his eyes darted around the room. "Henry, why would you want to learn the Russian language?" he suddenly whispered.

"Because—"

Reynolds shushed Henry by clamping his lips together. He slowly released them and gestured to Henry to speak quietly.

"Because I want to learn the language so I can work for the CIA when I grow up." Henry whispered back to Reynolds. Both Henry and Reynolds constantly surveyed the scene for any onlookers but Henry knew not why. He was just mimicking the actions of the adult as he thought he should.

"I can lend you a book but you must promise me two things. One, you never show or tell anyone about it and two, you don't use it to work for the CIA in the future."

"Why not?"

"Trust me, Henry, they are bad people who are trying to prevent a positive spread of political ideals. They are the true enemy Henry. Just promise me you will stop wanting to work for them."

"I promise," said Henry. He would never show or tell anyone about the book but when it came to part two of the promise, he lied. Mr Reynolds left the employment of the school not long after this and was never heard of again in Red Hill, New York or anywhere.

***

June 1953, Nebraska, US

The communists were at war with themselves. Inter-party fighting had occurred in East Germany as an uprising escalated through over seven hundred localities in the country. As the Soviets increased the East German way of life to fit the profile set by Moscow the East German people rebelled. Protestation grew against the large increases in work quotas for the brigades whilst living standards declined, and country-wide strikes were rife. It would take violent suppression by Soviet tanks to restore the peace. The day would become a celebration in West Germany until the 1990 reunification.

The news had caused celebration in the Miller household. Mary was in fine spirits and they were not chemically enhanced. She was becoming a changed person. Perhaps being forced to embrace sobriety with isolation was making her reflect on past behaviours and a resolution of change had made her a new person, determined not to regress to her former self. A self-pitying misery. She wanted to share all the good things with Henry. He was a fine boy and would make a fine man. This is how she saw him now. She could see him clearly and he was her everything.

At that moment though, the Henry she saw had a puzzled look on his face.

"Why are we celebrating when the tanks stopped the people?"

"It doesn't matter. It was a clear message that their way doesn't work and even more so the people don't want it. If most people don't want something then change happens. They can't force them."

"How will it work now then with three leaders?"

"It won't, Henry. Malenkov, Beria and Molotov will squabble and fight and nothing will get done. The Soviet Union will fall and communism will end. Life has just begun for you and it is going to be so good."

***

November 1958, Nebraska, US.

Five years had passed and nothing had changed. If anything, it had gotten worse. The squabbling leaders of the Soviet Union had been toppled by First Secretary Nikita Krushchev and he had just issued the West with an ultimatum to withdraw from Berlin within six months.

Mary Miller was unwell. She had been unwell in one way or another since 1944 but this was physical decline. Ever since her first attack, five years ago, had knocked her off her feet, she had never been able to regain her strength. Henry had been looking after his mother diligently and every night, he would bring her dinner and they would talk and laugh. A lot of recycled material would go back and forth in the conversations as no new memories are made when you are bedridden. Unless Henry had something new to report or something on the wireless had sparked debate. One recycled bit, that always had them in stitches, because if they didn't laugh, they would cry, was how they had thought the death of Stalin was going to be the end of the Cold War. Oh, how wrong they were and they mocked themselves silly with this.

Henry's day had been much like any other. He had been at school, which was much easier for him than it used to be as most of his tormentors had left at fourteen or fifteen. He was now rarely bothered or accompanied by anyone and that suited him just fine. Why bother with people if you have no need, he would often be convincing himself. Henry was an academic. It was what defined him. All those years reclusively in his room, reading and studying had given him a natural curiosity to understand everything. The high volume of knowledge also gave him a sense of superiority which, if he had any friends, would make them think he was a bit of an ass. He had stayed on at school to get as much education as he could. His ambitions to join the CIA had not withered and he knew to get chosen for such a prestigious post, he needed to stand out from the crowd.

After school, he had come home and tended to any farm or housework that needed to be done. Though this was very little these days as the farm was in a state of disrepair and the house really should be bulldozed. The natural decline had been happening over the years as Henry could never have possibly kept on top of it all without his education suffering. Perhaps it was selfish of him but, it is what made Mary most proud. She had been no use to him and, with no father, he had nobody to motivate or instruct him, so his self-determination was a blessing. Perhaps if life had been different, and he had friends in town, then he would have been led astray. Perhaps the treatment the Millers received over the years is what made Henry who he was. Perhaps it was a good thing in the greater scheme of life?

Like every other day he had prepared dinner for his mother and taken her tray in and, like any other day, more bad news came across the wireless about the Soviet expansion. An egg hit the edge of the window. Over the last few years, Henry seemed to spend more time cleaning eggs from the farmhouse exterior than doing anything else. It seemed to have become a role within the town for the children to inherit as the previous ones move on. As if it was a position in the local council and the work must continue.

"Henry, it's time."

Mary had been listening to Henry with great interest over the last few years as he would tell her his life plans. What she had always noticed, and what pleased her, was how little he deviated from his ambitious statements made when he was thirteen. It was always the same. School, University and then the CIA. There was never anything else. It was a fine determination and Mary knew it would hold Henry in good stead for the future. She hadn't known many men in her life but was sure they were not all so organised, decisive and deliberate. However, she had seen this positive attitude before in a man and that man was William. Though they had barely met, Henry had grown up with some great similarities to his father. The acorn clearly doesn't fall far from the tree. When Mary was living a life under the influence and control of chemicals it would pain and anger her to see William in Henry but now it soothed her. It brought her great joy to know she had been blessed with two great men in her life. She was proud of them both.

"I want you to promise me something, Henry. I want you to promise that you will go off into the world and never look back. There is nothing in Red Hill worth returning for. Now, don't you be worrying about me either. It is your time now."

"Not yet Mom, I need to look after you."

"Oh, I will get someone in to do what you do."

"Even listen to the wireless in the evening?"

"I quite like the idea of some peace and quiet." Mary offered Henry a reassuring smile. She wanted him to shine. She didn't want him worrying about her when he had a life to build.

"I'm sorry for what I did. I stopped you from having a childhood—"

"The town stopped me—"

"I stopped you first. Listen, never let anyone tell you no. If you want to do something then you go ahead and try. Don't let anyone say you can't do anything, ever. I'm sorry I ever told you no."

"You don't need to apologise for anything Mom. I understand."

"I think you do. Oh, and Henry, always be kind to girls." Mary said this with a wink.

Mother and son had made their peace and both went to bed with a warmth inside. Henry's warmth was a feeling of positivity and excitement about the direction his life was soon to take. Marys was caused by the overdose of the black-market mood pills she had been secretly administering for many years. The next morning only Henry woke up.

LIFE BEGINS AT LILY

July 1959, Kansas City Union Station, Kansas, US.

Lily had been flustered all day. It was a part of her personality that most people found endearing even if it made her disorganised and always running late. It was never a problem to her as people seemed to accept her apologies with those big eyes and charming smile. This acceptance was why she never tried to fix it. It never bothered her. But trains were not interested in charm. Trains were interested in timetables and conductors their partners in crime. If Lily was not on that train when the whistle went it would be a long wait for the next one and extra expenditure a student could not afford. She stood in line at the ticket office as she could see the train preparing to leave. The final checks were complete and the conductor began to close the doors.

'Excuse me,' said Lily to the gentleman in front, 'would you mind if I go before you as I am in such a rush?'

With a bat of her eyelashes, the gentleman obliged and Lily bought the final available seat. For anyone else taking this journey, it would mean sitting on their luggage in cargo. Though Lily was disorganised, flustered and always running late, things always seemed to work out fine for her. She was lucky like that.

The train had sat at Denver Union Station in Colorado for over three hours. This was not a scheduled stop for anything more than passengers to embark or disembark. Something had gone wrong with the engine and the railroad finally accepted it needed further investigation and an overnight stay at their expense. Lily didn't mind. It had become unbearable sitting in a tin can train carriage in the summer heat surrounded by other people's body heat. For most of the passengers, it was a rarity to travel by train and this current situation was alien. They didn't know the town and had not planned on any overnight stays but found themselves directed towards hostelries for the night. For the regular passengers who had experienced this situation before, their next course of action was clear. They must move. This was a foot race. There were never enough rooms to go round and so the unlucky latecomers would have to source alternative accommodation. A cost to themselves the railroad would never compensate.

As the regulars began to pick up pace, urgency soon spread throughout the crowd. The value of speed was obvious. All the passengers moved towards the town centre, dragging their luggage and children whilst dripping in sweat. It was a most uncomfortable time for all. Some of them dressed for the summer but not for athletics in the sun. Lily had felt faint on the train but had recovered in the fresh air and now found herself in the middle of a literal human race. Moving her whole life cross country meant she was weighed down by two large cases containing her meagre worldly possessions. Even so, she still found it thrilling. This was a quest and she was going to succeed.

Lily arrived at the hotel somewhere in the middle of the group. She was by no means first but everyone else had set off before her. That is how she saw it, otherwise, she would have romped home. Out of breath, she stumbled up the hotel steps as the door was held open. A young man practised his chivalry unnoticed by Lily who fell through the entrance and managed to secure the last available room. She was lucky like that.

Lily had come to university to make something of her life but at eighteen she was not ready for anything quiet. She wanted to live first and she wanted adventure. Lily had never been one for taking in current affairs or keeping on top of topical events, so her level of knowledge on communism, the Soviet Union and the Cold War was little to none. This is why she went forty miles north of Stanford to Berkeley University on a sunny day in August 1959. A lot of people on campus had mentioned some rallies up there and it sounded exciting. She had never been political. Not that she didn't have strong opinions on things, it had just never cropped up for her before. She was brought up in an orphanage which offered basic needs for children to survive and little more. There was no nurture, love or intelligent debate and so her political direction was yet to be decided. It was astonishing to all at the orphanage that one of their number had managed to complete high school let alone get accepted into Stanford but Lily was bright. This didn't stop her from being reckless and randomly visiting a politically charged rally just for a thrill. Book smart but not street smart.

To most people present the rally was emotional. Whether it was a drive to convert others or a heartfelt connection to the cause, these people were loud. They had something to say and they were angry. They were going to be heard by as many people as they could get to listen or simply to notice. Megaphones were not the only way of getting your feelings across and Telegraph Avenue, the main road leading to campus, was immersed in hand-made signs on either side. Socialism for All & All for Socialism kept appearing on the placards. Some scrawled on at the last minute and others meticulously designed to hit harder. Equal Rights for Everyone, Abolish ROTC, Time for Revolution and Free Speech were other repeated messages that Lily enjoyed. She felt like she was at a raucous art gallery. Cuba Libre, Cuba Libre, Cuba Libre chanted different groups as she moved along the street. The signs pumped upwards emphasising each chant. The protesting students agreed with the freedom socialism had brought to Cuba when Castro overthrew Batista. Long Live Free Cuba.

Lily couldn't help herself. She found the chants intoxicating and contagious. She didn't see any harm in joining in and was already swept up in all the drama. One little orphan wouldn't make a difference to anything. A young girl with eyes that screamed change thrust a sign into Lily's hands. She directed her into the group and before Lily knew it, they were all marching up the road. To where, she had no idea but she was warmed by the unity of the people and thrilled when she pumped her sign and cried 'Cuba Libre.'

A group calling themselves SLATE had arranged this march and a youngish guy with a megaphone called for revolution and reaction from all. The crowd that surrounded him echoed his sentiment and responded with concurring expletives. The atmosphere in the crowd had turned a little aggressive and Lily's curiosity was wavering. She was not feeling the passion of the group. It all looked quite exhausting and the physical side of it had bruised her arms. She dropped back until she was on the outskirts and was about to relinquish her sign when she found herself face-to-face with a random man. Inches between them. He looked oh so serious, Lily thought.

"Hey," said the man and stared at Lily.

He raised his eyebrows a little and enlarged his eyes. He seemed to be trying to say something without saying anything but Lily had no idea what it could be. She offered up a similar facial gesture as a natural reaction intended to convey a request for elaboration but it only resulted in the man increasing the emphasis of his gesture. Lily shook her head at him and he looked hurt. Perhaps he had noticed the sign in her hand because as soon as he read it, he launched into a lecture about the dangers of communism and criminals like Fidel Castro. Lily had not signed up for a lecture yet, so wasn't about to stand there listening to some stranger rant and force his opinion down her throat. Lily had been happy to ignore the fact the rally was doing this on a much grander scale as it was all bright colours, passion and youthful exuberance. But she had tired of that and this unwelcome rant was exhausting. She just wanted a coffee and to maybe relax on the grass.

"Bye," said Lily as she walked off on the stranger mid-sentence.

"Unbelievable," was the response but that was already behind her now and so was the rally.

Lily spent a few hours lazing on the grass under a large tree on the campus. It had been the perfect way to spend an afternoon. She had gotten lost in a bootleg copy of Allen Ginsberg's 'Howl' and had no idea what to make of it. She had been given it by a young lady who had told her it would get her juices flowing. She had been a bit naïve to what to expect and its content had shocked her a little. She had considered stopping reading but told herself she was a high-level scholar and she should read such things as it would open her mind to the human condition and help her gain greater understanding. Well, that and the fact it was rude. She felt the need to wrap it in a cover of a Spanish textbook and that excited her. Life was all about new experiences and she had definitely found some today.

THAT GIRL!

July 1959, Kansas City Union Station, Kansas, US.

Paint peeled and flaked from every surface it still clung to. Window frames had slipped their fittings and the rotting roof was collapsing into what was once the living room but the land had worth. With his mother's passing, Henry knew there was nothing left for him in Red Hill. The offer he had received was less than the true value but it was the only offer on the table and he didn't have the time to negotiate. He had been accepted into university. His course started in two months and he wanted to get to San Jose as soon as possible to explore his new world. This was not just a new world but the chance of a new Henry and a chance to leave the past behind him.

He had packed his cases and gone through every item in the house. He rummaged through all the cupboards and drawers but all he found was cheap and broken homewares. He was happy to leave this to be destroyed in the demolition. He had never been into his mother's wardrobe but he needed to clear it in case there was anything personal in there. He knew she would want this. The door had fallen off its hinges as he opened it and dusted erupted up. Once it settled, all Henry found were moth-eaten dresses that hadn't been disturbed in years. He didn't think his mother would like anyone seeing them and so bagged them up to be burned. Once the wardrobe was clear, Henry could see to the back and spotted a small table. He had never seen it before. The table had a small drawer with key a in the lock and it sat under some plastic covering. In all this dilapidation surrounding it, this table was preserved. It was looked after and seemed loved. If this was so coveted by his mother then he needed to know why and honour her memory.

Henry removed the plastic covering and unlocked the drawer. He gently pulled it forward and found it contained just one item that was also covered in plastic. He removed it to find a framed photo of a couple smiling back at him. Young and with their whole lives ahead of them. His mother looked beautiful in her white wedding dress and his father looked noble. This was the first time he had seen a photo of his father since his childhood. He had forgotten what he looked like. Henry felt this was something he should take with him and started to remove it from its frame but stopped. In the background of the photo was this farmhouse in all its finer glory. The paint job looked like it had been done that very day. Henry realised they must have celebrated their wedding here. Everything in the picture looked so perfect. So new. So cherished. Henry kissed the photo and placed it back in the drawer. He locked it up and replaced the plastic covering. He would leave them together in the place they were happiest. His mother's passing hit him hard but he was so grateful for the last few years together. He kept remembering the last advice she gave him.

'Leave Red Hill behind you and forget,' she told him, 'Live life and be all you can be, do what you want to do and don't ever let anyone tell you no...'

He wasn't going to let anyone even try and rain on his parade. He was going to do good things. He was going to study hard and join the CIA. He would serve his country and the global greater good.

'…and Henry, always be nice to girls.'

Though he had accepted less for a quick sale, the legal documents took longer than expected to be drawn up and it had fallen on the day he had planned to leave for good for the final handover. Henry had been incredibly organised with what he could, even with a lot of this procedure out of his hands. He was fully packed, though this was only one case, as nothing was worth keeping, and ready to leave at nine that morning and his train wasn't until three in the afternoon. Ten came and went with no further communication and before he knew it the clock showed eleven. Henry was getting edgy as he wanted to leave by noon at the very latest so he could commute to the station in a casual manner. He was starting a new life and wanted it to start calmly.

Henry's wristwatch hit midday and he was no longer in the best of moods as a car finally came over the horizon. He needed to sign their documents, collect his documents, action final checks, hand over keys and finally drop the papers at the land offices on the way to the station. He hoped the buyers would understand his urgency but then again, they had failed to do so already by getting here late. Of course, they needed one final walk around so they could pull at the house panelling and question the plumbing.

"You are buying this for the land and not the house," said Henry through gritted teeth. The buyers smiled as if to say well done, you caught us out on that one. Finally, at twelve-thirty, Henry was on his way to the station. This was now a rush and he was not happy.

Sweat dripped from his brow as he breathlessly joined the ticket queue in the hall. He could see his train making its final preparations on the platform but all he could do was wait his turn.

His first chance to try out the new Henry came a lot sooner than he expected. He imagined this would be a university persona nurtured over time and he would come out the other end a changed person but opportunity came knocking before he even left Kansas City Station. It was now twelve fifty-three and Henry was next in line when he felt a tap on his shoulder.

"Excuse me, do you mind if I go in front of you? I am in a rush," said a girl, "I will only take a minute but I seem to have a lot more luggage than you."

Though Henry was sweaty, breathless, irritated and in a rush, his mother's message to be nice to girls echoed in his mind and she did have a lot more luggage than him. He gestured for her to pass with a smile. She was good to her word and had completed her transaction and left the queue within a couple of minutes. It was twelve fifty-five and Henry was being served. After all this rush and worry, he could relax a little as he was going to have a few minutes spare.

"Cargo only now sir.' The ticket clerk said without looking up.

"But you just sold a coach ticket to that girl?"

"Last one sir."

Henry's first try at being nice to a girl landed him a forty-eight hour long train journey spent sitting on his luggage with his only comfort a pillow made from his own jumpers. By the time the train arrived at Denver Union Station twelve hours later, his legs had seized and he had a crick in his back. His mood had worsened over the journey but he refused to let it get to him. This minor discomfort was not going to be the feeling that set his new life in motion.

Henry stood on the platform feeling smug. He could see by the faces of the others who had been travelling cargo that he wasn't the only one. The coach passengers were still seated in their greenhouse of a carriage being roasted by the midday sun. Sweat dripped down them causing a puddle on their seats. A lot of them were new to rail travel and didn't want to risk losing their seats. There was a cooling breeze across the platform that the cargo passengers had been thoroughly enjoying. The train had sat at the station for almost three hours when the passengers were informed a fault with the train meant they would need to spend the night in town and continue the journey tomorrow. The train company would cover the costs and the hotel in town was expecting them. Finally, the coach passengers left their seats and were grateful for the fresh air.

The group trudged down the main road into town. Along the journey, word began to spread there was a possibility the hotel wouldn't have enough rooms for everyone and latecomers would need to find alternative accommodation. Henry was unaware of the circulating rumour but, being proactive, he was amidst the main flock approaching the town. He didn't imagine this would be the first time anything like this had happened and so the town must be able to accommodate a train full of unexpected guests. They must be heading to a sorting post and then split between nearby establishments. That made sense to Henry so he was not in the rush others appeared to be in. He almost pitied them as he enjoyed a leisurely stroll with his one case.

People had been rushing past Henry right up to the moment his hand was on the door handle. He had still not considered it might be a race for a comfortable bed. He had thought himself a little smarter, as he often did, and these people were in a senseless rush when they could enjoy the tranquillity of night. It wasn't Henry's fault that he sometimes had a sense of superiority. He could speak five languages by the time he was fifteen whilst most of his peers at school struggled with the one. Learning languages was something you could do alone and he was always alone.

A girl dragging her luggage whilst cursing in some very imaginative ways had caught Henry's attention. He was a little taken aback by her colourful use of language but also amused. The late-night walk to the hotel had calmed Henry and though he recognised the girl as the reason he had travelled cargo, he didn't hold it against her. Be nice to girls Henry, he thought and, with a smile, took hold of her arm and pulled the door for her.

"Thank you," she said as she rushed past almost dismissive.

Not everyone was as calm in a situation as him, thought Henry, this was the reason for organisation. He brushed it off before following in and taking his place in line behind her.

"Last single room here," said the clerk as the girl approached the desk.

Henry chuckled to himself at the irony of her taking the last of something twice in a row and him being the next in line both times. He felt it was a test of the new Henry and he was going to pass with flying colours. Anyway, he was happy to go to one of the other hostelries. He just needed to find out where.

"There are no other hotels," said the clerk once she had sent the girl on her way to her room.

"What are the rest of us to do?" asked Henry and the clerk pointed towards a scruffy-looking pair who had appeared at the door.

"Come on you lot, on to the truck. We have space for you all," said a man wearing a hat full of holes and hand-me-down overalls.

For about fifteen minutes the truck navigated a dusty back road that went from wide to narrow with no pattern or reason other than the work of Mother Nature. After feeling every bump, pothole and rock obstructing the road, they finally pulled up to a farmhouse. It was a lot better kept than Henry's and so he was relieved they had somewhere comfortable to stay. Others questioned how the residence could house so many for the night but Henry knew how large these places could be once inside. He also knew how warm each chair, couch and bed could be. He could still remember from those few years before things changed.

"This way," said the man, leading them from the house.

The group followed, all desperate to rest their heads now. The sun would soon begin appearing and it was going to be hot and uncomfortable wherever they were. So, the quicker they got down the more likely they were to get a little sleep at least. The man led the group to the back and lit lanterns to illuminate the hay-strewn barn. By this time of night, the bails and loose straw looked inviting. The people in the group who found themselves in the barn tonight were here because they didn't race for the hotel. They were not about to make that mistake twice and with a blur of activity dispersed towards the best-looking corners to curl up in for the night.

Henry was slow to react and found himself trudging to a remaining corner. There was little straw or comfort there and so he would be using his jumpers and clothes again. Henry was exhausted, so it was no surprise he found himself chuckling again. It was fatigue kicking in and the acceptance of the little he could do. He kept thinking back to holding the door and losing the last bedroom to the girl, he kept thinking of letting the girl in front of him at the train office and getting the last coach ticket, he kept thinking about his mother telling him to always be nice to girls and he kept thinking how smart he was. The last thought was entirely ironic as he fell asleep on a rotten, wooden, bug-filled barn floor. Somewhere deep inside Henry was a suppressed sense of humour. He needed it for the life he had spent.

Henry arrived at the university and settled in. He had not made it to any social engagements yet but was psyching himself up for it. It was difficult for him after his reclusive childhood but was determined this was to be another major part of the new Henry. So far, he had idled around the campus to find his feet and stumbled across a nice little café bar. He liked to spend his days sitting in a corner watching the world go by. He was more than watching, he was observing, investigating, learning. He was trying to understand the psyche of human nature and he was picking up on little rituals. He noticed the same people would bump into each other on a daily basis and go through a dance of phoney niceties, brief arm touches, and plans to meet up that would never, ever happen. He also noticed they would all just talk at each other. Nobody ever listened.

This was very much a student hangout. The groups huddled together in big conversation speaking of ideology and grand plans. How they were going to change the world and take down this government and that regime, oppose this, refuse that and protest everything. One morning, there sat a group adorned with military memorabilia like epaulettes or buttons and even a soldier's jacket. There was something about the items that the group wore that stood out. They were not US surplus. They all incorporated stars and red motifs in their insignias. Henry noticed the collar of one jacket displaying the badge of a Capitan in the Cuban Revolutionary Army. This strange get-up worried him. They spoke of revolution, as they often did but this was closer to home. Pro-communist protest marches at Berkeley's campus had been carrying on for a while now, almost daily, and they planned on joining in. The idea that some people wanted communism in the US upset Henry and he believed it was his duty to prevent this catastrophe.

Henry had expected the protests to be a small group of lost students who had turned up seeking a sense of belonging. He imagined he would have no problem connecting with them, educating them and turning them back in the right direction. Nip any thoughts of revolution in the bud. He would head to Berkeley this afternoon and by evening they would all be sharing coffee as they agreed upon the greater benefits of a capitalist society.

He arrived on Telegraph Avenue and was at once overwhelmed. This small gathering, as he had pictured, had engulfed the main road. From sidewalk-to-sidewalk groups of protesters clustered together with placards declaring their demands. It made no sense to Henry. A lot of what they demanded they already had. 'Free Speech.' Well, that was a given and a constitutional right. 'Abolish ROTC.' That seemed like madness to Henry. The world needs order and there will always be threats from other nations or other ideologies. We need defences and it is better to have educated servicemen in positions of power when handling situations of life and death. Idiots.

The large attendance at the rally worried Henry. There seemed to be a lot more people interested in a new direction for the country than he had considered. It felt like an invasion. Henry was a little relieved to see he wasn't the only one who thought this way. Dotted around the area were men in black ties, who stood out like sore thumbs, constantly taking photos with little regard of being inconspicuous. The powers that be had got wind of this attempted uprising and would end it before it began. Henry admired them. It amused him to think all this protesting did was make him more eager to join the ranks of the men in black. He doubted that was the desired effect. Safe in the knowledge that the authorities were in control of this situation, Henry turned to leave but found himself nose to nose with a familiar face.

"Hey," said Henry and raised his eyebrows as if to say, remember me?

The girl stared back at him as if they had never met. Henry enlarged his eyes to encourage her memory of the man who gave up a comfortable train seat and hotel bed on a forty-eight hour long train journey from Kansas but all she did was mock him. Had his mom been right all along about people, he wondered, but decided to put it down to just meeting a girl decency was wasted on. He saw the sign in her hand had a star emblazoned in red paint and the words 'Cuba Libre.' It all clicked. She was one of them. She wasn't being rude, she wasn't being ignorant, she was misled. She had fallen into the folly of the fresh student and was caught up in the desire for change. She was being brainwashed and so Henry told her. He must inform her why this direction was not the path she should take. It was his duty and she would thank him for it.

"Bye," said the girl as she walked off on Henry mid-sentence.

Unbelievable. What a wasted day, he thought, before remembering the men in ties dotted around the misguided youth. They are the smart ones and I am one of them, he mused to himself.

SIX BUCKS FOR DEVILLED EGGS?

Povtoreniye, povtoreniye, povtoreniye," said Professor Scott. Henry sat in a centre seat on the second row. He had wanted to be on the first row but that was full when he arrived and he had been early. He made a mental note to get here even earlier in future. He had been looking forward to this first lecture for what seemed like a lifetime. Not just any subject but Russian Language. Finally, he could learn in the company of other scholars without suspicious eyes being cast his way.

Repeat, repeat, repeat, he noted down in response to the Professor. Listen, repeat and memorise was the basis Henry had always used for learning languages. He had spent many evenings sitting in his room saying the same word over and over until it was lodged and filed somewhere in his brain. He had enjoyed times before where he could converse in French or Spanish with teachers at his school but the opportunity to use Russian had never presented itself safely until this faculty of academia. Knowledge is not something to suspect but a gift that can be used for the greater good. That is how Henry had always seen it.

As Henry sat there satisfying his thirst for knowledge and warmly imagining the future possibilities life could bring, the door to the lecture room clattered open disturbing the whole class. All

Henry could see was the back of a girl's head as she was scurrying around to pick up her textbooks that had strewn across the floor as the door hit her on the butt as she passed through. Henry went back to his textbook as the pile of books, bags and disorganised tardiness stumbled through the room to the nearest empty seat. The seat next to Henry.

"Can I sit here?" whispered the girl and Henry agreed without his eyes leaving the words on his notepad. It soon became quite a fight to focus as the non-stop noise of shuffling and digging was very off-putting.

"Sorry to interrupt but do you have a pen I can borrow?" Henry reached into his bag and retrieved a pen case revealing a selection of perfectly organised writing implements.

"Are they colour co-ordinated?" said the girl, "nice." Whether this comment was meant tongue in cheek, Henry certainly didn't recognise any sarcasm in it. Why would anyone be sarcastic about good order and control? It wouldn't happen and so the compliment landed. Henry finally looked up to thank the kindred spirit next to him and was surprised to see the girl who had been the recent scourge of his existence beaming a great big smile back at him as though this was their very first encounter.

"You?" asked a surprised Henry.

"Hi, I'm Lily."

"Do I not look familiar?"

"Sorry no," replied Lily, "I can be a bit of a scatterbrain at times."

"Unbelievable," said Henry as he turned back to his work. This word nudged a memory in Lily's mind and she clocked Henry as the young man who was lecturing her about communism at the rally. Lily was considering the idea of playing with Henry but there would be three years of university for that. Perhaps it would be wiser to concentrate on the class and make friends.

"I was impressed with your pen organisation," said Lily and then observed Henry to see what reaction would occur. She bit on her tongue with anticipation but soon saw a smile slowly appear on his face.

"Is that a smile I—"

"Tikho," shouted Professor Scott at the pair and Lily sank suddenly like a naughty puppy.

"That means quiet," said Henry. Lily leaned towards Henry and whispered she knew what it meant since she was taking this class and she really did find his organization skills a very attractive character trait and hoped it extended from his writing instrument storage to all facets of his life. All in perfect Russian. Accent and words. Henry was impressed. She was ahead of him.

"Tikho," shouted the Professor again but this time with more agitation in his voice. The smiles dropped from both students as being a class disruption was not the impression either of them wished to exude on the first day. It was very un-Henry-like behaviour but Lily had a natural mischievous side to her.

Henry listened intently to the lecture being given and was constantly making notes. As per his usual process for learning and developing a language, he would repeat to himself what the lecturer said and play with the intonation and accent until he had it down in his mind. He would do this in his head, or so he thought. In reality, he was speaking under his breath, audible enough for anyone sitting next to him to hear.

"Tikho," said Lily. Henry turned to give her a how dare you look but stopped as he saw the grin on her face. She was messing with him. Henry tried to stifle the amused look on his face but was failing.

"Tikho," said Henry right back at Lily.

"Tikho," said Lily without missing a beat.

"Tikho," said Henry through the side of his lips.

"Tikho," said Lily mimicking the Professor.

"Tikho," yelled Professor Scott. The pair sunk back down in their seats so that their faces were obscured behind the heads of the people sitting in front of them. They looked at each other and Lily mouthed the word Tikho at Henry and neither could contain their laughter anymore.

"Out. Get out. Both of you." Henry and Lily gathered their belongings and ashamedly shuffled out of the lecture room with heads down and faces red.

"You get one pass with me and you two have used yours. Let this be a one off." Henry had never really been in trouble before, well not through any fault of his own and now he had been excluded from his first lecture. This wasn't really his fault either though, he had been misled by the annoying girl. But he didn't care, he kind of liked her.

**

The lights of the Ferris wheel at San Jose fair illuminated the night sky. Henry stood at the gates staring slack-jawed at this novelty. A sheltered upbringing had meant that Henry had never seen a fairground in full swing and certainly not a beautifully lit Ferris wheel. He had seen pictures in papers before but they had all been black and white and so the extraordinary vision before him had never been translated well on the page. It wasn't possible. Though this was a first for him, he wasn't going to tell Lily that. It would bring up too many questions he wasn't ready to answer. It was only their first date and she didn't need to know about his isolated childhood. She needed to see fun Henry. This was how you made friends. Or so he had read in a book.

Lily grabbed Henry by the arm like a child leading their parent to the best section of a toy shop. It was rather fitting as she was taking Henry to the roller-coaster. It was very rare for fairs to have roller coasters so this was a once-in-a-lifetime opportunity. Lily brimmed with excitement to the point she could barely catch her breath. The route to the roller coaster had been perfectly planned by the fair as you had to pass an array of beautifully presented and brightly lit rides and games designed to capture your imagination and empty your wallet.

To the right, just after the entrance and behind the very large palm tree was an even larger helter-skelter. Beautifully painted pictures adorned the panels of the structure that cascaded down like a pirouette supporting the slide. This was easily enough to grab Lily's attention and she was soon nearing the top with one hand carrying a sack and the other dragging Henry.

Before Henry even established what was happening or where exactly he was, Lily had thrown herself down the snaking wood with reckless abandon and skidded onto the soft ground below. Henry was taking in the view that led down to the San Francisco Bay coast near the Alviso marina. It was new to him to be able to see so much and he had not spent much of his life anywhere near water. Another new experience in his new life.

"Come on Henry, I can see your petticoat from here," called Lily from the bottom. Henry liked how bold she was and how she always sought something interesting and exciting. He thought to himself how they could spend their weekends camping, visiting the coast, galleries, museums, community fairs, science fairs or any multitude of fun activities to complement and contrast against their weekly work. He would work in an office for the CIA and she could be, maybe a teacher, maybe at a university, maybe he should stop thinking like this, he interrupted himself, this is the first date. Keep your cool Henry, keep your cool.

The evening was shaping up well and the young couple were having a wonderful time. After the helter-skelter, they walked through the haunted house, which had been wasted on intellectuals like them. They knew the touch they felt was just someone working there and the ghostly images were light, shadows, reflections and photography tricks. The Waltzer had been fun and the roller coaster exhilarating. Everything that Lily had hoped for. The couple disembarked with tingles pulsating throughout their bodies. They did not know what to do with themselves and Henry's impulse was to grab Lily by the waist and spin her around. Lily's impulse was to squeal with delight. As they stopped their eyes met and at once they both awkwardly looked away. Standing in silence and looking sheepish they both desperately searched for something to say to break the tension which Henry did by gesturing to the enormous, colourful, elegant, illuminated Ferris wheel shadowing the couple and towering over the whole fair.

For the first time, Henry took the lead, pulling Lily to the attraction. Lily was hesitant but hid it well. They took their places in a carriage and Lily gripped the bar as the ride whirred and the carriage rose. Henry was blinkered to Lily's discomfort as he had an even greater view than the Helter-Skelter offered and could see for miles in all directions. He could see woods to the east, the city to the south and west and far out to the bay in the north. To Henry, it was like California had suddenly revealed itself with a teaser of what it had to offer. This was only San Jose he thought.

Lily was tucked tightly beside him and had gently curled up under his arm. Henry had continued to speak of all he saw and the excitement they were having, completely oblivious to the fact Lily was now under his arm. He was in his own world. This was all new to him and his eyes were being opened more and more the higher the wheel rose. By the time their carriage sat right at the top, you could barely see the ground and the people looked like ants. Well, they did to Henry who was embracing the novelty and they did to Lily who was clenching her eyes shut. When she pushed her face into Henry's chest, the penny dropped she was not enjoying the same experience he was. One of her hands had been permanently gripping the bar rail. It had not moved, it had not weakened its grip, and it was shaking.

"Why come on?"

"You can't let fear stop you."

"What about the helter-skelter or the roller coaster?"

"They are fast. Like ripping off a band-aid. This…well it gives you time to realise where you are." Henry curled his arm around Lily's shoulder and gently placed his hand on top of her one attached to the bar. Lily gradually released her grip and allowed her fingers to slide between Henry's and interlock. He pulled her tighter to him.

"It isn't so bad anymore," said Lily as she slowly opened her eyes and looked up to the stars in the sky, "they are beautiful."

"Yes, they are," agreed Henry as he looked into Lily's eyes.

"Cheesy line," said Lily with a grin, "but it worked." Henry took her gently by the cheek and they kissed.

***

Henry had been under the helpful influence of the shop assistant at the local menswear store in town. He had never followed fashion in any way and never had to dress up as smart as he needed tonight. He and Lily had been getting on famously and they had been on a few fun-packed dates since the fair but now it was time to turn it up a notch. Time to be adults. He was taking Lily to an uptown swanky restaurant. He wanted to look the part and 'blow her socks off' as he had described it to the shop assistant. He had one word for

Henry, 'Tuxedo'. He was also recommended to make sure his lady friend knew exactly what he was wearing so she could dress accordingly. Nothing would ruin the date more than if Lily were uncomfortable.

They sat across from each other in a beautifully lit and ambient restaurant. The table seemed to have more cutlery on it than anything else but they had read to work from the outside inwards, but either way, it was a little daunting. Right up their street. They were taking in the whole room and the very rare experience for students, only possible since Henry sold the farm. What a treat.

Lily's jaw dropped as she spotted Rock Hudson sitting on a table on the other side of the room. She nudged Henry to draw his attention to who she found but he was a little less interested. Yes, it was an A-list celebrity, yes it was a movie star but Henry was wearing a tux in a very classy joint and he would appreciate it more if she only had eyes for him. Lily soon realised her starstruck behaviour was possibly a little inappropriate for the venue and the occasion, so she took Henry's hand and told him that he was much more handsome. Of course, he didn't believe it but any time Lily said something complimentary to Henry, his heart swam. He was smitten.

This date felt a little different to the fun ones before. It felt like they were really going to decide whether to commit to something real together and therefore they needed to know a little of each other's background. Lily had gone first and told Henry all about her upbringing. She had told him how it had never brought her down by being an orphan as it was from such an early age, she didn't know anything different. She was just orphan Lily who lived with orphan Joanne and orphan Eve amongst many others. Nothing much was ever expected of any of them and any grand designs or ambitions they may have had were soon quashed by life at the orphanage. Lily was different though. She played the class clown. She was everyone's friend, she was a leader of fun and secretly, behind closed doors, when nobody was looking, she was a very intelligent scholar. She always felt like she had a photographic memory because as soon as she read something she just knew it. That is what brought her to Stanford.

Henry told Lily all about his upbringing in Nebraska and the childhood he had experienced. He didn't hold back or sugarcoat anything. He trusted Lily and wanted her to know where he came from. Lily, the orphan, who had never been expected to achieve anything, and had never known love or affection in any way, felt sorry for Henry. His upbringing and the relationship he had with his mother made her glad to be an orphan but she was not going to say that. She couldn't believe that people would be so cruel to this kind and wonderful man. Lily was smitten too. She wasn't going to let him know that just yet though.

"You didn't mention your father. What does he do?"

Henry's whole disposition suddenly changed. His chin dropped to his chest and his mind wandered. Lily had no idea what caused this shift. She knew she must have crossed a line in her enquiries but then again, shouldn't she get to know these things about Henry? She had told him all about her background and would have answered any questions no matter how personal. That is how they would show real trust and connection to each other. She took Henry's hand and his attention returned.

"He died on 6th June 1944 on Omaha Beach." Lily knew exactly what this meant as everyone did in that era. She knew why it had affected Henry so much but she could also see the pride in his face when he told her. Henry went on to explain that he hadn't known his father much but his memory had motivated his ambition. They agreed that he, much like all the other men who were there that day were heroes. They toasted all that died in the war, they toasted all that fought against tyranny, and they toasted Henry's dad, the hero. But there was something else. In the background. It was visible in a corner of Henry's eye. Something from a corner of Henry's mind. A detail that was being omitted here.

"I can see why he is your inspiration. Maybe you could follow in his footsteps?"

"I'm no hero. I could never shoot anyone. I would just imagine some kid at home waiting for his pop to return."

"But for the greater good?"

"I guess I'm not my father."

Lily wasn't going to push it. She had seen the effect on Henry when she first asked about his father and she was happy to have him back in the present. He had opened a lot to her tonight. That will do she thought.

The bill arrived and Henry's face turned pale. Not because it was more expensive than it should be. It was more expensive than it should be, excessively, but he was aware of that before he came. He was prepared to spend to give Lily a taste of the high life. Henry's face was pale and he tried in vain to hide it. He did not want the other diners to see, he did not want the maître d to see and he certainly didn't want Lily to see. Apart from the white in his cheeks, Henry hid his anguish quite well and nobody else in the restaurant was aware of the predicament. But he did not fool Lily. Perhaps she was just too close and could see the small beads of sweat forming on his brow or maybe they had made a strong connection or maybe something else. Either way Lily had enquired to the problem and she had a right to know that Henry couldn't find his wallet. This was very embarrassing for him. He had felt like eyes were on them the whole evening as if these youngsters didn't belong in this classy establishment. Or maybe it was something in their accent or body language that gave away their social class, either way, Henry was not going to be looked down so this could not happen.

"I will talk to them."

"Or?" said Lily gesturing to the exit.

"We can't. It's stealing."

"And six bucks for some Devilled Eggs isn't?"

Lily slowly and stealthily collected their coats from a nearby stand and casually put hers on. Trying to make it natural and normal so anyone watching would presume all was as it should be. She passed Henry's coat under the table.

"Lil?" pleaded Henry.

"It's a game, a game of dares," said Lily, "I dare you." She gave Henry a mischievous grin and before he knew it, she jumped up, rushed through the restaurant and was out the door. Henry froze as Lily had drawn the attention of the maître d, who now appeared at the table demanding immediate payment and issuing threats of police involvement. Henry sat there like a rabbit in headlights. Suddenly an eruption of noise came from the other side of the restaurant as crockery crashed to the floor. The agitated maître d, who probably should have found a job more befitting his temperament but finds some bizarre prestige in kissing up high society, has another problem to resolve.

"You wait here," he commanded as he marched across the floor.

Henry looked out the window at Lily who had hidden around a corner. She beckoned him to join her but Henry refused. He knew he had his wallet previously so it must be somewhere. He searched his pockets again but nothing. He looked back out to Lily, gestured for any helpful input and she waved his wallet at him. Clamping her hands in over-exaggerated prayer, she pleaded for him to join her.

"It's just a game," mouthed Lily.

Henry had no way of paying and the maître d didn't look the understanding type. He couldn't go to prison for it and how would have even known who he was? He was just a surname on a reservation list. And six bucks was daylight robbery for devilled eggs. It was now or never. The commotion was his cover, his distraction, his ally. Though not entirely understanding why he was in that situation or why he was doing what he was doing, before he could analytically reason these questions, he had run full speed out the door and down the road to where Lily was hiding.

"Why?"

"How do you feel?"

"We broke the law."

"Henry it is nothing to them. How do you really feel?"

Henry considers this for a while. He wonders if there is more to Lily than meets the eye. Should he be concerned? Then again, six bucks for devilled eggs made it feel like the restaurant were the crooks. Lily was right and Henry was smitten.

"Alive."

WHO CAN YOU TRUST?

W ith a spike stick in one hand and a refuse sack in the other, anyone would think Henry and Lily were in trouble with the law. It would be a smart assumption as most of the people in this community initiative program had been forced as punishment, but Henry and Lily were just doing some good. Lily had seen it advertised on a notice board on campus and knew it was something she and Henry could get involved in. Doing their bit for the greater good she thought.

Henry was a little wary of the company he found himself in. He was trying not to be judgemental and take everyone at face value but knowing that some of your colleagues are criminals made it harder to be so considerate. He kept reminding himself that nobody would receive this as a punishment for a serious crime, but they may have gotten into a bar fight because someone had knocked over their beer or their refuse sack or spike stick! He was a little concerned they were allowed a spike stick in the first place.

Not everyone was a possible threat in Henry's eyes. A little old couple were tottering around together slowly picking up little bits of trash. Clearly here as volunteers also. They were not the most productive and had to work together as one would prod and lift the stick for the other to peel. It was slow but every little helped. Lily had been her usual curious and energetic self, chatting with everyone. She was finding out everything and anything about everybody. Everyone has a story she would always say. It made Henry a little anxious to watch her just start conversations with random strangers who could easily be one of the criminals. He knew to let her be though. A beautiful bird cannot be caged and this was the same with Lily. Henry always knew that he had to accept Lily's natural curiosity and desire for adventure and never try to stifle it. If he did that then he would ultimately lose her.

Henry worked alongside the elderly couple and got to know a little about them. They were called Reuben and Agnes and originated from the old country. They hadn't elaborated on which country was the old country exactly but somewhere in Europe. A lot of European accents sounded quite similar when speaking English and even Henry, a multilinguist who studied languages, didn't always find it easy to decipher. The three of them had worked their way down an alley slightly off the beaten track, out of view from the main road and the plots being cleaned up in the community project. They were not alone in the alley. Against a back wall at the bottom end were a couple of student communists who were flyposting propaganda. Designed to be visible from the road and stir reaction. They intended to draw attention to their cause long after they had vacated the vicinity of the poster but it had already caught the eye of a couple of police officers who did not share the same belief structure towards communism and, in no uncertain terms, demanded the immediate removal of the material. A sense of smugness came across Henry as he watched the communists try and argue their case.

"Listen to the man, Reuben, they never learn," said Agnes.

"They have a right to peaceful protest," agreed Reuben, "Go and help them, Henry. I would if I was your age."

"Help them? I don't think the police need my help."

"Tsh, you just don't get it. It doesn't matter what the person believes in. They have a right to their beliefs. My Reuben would have been right over there in his day."

"So, you are commies?"

"No Henry. They have always been our enemies. We hate them as much as you do."

The conversation between the police officers and the protesters seemed to have met a stalemate. Neither were backing down and it appeared this was going nowhere. An atmosphere was growing and could be felt all the way down the alley. Henry watched the situation intently whilst trying to be discreet. The blood ran from his body and his muscles tensed as he witnessed the officers do something that destroyed his lifelong belief in authority in a heartbeat. The one thing no protester or anyone ever wants to see police officers do. They removed their badges.

This was about to get very brutal for the protesters and they didn't seem wise to it. Henry did not like violence. He did not fear it, never wanted to witness it and if he could prevent it in any way, then he would. Henry tentatively moved towards the stand-off but before he got close the action erupted and batons came crashing down on the protester's skulls. What makes an altercation like this nothing like the movies is the fact that when heavy wooden clubs, designed to incapacitate, come crashing down on human skulls, the people collapse to the floor, receive a few more strikes and then are completely out cold. It is quick, it is barbaric and it can have lifelong lasting effects.

Henry stood about twenty yards from two police officers who stood over the bloodied mounds of two protestors. Their attention turned to him. He was doing community work so there was a good chance he was on punishment duty. Nobody would believe the word of a criminal over two officers of the law. He was not welcome here and was about to go the same way as the protesters. The officers approached Henry menacingly.

"Hey Pig, back off." A yell came from down the alley. An aggressive but determined one. The yell came from Agnes. The officers stopped to survey the scene and just find out who else was around. An elderly couple could be more persuasive and were certainly more of a risk to the credibility of the officers than two commie protestors and a criminal. Also, who were they? Whom did they know? Who else was around? The officers decided they had done all they could today. They had cracked the skulls of some commies so they could dine out for free tonight with that story. They were in that circle. They returned their badges to their uniforms and departed the scene. Henry was shaken and slowly made his way back to where the elderly couple were.

"You go back and find your girl. We will see to them," said Reuben gesturing to the students already being aided by Agnes. Henry stumbled back to Lily and filled her in on the events as she soothed him.

"I was very surprised to see you with those two. I just didn't think you would have given them any of your time."

"Why do you say that?"

"Reuben and Agnes? They are the only ones here working as a punishment."

"They are the criminals?" said Henry surprised, "that little old couple?"

"Yes. From what I heard they have been spreading Nazi propaganda."

"But they look so fragile and gentle."

"Everyone has a past Henry."

DATES, DARES AND THE CHAIRMAN OF THE BOARD

It was an evening for lovers. The atmosphere was indescribable but if surrounded by it, in love and with that special person it will encompass you. A warmth like no other. As if the sun itself had taken residence in your soul. That is exactly how Henry felt and this poetry was how he expressed his feelings to Lily. Well, so far, he had only said it in his head and not out loud. He was working up to it. Considering Henry's upbringing taught him zero social skills; he was particularly good at dating. Well, he had only been doing it with Lily but she seemed happy to him. She always seemed happy as long as they were doing something. As long as they were living life. Henry was more than happy to participate as college was the time to have adventures and be a little reckless. You get it out of your system young and then, after graduation, you get the job, the car, the children and the three-bed semi in the suburbs with the white picket fence and perfectly even green lawn.

His mom's words from her last days were always fresh in Henry's mind. Be nice to girls. He was sure it was this but he also felt this seemed a little specific. Maybe he was remembering it wrong. It wasn't even that long ago and here he is trying to recall his mom's last words of advice. Perhaps she said to be nice to everyone and in particular girls. It was definitely about being nice and certainly contained girls. Just be nice to people as they aren't so bad. That will do as a motto and a way of life, thought Henry, holding the door for a couple as he and Lily left a restaurant. But they could have been Nazis or commies. How can they just live so brazen with it? How can you ever know? How come there were so many people out there who have beliefs that conflict with decent society and put people with other beliefs at risk? What about those police officers, if you can't trust the police who can you trust? Jesus, Henry's mind was all over the place.

"I know something that will help you relax," said Lily. She was not blind to the fact Henry was overanalysing everything. One day of doing some good had really left a mark on Henry and if they could go back in time and not volunteer then Lily would have preferred it. Shows what doing good can get you. No, you mustn't think like that she told herself.

"Come on." She took Henry by the hand and dragged him to a night spot off the main road. Confidently strutting forward as if to appear to belong, so nobody would give a moment's thought they were only eighteen. Before entering Henry hesitated and stopped fast. The look on his face was obvious to anyone who knew him, he was questioning right from wrong. His moral compass was spinning and he was working out where it was going to land. It was all just a pointless charade though as he would do whatever it took to please Lily. And Lily liked to be reckless and the feeling of doing things you shouldn't thrilled her. She was in no way bad though. Lily did have a moral compass and would never do anything that could in any way put anyone else in a position of danger or could have negative consequences for random strangers. No, she would just push the lines everyone has before and trying to get served a drink at a bar when underage is a rite of passage. Every parent who tells their child they must never do this has of course done it themselves. Lily knew this and she never had parents.

"I dare you," whispered Lily with a huge grin on her face. Henry's face softened as he lost himself in the high beam of the toothy smirk. Guiding lights to mischief for Henry. He had started to accept they were always going to have this effect on him and even when they did settle down, he would have to often follow the smile to keep her happy. They entered the establishment which had a jazz group performing and walked straight to the bar. It was only a Monday so the place was rather empty. The jazz band had a trumpeter with extremely powerful lungs. He looked like he could inflate a hot air balloon in one blow and the noise he could get out of the brass instrument was very loud and quite screechy. By design of course.

The effect it had on the couple was the bartender struggled to hear them. He hadn't carded them or even questioned their age so it looked like this would be a successful dare and even Henry felt a little excited. As Lily shouted out for two bourbons on the rocks the band came to the end of their song. The noise of a screeching trumpet was suddenly replaced with the noise of a screaming girl wanting liquor. The scream caught the attention of a weary academic whose only pleasure in life was his highly valued moments away from his students. Drinking hard liquor and trying to forget the wrong choices made in his life that led him to being a university professor. Not that it wasn't a well-respected and high-end career, it was just not for him and never had been. Professor Scott wanted to be a pilot, an explorer or a spy but those dreams died when he was suddenly forced to grow up and get married. Still, he loved his son and wouldn't swap him for anything in the world but he did not need students in his bar ruining his drink-fuelled daydreams.

"You can hold those bourbons, Earl," said Professor Scott as he appeared beside the suddenly panicked couple, "Come back when you are twenty-one."

"Oh, is Bourbon alcoholic?" said Lily feigning surprise, "I didn't realise." Professor Scott was having none of it and marched them out of the bar with a severe reprimand and a strict order that they were not to come back in again until they were twenty-one. Henry and Lily knew he wouldn't take it any further and it was just an inconvenience for all they had walked into his bar. Professor Scott knew he wouldn't take it any further as he had only kicked them out since it was his duty of care as their professor, and so expected of him. Anyway, he had tried to get served when he was underage too. Just like everyone else.

With their luck out on the bar front and feeling a little shaken from having been caught by their professor, Henry and Lily felt it may be wiser to opt for more sensible entertainment tonight and agreed on a trip to the cinema. 'The Wreck of the Mary Deare' was still showing and an action-packed film like that was perfect for both of them. Even more so for Lily as she had a thing for the older gentleman, though she wouldn't let on to Henry, and Gary Cooper and Charlton Heston both hit the spot. Walking under all the streetlights, it was clear the evening was brightening up. In fact, it was becoming very bright.

Much brighter than the streetlight's normal illumination. In the night sky, a couple of spotlights crossed each other again and again, drawing attention to a large crowd of people who all decided tonight was a good night to take in a movie. As the couple neared, they realised this was not a surprising queue for the ticket booth but an excited crowd gathered outside. They were all there to try and steal a glimpse of one man. The chairman of the board, Mr Frank Sinatra.

There was no chance the couple would be taking in a movie tonight as the cinema was completely closed to the public. It was a huge event in the Hollywood Diary. Not just any standard premiere which happened most months but the long-awaited release of 'Never So Few.' For the last couple of years, Sinatra had only made two films per year and so his legions of fans were getting less of a fix than they had been. They were out in force tonight, standing behind a red velvet rope. This was as close to the cinema as Henry and Lily could get tonight. Their path blocked by the crowd, the rope, the press and quite clearly the door staff should they try and get by. Accepting defeat Lily turned to head home.

"Where are you going?" asked Henry.

"I don't know but we can't do anything here."

"You failed at your last dare though."

"So?"

Henry gestured to the line of expensive cars dropping off invited socialites who were fillers for important events but, fully aware of this, always felt very important to be part of it. They weren't. The couple were not dressed in a Tuxedo and evening gown, so there was no hope of getting in as guests, but they were smart enough to be part of someone's assistants and there was a gap between two of the cars which would provide cover if a couple of people were to slide through at the right moment.

"It's just a game of dares," said Henry, "I dare you." Lily smiled. That was all she needed to hear and the dare was on. Henry was as much a part of it as her and would have to play his role convincingly. Lily was always so good at inventing a character and completely losing herself in the performance of her creation. She had been keen on theatre all her life and loved to play make-believe but make it real. Henry just knew what Henry knew and that was generally what books had told him. He knew the idea of performance was to play the truth regardless of what it was. So, if he was to convince anyone he was somebody else then he had to fully commit.

The couple waited for the perfect moment when the crowd was distracted by the sudden burst of flashes and rush of security at the arrival of Gina Lolobrigida and darted through the gap between the cars. They positioned themselves in a group behind Miss Lolobrigida, as if part of her entourage, and followed towards the main entrance. As they were about to walk through the huge doors, a large black sleeve thrust in front of them. With a suspicious look, the doorman blocked their path and asked where their passes were. Lily spotted that all members of the entourage were wearing a pass around their necks signifying they were meant to be there. Without missing a beat, Lily's improvisation skills kicked in.

"You are kidding?" she said indignantly.

"Not at all, I—"

The doorman was quickly cut off and shot down as Lily feigned incredulous disgust at the most insulting insinuation ever bestowed on her. The volume and magnitude of this act would have such severe consequences for the man that he was unlikely to work in this town ever again. He may as well have been booking his train back to Idaho because he was not going to recover from this in any way. The shame he must feel to know he must return to his hometown as a failure. This is exactly what Lily wanted the doorman to think but unfortunately, though she was very sincere in her performance, he was quite used to chancers trying to get passed him and very secure in his job.

"Where is your pass?" he asked firmly as he cut off Lily mid-flow.

"For crying out loud. We are Sinatra's people. We don't have a pass as we were swapped in last minute as his other assistants dropped out."

"Why did they drop out?"

"I don't know. I'm not their keeper. Why don't you go and ask Mr Sinatra?" said Lily, "he sure loves being disturbed at such events."

"He isn't here yet. Why don't you know that?"

This approach seemed to have backfired on Lily. She had presumed he would already be there and the doorman would in no way go and disturb Sinatra at an event. She could then play on his insecurities. All she needed was for him to doubt himself just the smallest amount and then she would hit him with the question of what kind of person in their right mind would use Frank Sinatra's name for something like this. He wasn't someone to cross. Lily had a reckless nature. They were at an impasse as a large black limousine pulled up and Old Blue Eyes stepped out to the largest of cheers. The people had come for him and he was making sure they got him. He knew how to play a crowd and he knew the value of the fans. So, when he approached the entrance where Lily and Henry had been shoved back behind the doorman and Lily wriggled through to tell Sinatra that they had made it and all was good, he just thought she was a well-wisher supposed to be this side of the rope. Which is why he responded so cordially.

"Glad to hear it, kid. I will see you inside," and in he walked.

Lily glared at the doorman. He was starting to break. He heard clearly what Sinatra had said to this girl and he did not want to annoy Sinatra or his days around here really would have been numbered. The story seemed legit and the huge-framed doorman, the gatekeeper to the rich and famous humbly opened the door and apologised as he gestured the couple in. They felt like royalty. Like all children who find themselves in a situation where they are surrounded by adults with reputations for behaving irresponsibly and caring little, they were free to blend in and so headed straight to the open champagne bar.

***

Henry was smiling. A big beaming and uncontrollable smile. It went from a grin to a smirk to the toothless gum lip of the elderly and back again. He was looking at Lily and she was not fairing much better. Her eyes could only be described as squiffy and her hand was constantly being employed as an emergency giggle muffler. Neither of them could have told you how much champagne they drank that night and it was premium quality. And unlimited. The bus came along the street and Henry and Lily had to compose themselves or they were not getting on. They held their breath, stood tall and adorned their faces with a serious look. It was clear they were a little worse for wear but the bus driver, much like most others, didn't really care. The conductor was a different adversary entirely. He got on the bus at the corner of Sunset and slowly worked his way along the passengers. He didn't look at them or speak to them any more than necessary for his position and was happier when the passengers would pre-empt his request and have their tickets held out ready.

Henry and Lily did not have tickets. They had got on in a rush as the next bus wasn't until tomorrow and they were not thinking straight. They were not the first people to ever do this, drunk or not, and the transport companies always had an alternative plan for this situation. Henry had his wallet and could just buy two tickets from the conductor. Problem solved.

"Tickets please," said the conductor in a tone that showed his frustration at having to ask. Henry drew his wallet out and dug inside until he withdrew a five dollar bill. More than enough but he couldn't manage counting change at this moment so would trust the bus conductor to do that.

"Tickets please," said the conductor in an even frostier manner and his annoyance was increased when Henry once again wafted the bill in his face.

"Not money. Tickets. Tickets. You, kids, are all the same. Forgotten to get your ticket before you got on. Think that's fine. Think I will sort it out for you. No. Not on my bus. You think I am going to wipe your asses for you?" a much more sinister inflection coated his words. "Looks like I better call the police," he sniffed the air around them, "and have you been drinking?" he smirked, "this isn't going to go down well for you."

Whatever it was that put the conductor in such a mood that night, or perhaps a series of events over a period of time, or maybe he had been dealt a whole shitty hand, Henry was not going to let him take it out on them. Alcohol had a strange effect on Henry that he only discovered that night, it made him more reactionary than Lily and also allowed him to care less for all potential consequences. The bus pulled up at the next stop and before the people could climb on, Henry grabbed Lily by her hand, pushed the red-faced conductor aside and jumped out the door. Lily came flying after like a kite in his hand.

They were out the door and down the street before any of the other passengers could memorise their faces and before the slow-footed and slow-witted conductor had any hope of chasing them. They may not have got all the way home but when they ran into the park and found themselves staring in wonderment at the midnight sheen of stars laying restfully across the tranquil pond, they felt it had all been fate. This setting was so perfect. Like straight out of a novel. They sat down on the bank and looked out across the glistening water.

"Will we always have adventures?" asked Lily. Henry smiled, wrapped his arm around her and pulled her gently to rest in his nook.

"Even after graduation?" Henry pulled her in tighter and kissed her gently on the forehead.

"And more games and dares?" Henry caressed her cheek and tenderly kissed her lips.

"Well then, I dare you to love me," said Lily.

"I already dare," replied Henry as he took his love in arms and they softly sank into the grassy banks and their embrace.

ANOTHER DOOR OPENS

August 1962, California, US.

Henry had been staring at the officially stamped envelope for at least thirty minutes. As if he could determine the sentences within said exactly what he wanted through this ritual. It was also through nerves. He had been waiting for this day since the first time he discovered what communists were. All the abuse he had suffered as a child and the destruction to his mother it had all caused. He had worked hard. He had suffered and he had toiled. This was the well-deserved pay-off he had coming his way but what if he didn't get the answer he wanted? No, that would be foolish, thought Henry, I have everything they need and look for. I am a perfect fit.

"If you don't open it, I will," said Lily as she playfully made for the envelope. She was feeling the tension just as much as she was waiting to be able to sing about what her man did and how proud she was of him. Of course, it wouldn't actually be wise to advertise this line of work and Lily would need this explained to her and the possible repercussions of loose lips through pride. Lily was reckless but she was in no way stupid.

Nearly three thousand miles away across the US, in an office in Arlington, a recruitment process was being concluded. From the vast number of applicants received annually from graduates all across the nation, the list had been filtered down to the very best candidates brimming with the perfect mix of subservience, learning potential and prerequisite skills. The prerequisite skills in this line of work could vary between the bullet-pointed necessities of at least one second language, though one was never going to get you through this process against others with at least three or four, to the between-the-line desired benefits to the employer such as having limited family. No living family was solid gold for an applicant and may well get him offered a position regardless of the other skills. He could learn the rest and was in no rush to ever leave as he has nowhere to return to. Perfect material.

Henry's application had gone through this process in the last few months. This was not the first envelope he had received but he knew it would be the last. One way or another, this envelope contained his future or lack thereof. There are many stages to this recruitment. The system must be precise and nothing can slip through, but of course, things always do. Henry's file had passed through many hands as it would either be green-lit or red-crossed. It had landed on the desk of final deliberation. A standard desk in the office in Arlington that housed an in-tray, an out-tray, a cigarette lighter, scotch in the drawer, a pile of files in the centre and an inscrutable son-of-a-bitch looking for any reason to destroy the dreams of the young. The file on top showed Henry's image in the top left and another file paperclipped to it displayed the name, William Miller. A stamp came crashing down on the file, dripping in red ink, leaving the word rejected planted across the application of Henry Miller. The accompanying notes simply said 'Communist Connections' and were signed by Special Agent Croft.

**

A glass of bourbon, with two near-melted cubes of ice, had been sitting full for a while. It had been looked at, it had been stared at, it had been scrutinised and investigated from every conceivable angle. It had been sniffed a couple of times and a tentative lip had serviced the glass rim. Yet still, the glass remained at approximately the same level of liquor, bar the water from the ice cube, as it was when the bartender served it. Henry was lost in it. He could not quite compute what had actually occurred and what would happen next. He was seeking answers in the drink but not in the way most do. He just stared at his reflection amidst the treacle-coloured bourbon glass. Hoping for an answer from a mute oracle. Everything he had ever learned had been for this future. Everything he hoped for was based on this fundamental position of employment and the opportunity to do something positive for the greater good. It was also the only way he could envisage removing the eternal chip from his shoulder and make up for his childhood.

"Try not to think about it," said Lily with a sympathetic hand on Henry's shoulder. She had felt the crushing blow as much as he had when they opened the envelope a little over an hour ago. She wasn't feeling in any way good about it but had only been hopeful of this ambition for Henry once she met him. Henry had this dream since the moment he could dream.

"You have so much to offer. Screw them."

"It's bullshit. He was at D-Day," growled Henry.

"I know. He was a hero. They all were," replied Lily as she gave Henry a tight hug. She had never expected to be involved in such a melancholic situation wearing a mortar board and gown. This is a party and she needed to get Henry to snap out of it. He could growl and snarl and moan and grieve later and then once that was out of the system make his next plans. Until then they were there to celebrate and see where the night took them.

"He was a hero," agreed Henry and finally downed his drink. Professor Scott approached with three more glasses and a twinkle in his eye. He was at least two sheets to the wind and would clearly hit three very soon.

"So, what next for you two lovebirds?"

"World domination," joked Lily.

"You are language students, not political superpowers. Well, whatever you do, make better choices than I did."

"You have a great job Professor."

"Ha. I had no choice. One mistake when I was young and drunk and I have been stuck with her ever since. I had dreams, but, oh well, what I am saying is never give up on your dreams. I think that is it."

"What if your dreams are already dead," said a melancholic Henry.

"At twenty-one? Give me a break." He slaps Henry on the shoulder and Henry forces a smile as the professor looks back at his table.

"Look at them all. So stuffy. So boring, so devoid of life. Oh, I wish I sat where you two did. Look, I have one final piece of advice for you before you go out into the world. Make bold moves. In life, no matter where you are, who you are with or what is going on, always remember, you only get one go at it."

And with that, University was over.

"Just one go, Henry," said Lily and raised her glass. Henry's mood had surprisingly been lifted by the professor's drunken pep talk. Maybe not quite the reckless abandon ideals of the 'you only live once' brigade that Henry was sure would have hit home with Lily, but more the fact that he wasn't in any way stuck. He wasn't being forced by social stigma to act in any particular way or progress in any standard path. He had gone through all that when he was young. Society was not necessarily something you should permit to dictate your life. As long as you weren't hurting anyone then find your own path and he could. It was a sudden realisation that he hadn't lost his dreams or his chance at all he wanted, he had been given a greater opportunity. He had been given freedom.

Henry raised his glass to meet Lily's and toasted to the future in French. It was the beginning of a game they had played on and off since they met. Randomly conversing with each other in many languages to see who could stump who first and they also liked to watch the reactions of the people around them. Usually, they were in awe. This is what Henry and Lily perceived the looks to represent but there was equally a high chance that the looks were condemnations from others to the self-indulgent and smug behaviour the game exhibited.

Lily toasted back to the future using her German. A conversation of short back and forth sprung forward with Russian, Spanish, Italian and Portuguese, though the last few have such similarities the couple would possibly call a forfeit dare if over-used. They would use Chinese and Japanese from time to time though they were in no way fluent. They had just toyed with these languages together whilst competing in this game. They did not take any lectures on them. They just seemed to absorb languages so well that everything they heard or read just stuck. Once it was in, it was always in.

They spoke of the future; they spoke of adventure and they spoke of love. Everything they said they would do was always prepositioned with the word 'we'. They were a unit and would always move forward as one. At a junction in their lives where they could do anything, go anywhere and be anyone. The bourbon was relaxing and Henry was in a much better mood now. They toasted to freedom and opportunity and at that moment it came knocking.

A well-dressed man, in a tailored suit carrying a briefcase, interrupted by telling them they made a beautiful couple. Normally a well-received comment but not when it is said in French and repeated in German, Spanish and Russian. This interruption was designed to make it clear the conversation intruder had been eavesdropping on their whole conversation. All students at the graduation party could speak two languages with some speaking three but none could compete with Henry and Lily when it came to being multilingual. Who the hell did he think he was?

"Apologies for the intrusion," said the interloper in an upper-class British accent, "permit me to continue in English as I have used up most of my foreign languages with that one sentence."

"Arrogant English prick," said Lily in Russian so she and Henry could enjoy their private code without the arrogant English prick understanding them. The man seemed to react with a spit of his drink on hearing these words but was adamant he did not understand a word of it. The timing of his reaction must have been a mere coincidence.

"Allow me to introduce myself, my name is Stan and I am here to recruit new employees from language graduates. I go around to a lot of these events and just listen in for a bit and see if I can gauge the standard and number of languages a graduate can speak and then hone in on the multilinguists like yourself."

"Very flattering," said Henry, "may I ask why you don't set up at the graduation fairs like most employers?"

"What I offer is not a career so much as an opportunity. A year out before you settle down into your lifelong career. So, for this reason, I'm not permitted to set up at the fairs."

"Sounds sceptical," said Henry.

"Like a gap year?" said Lily.

"Yes, just like that. We find a lot of graduates want to take a year to do something different and have a break instead of jumping straight from study to work. There is nothing to be sceptical about. It is just facilitating corporate investment events all around Europe. A chance to travel, see a bit of the world and then come back and go into your chosen fields."

"Europe?" squealed Lily.

"All over," replied Stan.

"I apologise for being a little standoffish with you. Just a little bad news earlier. I am Henry and this is Lily."

With introductions fully made the three of them discussed the opportunity further. Stan explained this was not a lifelong choice or a career decision and he explained that it was not something that got offered to everyone. What they look for is the best of the graduates. The people with the most languages had the greatest value because they could converse with guests and investors in various countries. With the European languages that Henry and Lily had demonstrated, whilst playing their game, they would be considered highly skilled and extremely desirable. Anyway, they could always leave after the first event if it wasn't for them. Nobody was holding them prisoner, joked Stan. The decision was entirely theirs of course, but what did they have to lose by trialling an event?

"Well, I hope to get a yes from you but I will only know if you turn up. The offer is out there and, if it is a no, then I wish you all the best whatever you choose but, hopefully, I see you Monday week in Monte Carlo." With that, Stan finished his drink, picked up his briefcase and left. He did not approach any other graduates and this did not go unnoticed by Lily. Stan made sure of that.

"Monaco Henry," said Lily, "this is adventure."

"I'm not sure Lil, something felt off with him."

"He is just British; they are all like that I bet. Come on Henry, we only get one go at life, remember?" Henry knew this was adventure and he had promised Lily it. It was only a trial event and they could come home if it wasn't for them. A little travel did excite him though. He had never been to Monaco before. He had never left the country before. Lily sat next to him beaming a pleading smile. They both knew which way this would go.

THE FIRST JOB

August 1962, Nice, France.

It was a beautiful summer night on the Cote d'Azur when Henry and Lily flew into Nice airport. The temperature was in the low twenties and the sun was setting perfectly, leaving a warm shine across everything it touched. A slight coastal breeze made it feel as though they had arrived in paradise. In some ways they had. Neither had ever left the States before, so the novelty of being in a foreign land was not wasted on them. From the moment they entered the arrivals lounge the excitement they had felt became a reality. It was the little differences that really made it. The posters and signs in French and the fashions adorning the people in the airport. The women were so chic with their large sunglasses and chiffon scarves and the men so debonair in their summer tailored suits. They could see how Stan would fit in well here.

They felt even more special when they saw their names on a sign being held by a chauffeur. After introducing themselves, which may have been unnecessary as the wide-eyed looks on their face made it quite clear they didn't quite belong here yet, they were being led to their vehicle. Instead of exiting to a car park, they were taken up some stairs. Perhaps car parks were built at the top of airports in Europe they mused. The wonderment continued as they reached the roof and realised it homed the helipads and their chauffeur was a pilot. Flying up the eastern coast of Southern France leaving a dark shadow scything over the Mediterranean, the coupled gripped each other's hand, continually directing each other's attention towards a new view to take in. Everything from the architecture of Promenade d'Anglais to the boats lolling on the calm sea. This moment was one they would never forget and they knew at once they had made the right choice.

They landed on top of a beautiful tall old building and descended only one floor to the penthouse where Stan was waiting. They entered with their jaws still on the floor, as they pretty much had been since the moment they arrived in France. It was even more glamour and luxury and Stan certainly suited the surroundings. He held court in the middle of the room as a butler brought forward a tray of champagne flutes. He took them off and passed them one by one to the couple.

"Welcome to the high life," said Stan. Henry and Lily said nothing. Not through being rude, just because they were simply trying to compute it all in their heads. It was all so much and that is exactly how Stan wanted them to feel. Every part of this journey was part of his show. All designed to impress and make every single recruit believe they had made the right choice. Once they had touched down in Nice, the show had begun. This was the life for them. It was one big show.

"Let's get down to business. The job is tomorrow evening and you two need to be briefed and ready." Stan opened his briefcase, making sure nobody saw the combination or full contents, reached in and extracted two files. One for Henry and one for Lily entitled Monsieur and Madame Gavriete. The couple opened the folders to find their own faces looking back at them. In an official promotional prospectus for the event. Their images but the names of Monsieur and Madame Gavriete tagged onto them.

"Please read the information," said Stan as the couple looked to him for confirmation it wasn't a mistake. Monsieur and Madame Gavriete cordially invite you to an opportunity to be part of the future, began the prospectus. The Gavrietes were an incredibly wealthy family with ownership of large amounts of infrastructure within the oil industry. The current Monsieur Gavriete had only recently inherited the position and business through the death of his father and he wanted the feeling of karma that could be offered by philanthropy. Something his father would never have considered. He was still a businessman though and so he saw it charitable to open his ventures to entrepreneurs as investment opportunities. The model of an unselfish, modern business mogul. Capitalism in its finest form and something Henry thought highly of. Stan could see approval growing on Henry's face as he read more and more about the Gavrietes. They were his sort of people but why did they have a photo of Henry and Lily?

"The modern mega-rich are often reclusive people, for security and standard of life really, so it is quite common at these events to have stand-ins play the role. So how are your French accents?" asked Stan. Lily looked excited but Henry was a little more reserved. Even if they are reclusive, surely people know what they look like and would accept advisors at these events instead of the actual Gavrietes. Something just didn't sit right with Henry. It was only a trial job though and, seeing how keen Lily looked, he would keep his reservations to himself until after the event.

Trying to keep an open mind, the group said their goodnights and Henry and Lily were escorted to their premium suite where they boned up on all information contained in the files and polished their regional French accents. They had dinner brought to the suite. It was some of the finest fayre the South of France had to offer and then they sank into their enormous four-poster bed where Lily, surrounded by such opulent luxury, drifted off quickly. Henry was wide awake. There was something about this job, something about Stan, something that just kept niggling at him.

The event was in full swing in the most decadent of rooms Western society could offer. Elaborately designed and decorated to be a middle finger to the Eastern Bloc. The heaviest of cream drapes flowed from the fifteen-foot ceilings on either side of exquisite 18th-century Louis XV regency windows. Gold trim laced the walls as an ostentatious equivalent to a dado rail. Gold-laced royal blue wallpaper below the rail and expensive paint above designed to be a mere backdrop for every painting adorning the walls, so perfectly presented with their lights tailored to each.

Event staff dressed in tuxedos mingled with guests, offering a platter of Dom Perignon, Russian Caviar, Italian white truffle and Serbian Pule cheese. There was a lot of female event staff also present, in the most divine cocktail dresses, but they were not offering any of the fine cuisine, they were there to offer possibility. Possibility which would encourage all the male dignitaries, power players, tycoons and wealthy wannabes to drink, enjoy and ultimately invest. After they had got the investment, the planted ladies would slip a small dose into the guest's drink which would leave them with about another hour of mingling before they must rush off to bed immediately as they suddenly felt tired. Thinking they had just taken advantage of the free food and drink a little too much they wouldn't question it and then the ladies were safe from possible harassment.

A very questionable operation but a lesser man would not have put such precautions in place to protect the female staff. A lesser man would have just expected them to oblige in whatever whim the investor may have. Stan did look after his people, in his own way.

A group of wall street types, all slicked hair and expensive watches designed to capture attention and ignorant of the meaning of subtlety, stood with Madame Gavriete as she explained the investment offer available. Lily's accent was perfect and she had transitioned into the wife of the wealthy French tycoon flawlessly. The group hung on to her every word. Perhaps the drink was making them more susceptible to the idea or perhaps it was aided by the provocative choice of dress Stan had supplied but either way they were putty in her hands.

Henry was finding it quite easy to convey the offer also. For all his moralistic digs from his conscience, he knew that he had promised to see this through and his concerns may be misplaced. He doubted it but the sensible thing was to have all the information first. He began conversing with a group of delegates from Saudi Arabia, an attaché of King Saud, always looking for investment opportunities to advance the wealth of the kingdom. They were very keen to know more about the background of the Gavrietes as they had never heard of them prior to this event. Henry was prepared for this question though as the answer had been included in the file as it was likely to be asked. Henry had thought this a little suspicious but the answer seemed believable. The Arabs were aware of a historical family of influence in France but they had faded out around the middle of the 19th century.

"That was my great-grandfather Claude whom you last recall from history. My grandfather had a suspicious and almost paranoid disposition and so when he inherited, he installed divisions working for the family under different names so that he could be left in peace."

"A bit like the mafia?" joked one of the Arabs.

"Not quite," laughed Henry. "We are trying to bring back transparency."

As Henry left the group, having secured the investment target bestowed on him, he couldn't help but question how he was expected to claim the modern Gavrietes were trying to be more transparent whilst, according to Stan, they were recluses and that is why Henry and Lily were playing them. It just didn't add up. Something felt off.

A Russian General had been enjoying the food whilst observing the room from the distance afforded to the corner of such a large space. An intelligent man, he abstained from drinking any of the champagne as he wanted to keep a straight head during proceedings of such great value. He could relate to the Arabs a lot more than the Wall Street show-offs. If anything was untoward at an event like this, the Wall Street types would be the perfect marks. He had watched for long enough and evaluated everything was entirely above board and a real opportunity was on offer, so approached Madame Gavriete.

Lily had also evaluated the situation and had quickly concluded this was a scenario for flirting. It was clear the General would be responsive as he greeted her with a kiss on the hand and a compliment on Madame Gavriete's appearance. This encounter had not escaped the attention of Monsieur Gavriete and Henry was beginning to feel a little annoyed by the spectacle developing in front of him. He knew he would be in trouble if he was to interrupt as a jealous lover but then considered the perspective of Monsieur Gavriete. He was him. Whether it was coming from Gavriete or Henry, it was completely acceptable and conceivable that the man about to approach the General and Madame Gavriete could be a little ticked off by the flirting.

"It offers the kind of return that could promote a General to a President," said Lily as Madame Gavriete in intentionally imperfect Russian.

"Perfect pronunciation," responded the General in his mother tongue and kissed her hand again. This was too much for Henry and he could keep his distance no longer. Approaching the conversation, his expression was very clear and the General could see he may have overstepped the mark but he felt secure in the knowledge it was unlikely Gavriete had understood a word of the Russian conversation. High breeding like his did not learn Russian as a second language but Madame Gavriete had married into the family and so had learned languages that may be a benefit to her future.

"Your wife is as beautiful as she is intelligent. You are a very lucky man Monsieur Gavriete," said the General, in French, attempting to appease his host.

"Perfect Pronunciation," responded Henry, in Russian, as Monsieur Gavriete and this was enough to startle the General who realised he had underestimated the monsieur and the message was clear. Back off.

The event concluded and once all investments were collected and signed off the staff were invited to finish off the remaining food and drink. It isn't many jobs that allow their waiters to polish off thousand dollar bottles of Dom Perignon. Stan did look after his people. Henry and Lily shared a couple of bottles with Stan. They were all quite tipsy and their words were slurred. Stan could not hide his eagerness to hear their thoughts.

"So, how did you find it?"

"It was such fun," said Lily.

"And you Henry?"

"'Lil, could you please grab some more drinks for us?" Lily went to get more champagne for the already rather intoxicated group. Henry watches until she is out of earshot.

"Listen, Stan, it isn't for us," said Henry with the clarity of sobriety, "I thank you for the opportunity but we will be returning home tomorrow. Please don't try and talk me around as you did promise we could try it out on a trial basis and we have done that. We have given it a full go and waited until the end to make a considered decision."

"I thought you were drunk," said Stan.

"No, like everything else here, it was all an act." This amused Stan and he toasted Henry.

"I understand and I appreciate your honesty. I thank you for giving it a go and let's enjoy these drinks before we go our separate ways." Lily returned with a bottle of champagne and the trio settled in for a while. They talked about the people who came to the event and joked about what it would be like to have such money to invest or even play with. Together they daydreamed of the glamorous high life and admit it does have a huge appeal but the ethical cost is too dear.

"I don't have anywhere near as much money as these people but capitalism and ambition mean maybe one day I can," said Stan.

"That does sound good to me. You reap what you sow," said Lily.

"As long as I have Lil then I would be happy to live on the breadline," said Henry as Lily groaned at the corniness of the comment though, of course, she loved the sentiment.

"You reap what you sow," toasted Henry and they clinked glasses.

"You must excuse me now as I have some final event details to attend to. Enjoy the champagne, the food and the rest of the evening. It will all be thrown if not consumed so go crazy." Stan places a further fresh bottle with the couple and bids them goodnight.

***

Henry had been up a while. They continued drinking the free champagne into the early hours and he had a sore head. At least he was up though as Lily was laying on the bed almost comatose. This was the reason he was up and she wasn't. He knew there was no stirring her right now which worked perfectly for him. He wasn't convinced she would agree with him to leave after this trial but he knew it was the right thing for both. So, he had decided to get all the packing done and when she awoke later on, he would say that Stan had already left and would be in contact at some point. He didn't like the idea of lying to Lily but then again it was for their greater good and so he could justify it.

Everything was packed and ready to go. All that was left to do was to wake Lily, send her to the shower and let her get ready in her time. No rush, all calm. An easy journey. He opened the room safe to collect their tickets, money and passports but the safe was bare. He was adamant that they hadn't retrieved them yet, unless, they had done it the night before. It was all such a haze but quite likely which would mean they would be in the luggage somewhere. Which would mean he would need to unpack everything and start again. He slammed the safe door waking Lily. Henry explained the situation but Lily was also none the wiser. Her memory was just as bad as Henry's from the previous night. The couple slowly started to unpack their luggage and scour their bags. Every pocket, every compartment, between each item and in their document wallets. This was unlike them. Well unlike Henry. He would have had all these items located together and, if not in the safe, then they would be in a document wallet. Securely in locked luggage but together and easily locatable for them.

About ten minutes passed and the couple reluctantly concluded the worst had happened.

"We have been robbed," said Henry on the phone to the front desk, "send the Gendarmes s'il vous plait." It was only a few moments later when there was a knock on the door. That was quick, thought Henry, before considering it was more likely someone from the Hotel to obtain further details before calling the police. When he opened the door, it was neither the police nor the hotel. It was Stan.

"Oh Stan, we have been robbed," cried Lily.

"Oh dear," said Stan "what did they take?"

"Money, tickets, passports, everything to travel with. We are stuck," said Henry, "we have to just wait for the police." The trio sat down and waited for the knock on the door and the authorities who would be able to resolve this situation or at least assist the couple. Ten minutes passed, twenty minutes, thirty minutes and nothing. Henry was getting impatient. The longer they waited the less likely the crook would be found or more importantly the items which would leave the couple stuck in France indefinitely.

"Oh, forget this. I am going to call the police myself." Henry picked up the phone and started to dial as Stan calmly pushed down the hook switch and cut the call.

"I wouldn't do that if I was you," said Stan in a very matter-of-fact way. Henry looked at Stan and realised his gut feeling had always been right. This man was no good.

"And why's that Stan?"

"Because I stole your passports."

"Even better reason to call them then," said Henry as he attempted to dial before Stan pushed down the hook switch again.

"How are you going to explain your actions to them?"

"Our actions? What actions? We haven't done anything wrong."

"Haven't you?" said Stan before explaining the true details of what they had involved themselves in. Monsieur and Madame Gavriete do not exist and never did. When the investors realise they have been duped they will not be happy people and nobody wants to upset power brokers in America or the Saudi King or a Russian General amongst others. A lot of powerful people have been conned and the only faces they can relate to this swindle belong to Henry and Lily. In case they did fancy attempting to get home and have their government assist them all they would find waiting would be life in prison. Their passports were currently on their way to the FBI with a detailed breakdown of the structure of the event. Every single border patrol and customs officer would be on alert to await your re-entry attempt. Interpol would be all over Europe looking for Henry and Lily. There was nowhere to hide.

"I can offer you an out though?" said Stan.

"An out? How the hell can we have an out? Once we are in public, we put ourselves at risk of being recognised," argued Henry.

"Not at all. I changed the photos in your passports. They still contain your names, addresses, personal details and all that, so you cannot simply be yourselves back there anymore. You can be someone here though."

"Yeah, and who is that exactly."

"Anyone. Anyone we come up with. I can make you anyone at all."

"I don't understand, what is happening," asked Lily.

"He tricked us Lil, he scammed us. Now we work for him."

"You don't work for me. You never did. You were hand-picked by the organisation as you have something to offer. The same as I was before you and others will be after. There is no stopping it."

Stan picked up his briefcase and sheltered it as he entered the number and opened the case. He retrieved two passports and handed them to the couple. Lily studied hers. Henry barely gave a glance and threw his to the floor.

"What's this?" demanded Henry.

"The only real opportunity. Look, I am sorry for how the system works and how we find ourselves here, I truly am. But your only other option is to try and make your way back to the US, hoping every law department and jurisdiction throughout Europe and into the US believes your story or is at least willing to investigate your claims. Do you really trust the integrity of the authorities?"

A few years ago, Henry would have said entirely but after the events of the little cleaning day, he had come to realise not everyone in uniform could be trusted to serve and protect.

"Stay with me. You will be safe I promise," said Stan as he picked up Henry's new passport and passed it back to him. Henry snatched it from Stan and opened it to see another new name next to his photo.

"Hannes Volz," questioned Henry.

"And Agathe Kreiner," added Lily, "you have made me two years older."

"Well next time I will make you two years younger mon amour," said Stan.

"I wanted to do good in life. That was all. I wanted to join the CIA and aid the greater good," cried Henry.

"But they didn't want you and since you were rejected for communist connections you became hot property to the organisation."

"How did you know that?"

"The organisation knows everything Henry, that's how they catch us all."

"He wasn't a commie, he was a hero."

"Anything you say Henry, but here we are," said Stan, "look it never sits well with me, the MO of the organisation but I have no control over it." Stan reaches back into his briefcase and pulls out a couple of document folders for the couple. "I truly hope I see Herr Volz and Fraulein Kreiner in Vienna but if I don't, I wish you the best of luck with Interpol and the FBI. Sincerely."

PARTY PROPAGANDA

September 1962, Vienna, Austria.

Winter settled on the ground as the plane skidded along the runway at Vienna International in Schwechat. It had not been the most pleasant of flights, due to the changing seasons, and with Henry and Lily being very new to international travel the turbulence had left them nauseous. Of course, it was exciting at first but once the attack on their sinuses kicked in, their bodies were unused to the assault and never learned how to counteract it. They were very glad to stumble off that plane and into the new airport buildings. Something about new things, relatively new since the building was only a couple of years old, had a way of making you feel positive. If you felt defeated and something new arose, it offered inspiration to push on. A two-year-old building caused this effect on Henry and Lily and, whilst it excited Lily to see what came next, it worried Henry about what could come next and reminded him they were not there of their own free will.

As they walked the tunnel approaching the terminal, they soon saw a large group of police officers and uniformed officials waiting at the end. Police uniforms were easily recognisable, and Interpol agents were as conspicuous as the men in black at the Berkeley rallies. Stan was wrong. He clearly wasn't as good as he thought at forgery and certainly not smarter than The Man. Thoughts rushed Henry's mind at a rapid pace. Was there a different way? Should they run? How can he get Lily out of here? There was no chance of success in a physical escape, leaving emotional pleas or lengthy explanations as their only resource. Why would they listen though? Who are they to the authorities but an arrest and accreditation at work? They had been spotted.

The police started to move towards them urgently as their hands flicked open holsters and removed sidearms. The lead officer blew his whistle and everyone stopped still. Henry's heart was beating like the hooves of a racehorse and Lily had cottoned on by the sudden force she felt from the squeeze of Henry's hand and the warm damp of his sweat. As the police neared the couple, they slowly raised their arms ready for the inevitable but the officers ran straight past them. Straight past to the man behind who was already face down on the floor, cuffs on his wrists and an illegal firearm confiscated from his jacket. Standing in the terminal where the officers had huddled was a driver holding a sign. They were not recognised by anyone or paid any attention to. To all observers, they were Herr Volz and Fraulein Kreiner as that is what the sign said.

Outside, waiting in a black limousine was a subdued Stan. He was lacking his normal pzazz and Lily enquired about it immediately. He almost looked depressed and, although she wouldn't admit it to Henry, she quite liked him. He didn't seem the 'bad sort' Henry thought he was and she was genuinely concerned to see him like this. Henry couldn't care less. As quick as Lily had asked Stan how he was, Henry cut her off by demanding to get straight to the point and know what they were being forced to do tonight.

"Political," said Stan and handed the couple a file each before immediately returning to the window he had been staring out.

"Is this all?" asked Henry as he looked at the thin file that contained only information about the German identities but nothing about the job.

"You will receive the rest of the info when we arrive."

"What a waste of time, we could be—"

"Oh, don't start Henry. Not tonight. Not this time. Just do the job. Please." For a moment Henry felt for Stan too. His tone and body language seemed to suggest the demoralisation of a broken man. Something weighed heavy on his mind and Henry decided he would make it easy for Stan tonight. He would do exactly what is expected without complaint, attitude or disapproval. He managed to stick to this, for about five minutes until the limousine pulled up at a geometric concrete compound decorated with red banners adorning a hammer and sickle motif.

"Communists?" balked Henry.

"Yes Henry, communists."

"Well, I hope we are bringing them down."

Stan let out a long sigh. He knew this was going to happen. In the brief time he spent drinking with Henry in Monte Carlo, he had gotten to know how anti-communist Henry was. He knew his background; he knew about his hero father and he knew about the terror of communism. It was all Henry had ranted about after celebrating capitalism and the wonderful Gavrietes. Surely, his opinion of the non-existent couple designed to separate the rich from their wealth must have changed. Perhaps denting his strong convictions and belief in capitalism. It was all irrelevant right then. Stan had to get Henry in line before they arrived and time was not on his side.

"No, no, no, no, no. It is against everything I believe in. Politically and morally."

"Don't give me this shit Henry. They are the client and this is the job. You do what you are paid for and leave your morals at the door."

"Paid? Like we chose to be here in the first place?"

"And I did?" growled Stan as he and Henry stared at each other. There was no time for a full-on debate or argument about values and hardship and Stan knew this. They must fall in line and do the job as their lives depended on it. They needed to realise the real danger of the predicament they were in. Stan knew he needed to be more heavy-handed with whoever he handled for the organisation but it did not come naturally, and people could see right through him. Henry continued to stare at Stan in defiance but Stan's stare soon shifted to a plea and Henry's stance softened. Something in Stan's eyes told Henry much more than words ever could. It was desperation and fear. A great fear. Henry felt nothing for Stan but pity. He thought he was a weak criminal being controlled and probably his weaknesses were what got him in this position in the first place. A chancer. A common opportunist thief and conman. That was all he was. Still, Henry pitied him.

"Ok," said Henry.

The grand room was alive with guests socialising and mingling as they all tried to establish where they stood within the event hierarchy and whether the person, they spoke to offered any worth to them. Or was there someone better just over their shoulder? Lily was in the thick of it giving a fine performance as Fraulein Kreiner embodying a representation of socialist beauty. Acting like she was of the people and for the people. The flirting was something Henry was begrudgingly learning to accept. He had received a stern ticking off from Stan for his jealous interruption of the Russian General and kept reminding himself it was just an act. Lily knew Henry was struggling with it and would always find a safe moment to give him a reassuring look. Just the slight upturn of the corner of her mouth whilst her marks were distracted by her legs. She was evidently enjoying the work and took to the whole situation with worrying ease. It was her reckless nature taking over. Something that could eventually get her in even more trouble than they were already in, though Lily didn't seem to notice or concern herself with it. Henry worried enough for the both of them.

"She seems to be getting into the swing of things," said Stan as he and Henry observed the room from the side.

"When can we leave?" asked Henry.

"When they let you."

"When will that be?" Stan ignored the question as he knew he had no answer and didn't want to lie. He thought of asking Henry to consider the fact that they had never let Stan go yet and so more than likely the couple were in for a long stay. He bit his tongue as he saw no benefit in a melancholy Henry and so waited in silence and feigned distraction long enough to naturally move things on.

"Have you learned the info?"

"Yes."

"Are you going to pass it along verbatim?" asked Stan but got no response. Henry was now trying to allow this moment to pass without having to give an answer and possibly lie.

"Henry?" demanded Stan. He could not let this slide without an answer. They could be in a lot of trouble if Henry let his beliefs get the better of him.

"Henry?"

"Yes. Verbatim," snapped Henry as he turned into the room, "you know one day I will run."

"I know. But will she?" said Stan as he watched him go. Stan found reassurance in the transformation unveiled in the short journey into the event. Henry had been learning, from Lily or TV or maybe reading, the art of acting and his characterisation detail was down to a tee. Just a simple slide of his body weight onto his right leg had raised his posture to give the appearance of an efficient and upstanding East German citizen. The reassurance in Henry's abilities hid the turmoil behind Stan's eyes.

Stan had been mingling himself. It was no coincidence that the guests he had conversed with happened to be in earshot of Henry or Lily. Listening to Lily hold court was like hearing a master manipulator mould putty in whatever way pleased her whims. It amused Stan how she could play with these men's emotions or libido. Whichever it was, she was very much in control. Fools, he thought. Why were men so often led by their basest desires or dreams of some idyllic retirement with a young beauty? Sure she would enjoy the boring existence these people could just about muster. They didn't know Lily at all, but then again, they were talking to Fraulein Kreiner and they didn't know her either. Stan knew her and it made him feel superior to all these caps, shoulder pips and dignitaries. It was nice for Stan to have a moment feeling superior as, although he would act it, it couldn't be further from the truth.

As reassuring as it was listening in to Lily work, it was not the same when checking in on Henry. Stan never expected it to be and was unsurprised to find himself desperately willing Henry to finish scripted lines at the appropriate opportunity. Henry seemed intent on keeping all his conversations casual. He didn't mind that. Well not as much. Henry was suffering from a crisis of conscience. All he kept hearing in his head was 'commies', 'you are speaking to commies.' It was taking him back to his childhood. He could hear the townspeople in Red Hill beating him and his mother with the stick of communism. These people broke his mother. This system deprived him of childhood. These ideals had been ruining his life. It was starting to wear heavy on Henry and the forced smile he was fighting to keep in place was starting to scrunch up. He could feel his teeth grinding and his hands tightening. He was so much more than just uncomfortable in his surroundings. If he wasn't a pacifist then his natural urges would be to lash out but when that goes against everything you believe in too, you are at an impasse. A tense impasse.

Henry could fight it no more and felt compelled to educate the congregated group on the errors of their thinking. Cutting off a highly decorated member of the former Red Army in mid-sentence, Henry erupted into a tirade discrediting communism, Marxism, socialism and all those who had any pre-conceived, or even experienced belief, in such systems. The group surrounding him were shocked. Not just at what had been said but where it was said. Did this man have a death wish? Even if you do think differently, sometimes it is better to keep it to yourself. A considerate bystander tried in vain to get Henry to stop as he watched the officer grow more agitated and enraged by this vitriolic spiel being forced down his ears. Stan was nearby with his back to the small group, desperately trying to join without drawing any attention to himself. He needed to get Henry out of there, now, but before he could find any natural opportunity, Henry took it too far and stated communists were no better than Nazis.

With a click of the Officer's fingers, two Soviet military police apprehended Henry and escorted him from the room as he continued to protest and attempt to encourage his captors to defect. Henry was too stubborn and blind to the ever-so-clear danger he was in. This was where Henry was reckless. The room was very busy and the conversation volume had masked the events of Henry's removal. It was done with great stealth, to go unnoticed by the guests and not dampen the mood of the event. It meant Lily, in full flow on the other side of the room, was also unaware.

Henry was taken to a room in the basement and cuffed to a table. One eye was fighting to stay open as its muscles had been crushed by blows, he was bleeding from his mouth and his nose was broken. He had been dealt a severe beating intended to make him either rethink his belief system or at least where it should be vocalised. If they hadn't achieved either of those then at least they had punished the enemy. There was a knock on the door.

"That will be the Deputy Chairman of the party. You really chose a bad place to speak your decadent views," said the guard as he moved towards the door. The second guard was unnerved when his comrade held the door open ajar instead of fully opening it and saluting the Deputy Chairman. A muffled conversation occurred before the guard turned to his comrade in the room and told him to remove his pistol, unload the ammunition and place it dismantled on the desk. His comrade questioned this, but, inferior in rank, soon did as instructed. The guard slowly backed into the room as the barrel of a pistol entered attached to the forehead of the guard. At the other end was Stan. The two MPs were restrained to the table with their own handcuffs and silenced with their socks and ties creating makeshift gags. Henry was shocked. One thing he never expected was Stan to come to his aid. Or anyone's aid. He hadn't pegged Stan as someone who would do anything for anyone unless it would benefit himself. This was more than just going out of his way for someone, he was risking his life for Henry. Had Henry always gotten Stan wrong? Stan did look after his people.

"Well, are you coming?" asked Stan. The two men shared a natural impulse to run but their natural impulse was deceiving them. They could not draw any unwanted attention. More than likely word of what had occurred would have been kept between a minimal few as the idea of people thinking differently was not something the Soviet Union liked to even admit existed. It would be completely on the down low and, as long as they stayed calm and played it cool, they could make their steady escape. Keeping a cool head was more important than ever as they were not going down back corridors, through basements, staff areas, or out through windows.

The only available exit was across the main lobby of the building. Between the multitudes of people mingling and networking. Past the members of the Austrian Bundespolizei, the Stasi and even the KGB present amongst the members of the KPO, SED and CPSU. Through all the MPs on duty and out the main doors that were framed with the red banners. With their hearts beating to the double and beads of sweat dripping from their brows they strolled across as though without a care in the world. Not a part of them looked out of place, if nobody looked too closely, and they were nearly out the door.

"Halt," came the command from the Deputy Chairman. He had not risen to the position of power he held by letting anything get past him, and he knew exactly who they were as he had witnessed Henry's outburst first-hand. He was not a forgiving man. Mercy had never proven any positive results to him. With the word ringing in their ears, the two knew the only way out now was to run. Yes, it would draw attention to them, but they were close enough to get through the door before anyone could react. Hoping the crowd would slow the chase of any officials, and knowing it would prevent the use of pistols, they ran through the crowd, out the doors and across the courtyard to the limo. Within less than a minute from when the word 'Halt' rang around the lobby, the two men sat in the back of their escape vehicle as the rear wheels skidded on the gravel before careering out the main gates.

The limo was not ideal for a getaway. The length made manoeuvres difficult, especially in city traffic. However, it was making good progress, considering, but was not alone. Two black GAZ-24 interceptors were in hot pursuit. It was to be an interesting escape as the interceptors could not draw attention to themselves as they didn't hold jurisdiction here. One dangerous photo taken by one stealthy person could bring up all kinds of questions the Soviet Union would rather not answer. It was going to take highly skilled driving to be inconspicuous in a black luxury stretch limo or a black GAZ-24 interceptor favoured by the KGB.

"Lil," panicked Henry.

"Don't worry she is out, she is safe," reassured Stan, "trust me." Henry found he did trust Stan and took comfort in his words. The limo had been driven expertly and had soon weaved through the city traffic and was heading to the city limits and the surrounding Schwarzenbergpark wood. The KGB cars had gained ground on the limo. Though a more powerful vehicle, the stretch would need perfectly straight roads to put any distance between them and this was not the place for that. The two GAZ-24s moved into position on either side of the limo preparing a pincer movement. Now was the time to react. A moment longer and the two units would be in position and the limo forced to stop. With perfect agility and expert skill, like something straight out of a stunt show, the driver yanked up the handbrake and pulled the wheel hard to the right causing the limo to spin in the centre of the road.

The bonnet deflected one of the units wide to the left and the black GAZ-24 smashed head-on into a tree. The other unit avoided the spinning limo but to the detriment of careering off the road and down a bank into the wood. The KGB unit managed to regain control of the vehicle and slowly climbed back up to the road only to find the smashed-up car of the other unit and their dazed comrades stumbling around. The limo was nowhere to be seen.

There was a calm, quiet atmosphere in the car. They had escaped the imminent danger and would soon be at a safe house. Stan had regressed to staring out the window. He was deep in thought and something weighed heavy on his conscience. Henry was looking at him, trying to find the perfect words to express his gratitude, but, more than that, apologise for having Stan wrong. He knew Stan had been the one who had picked them up in the bar but, had it not been him, it would have just been someone else. Henry doubted they would have been as considerate a captor as Stan was and never would have even considered coming to his rescue. Though Stan seemed to have accepted his position in life and enjoyed a lot about his work, he wasn't a standard criminal. He had a major flaw to ever making it to the top of any criminal game, he put others first.

"Why did you help me?" asked Henry, "I ruined your plan. I cost you money."

"Some things in life are more important."

"More important than money?" asked Henry.

"More important than anything," replied Stan without moving his eyes from his distant focus out the window, across the land and somewhere unseen in the back of his mind. Henry knew exactly what Stan meant and saw they had some real common ground. A certain quality in a person that Henry could really relate to and admire. He had this quality himself and was proud of it. It was the basis for what he thought, felt and how he acted towards others.

"You don't like communism either," said Henry with a warm tone. A small smile appeared on Stan's face for a moment. Only a moment but still long enough to give Henry confirmation.

"And Lil?" asked Henry. The limo driver divider lowered revealing Lily behind the steering wheel. Henry was shocked. He had no idea she could drive, let alone drive to such a skilled level. He also thought she had been necking glass after glass of champagne.

"I was just playing the role. Do you think I would get drunk at an event where you were so likely to go rogue? You do have your braindead moments when you feel you are being wronged." Henry was just about to try and argue this point but Lily was not about to let him get a word in. He should be grateful and only grateful right now. 'Stan kept supplying me with lemonade-filled flutes. Tipsy men don't tend to notice small details like that when they are busy staring at my chest.'

"But that driving, it was incredible," said Henry in awe.

"There is a little more to my childhood than you yet know."

"I'm impressed. Thank you."

"Don't just thank me. Thank Stan. He had this escape planned before we even began. He knows you well," said Lily. Henry agreed, he had connected with Stan but still hadn't managed to simply say 'thank you.' Stan had been oblivious to the conversation as he was too far in his head until he was interrupted by a hand gently resting on his shoulder. He was a little surprised to see any kind of affection from Henry but glad to think that maybe he was finally being seen for the decent but unfortunate person he truly was.

"Thank you, Stanley," said Henry.

"Stanley?" enquired Stan before realising his mask may slip, "oh yes of course. Stanley."

ALL THE GLAMOUR OF CRIME

October 1962, Europe.

Landing in Rome's newly built Leonardo Da Vinci airport, the couple chuckled as they realised the play on words in the dossier they received. It had informed them that it was to be an artful affair where they would be rubbing shoulders with the high end of Europe's cultural sect. Dress accordingly. The couple looked straight out of a Fellini picture. They had perhaps taken the instruction a little too literally but in their large dark glasses, open collars and large light hats they pulled off glamour, albeit in a slightly overstated way. But if there was one group of people who wouldn't judge them it was the cultural sect. Anything goes. The event was a resounding success for all involved and everything was beginning to fall into place nicely. Henry had started to enjoy himself. It helped that he no longer saw Stan as the enemy. He had accepted there were greater powers in play they couldn't do anything about. It was in the shadows and invisible to them all but at the same time always present. So why fight it?

From Rome, they flew to Brussels, and from Brussels to London, London to Lisbon, Madrid, Zurich, and Paris again and again and again. Each visit was an event and each event had just become a game they played. The simple aim was to see who could enjoy it the most. The couple found fun in further developing their characters even, giving them ticks or limps, and practising their perfect language and accent skills. Stan enjoyed the ease it all ran with and the celebration after. They would always get adjoining rooms and would drink and laugh into the early hours of the morning. More often than not, Stan would fall asleep in a chair in the hotel room with the couple. They should have saved money by not bothering to book two rooms but, just in case, they always did. Lily would always suggest to Stan that he may meet someone and need his own room and Stan would laugh at the suggestion. Lily never noticed what lay behind the forced laugh. Stan would only want one woman in that room with him and that was one woman he could never have. Get those thoughts out of your head he would constantly tell himself. Don't risk it all. He had friends. Real friends which he had lacked for so long. The idea of a person he could actually trust was so novel to him and having a kindred spirit like Henry felt like having a brother. No, he was not going to risk any of that. Henry often remarked that he may still run, but it was always in jest.

"I could do a Konrad Schumann," Henry would say, "just a quick hop over the wire and I am away," but then he would wink, smile or chuckle. He wasn't going to do anything of the sort and neither would Lily want to. He wasn't going to leave Lily alone with Stan. He had grown to like Stan but was not blind to the lingering looks and the subtle body language that would give Stan away. Still, he didn't blame him, he wouldn't blame any man for desiring Lily but he was never going to be so arrogant to become complacent. He always thought when you are in love with such an amazing woman you can never trust anyone else fully. Always hold back a touch.

The group arrived back in Monte Carlo on the 16th of October and were reminiscing about the first job they did together. They skirted around the details of how it ended and the situation they found themselves in the next day. Let sleeping dogs lie. They had moved on and had each other's backs now. The work they were here to complete was not scheduled until three days and this spare time was theirs to do as they pleased. In the days they would laze by the beach, grab some lunch in the old town restaurants, have a glass of wine or two and just generally take it easy and take in the area. However, the nights in Monte Carlo offered great opportunities for people with certain skills to make a lot of extra money.

They were not gamblers. Not even Lily. Though she was an impulsive person, she was still incredibly intelligent and everything she did was decided by calculated risk and reward. The other two would always take the sensible path of least resistance if possible. They would only ever gamble or take a risk if there was no other option open to them. They all possessed certain skills. Talents, education and experience. It was not in poker or roulette but in the art of deception. They could make you believe they were whoever they said they were. From wherever they wanted you to be, with precise accents, fluent languages and the smallest of details when it came to mannerisms and local customs. After a rocky start, they had taken great pride in their work. They could even make each other question what they knew of themselves. It was truly an art.

This is what Stan planned to utilise in an idea he had to obtain a lot of money from the casinos without risking a dollar or playing one of the house games. He withdrew a newspaper cutting from his jacket detailing an upcoming high rollers game at the casino. It was to be attended by Europe's wealthiest and elite. Stan had a game of his own called 'The Honey Trap.

"Do you know how it works?" asked Stan.

"I have heard of it," replied Lily. Henry said nothing. He walked into the other room, put his coat on and held Lily's out for her. Lily liked it when Henry played the traditional gentleman role and followed him inside.

"Lil?" called out Stan and Lily walked back out to him.

"Though you are both my boys and I love you both dearly, only Henry gets to call me Lil." She patted Stan on the hand and returned to Henry who was holding the door for her. He ushered her out the door as Stan watched feeling a little left out.

"Sorry Stan, sometimes three's a crowd."

The couple walked arm in arm in the light of the moon. The sounds of life were in the hills of Monte Carlo and they were walking by the sea. It was a beautiful still night. The sea was calm and lapped gently at the shore. The peaks of the small waves glistened from the moon and the rattles of the lines on the yachts were like a symphony. The couple took in the majestic sites the marina had to offer with such wealth and glamour on show at every turn. Though Henry had never been a rich man in any way, he believed in hard work bringing reward. He had never considered the wealthy having gotten their money through any corruption until the last year. This work really opened his eyes to how capitalism can be manipulated by some.

Still, he did not blame the system. It was the fault of the person and you would always have these types of people in all walks of life. Each rattle of the line against a mast reminded Henry of the times they had elicited wealth from the pockets of the mega-rich. The money may well have then gone to the organisation but at least they don't pretend to be of decent standing in society. Whoever they are, they are clearly brazen of their criminal status. They would always be around. Always operating in the shadows.

"Look at these palaces. Are we going on one?" asked Lily but Henry said nothing. He led her down a jetty that housed floating palace after floating palace, each one grander than the last. They were breathtaking to behold and the extravagance was almost embarrassing to view. It was a thrill. It was a lip-biting sensation that you felt guilty for. You must look away less the devil takes your soul. But we are only human, all of us and this banquet of wealth was an orgasm for the eyes. At the end of the jetty, in the last birth was the largest of all the luxury vessels. It was called the 'Lady Guinevere' and it looked like it must be owned by real royalty. You could easily host one hundred guests on board.

Lily's eyes lit up as Henry turned towards Lady Guinevere and gently led her up the gangway. All the glamour of her surroundings hit home as she reached the deck and realised, she was entirely underdressed for such a location. Were they going to dinner on the boat? It looked a little dark to be expecting anyone so perhaps it was something else. Lily didn't want Henry to see she was uncomfortable as she didn't want to ruin whatever he was doing for her. She loved his romantic side when it came out. A member of the crew wearing a bow tie and white jacket greeted them on the stern deck and led them around the edge to the starboard bow.

Still, nothing had been said by anyone. Everything was suggested in slight glances, body language and facial expressions. What was Henry up to, wondered Lily, who could barely stop biting her lip. At the front of the vessel was another gangway that led down to a floating surface which housed a beautiful old-fashioned rowing boat, decked out in a variety of blankets, cushions, and throws with a bottle of champagne on ice and a picnic hamper for two. This is what Lily called romance. It was never about the price tag with her. It was all about the detail.

The couple had been gently lazing on the rolling Mediterranean for a couple of hours. They had finished their picnic, drank their champagne and laid together with the rhythm of the sea. Wrapped in one of the blankets and looking up at the stars. Lily was in Henry's arms with her head resting on his chest.

"I always feel safest here," said Lily. Henry was a little confused by the comment as, to the best of his knowledge, this was the first time they had spent time on the Med.

"Right here," said Lily and drew a circle on his chest with her finger, 'always hold me close.' He drew Lily in closer and placed a gentle kiss on her head. That meant so much to Henry. Those words, that moment and that gesture. He had been concerned. He had never felt any anxiety before when it came to Lily. There were so many other fellas on campus during their university days but he never worried. He knew what was different now. She was having the time of her life. She was getting the adventure she always craved but Henry sometimes struggled to join in with all the fun. Something just held him back sometimes.

Then there was Stan. The gatekeeper of adventure. The one who offered the thrilling life and came through. The man who can create people. Make you whomever you want to be and do whatever you want to do. Freedom. Henry could understand the appeal and the fact he was also extremely charming with a beautiful English accent just made things worse in Henry's mind. He didn't want to mention it to either of them though as he did like Stan regardless. He was his friend.

"Will we always have adventures?" asked Lily. Henry smiled and kissed her on the forehead.

"I know it is a little crazy that we are in the situation we are in but I am so glad I am in it with you," said Lily. The boat slowly started to move back in. It was tethered to the Lady Guinevere and the crewman was gently winching them back in, giving them enough time to get themselves together and above all get dressed. This was not a usual excursion that people could buy whilst in Monte Carlo, this was something Henry had snuck off to organise earlier and had dropped the sailor a sizeable number of francs. It had been worth every penny.

The couple arrived back at the hotel room, gently unlocked the door and snuck in like two naughty teenagers who had broken curfew to visit Lover's Lane. They found Stan asleep on the balcony where they had left him. There was an empty bottle of champagne on the floor with a half-drunk bottle of port nearby. Henry came out with a spare blanket and softly draped it over Stan. Stan pulled the warm material up to his chin and in doing so dropped what had been resting in his hand. Lily bent down and recovered the fallen article. It was the newspaper cutting advertising the high rollers game. All screwed up and prepared for discarding. Any preconceived ideas Stan may have had for Lily in any other way were something he had accepted would never be.

"See," said Lily, "he knows." Henry smiled and walked back into the room. He wasn't tired yet and turned on the television. A news report was coming straight out of Washington.

"The US once again finds itself in a standoff with the Soviet Union," said the newsreader, "President Kennedy and his administration have discovered Soviet ballistic missiles in Cuba. Less than three hundred miles from US soil. Agreements had been signed at secret meetings between Nikita Khrushchev and Fidel Castro in response to US arms being deployed in Italy and Turkey. It seems we are the closest to nuclear war we have ever been. This newsreader, for one, hopes that sanity can be restored amongst these world superpowers for the sake of humanity."

GIVE MY REGARDS TO KHRUSHCHEV

October 1963, Barcelona, Spain.

The group toasted in anticipation of another great success. These events had become second nature to them and always ran as clockwork. Stan's precise planning was the perfect preparation and Henry and Lily were experienced old hands now. In another lifetime they could have been spoken of in debates over the greatest actors, but in this lifetime, they were conmen. Pure and simple.

"How do you do it Henry?" asked Stan, "what I mean is how do your capitalist values and morals permit you to take from the wealthy?"

"What choice do I have?" replied Henry.

"I would have believed that at first but now I am not so sure."

"These people aren't capitalists. They haven't worked hard or intelligently. They oppressed others to get where they are. That is how I can do it."

Stan passed the couple their dossiers for the event. Signor and Signora Ragenta. He was as quick as she was beautiful said Stan, tongue in cheek.

"Any of that and our friendship will be short-lived," joked Henry.

"I'm just teasing," said Stan as he winked at Lily who laughed. Henry didn't mind. He was reassured now. He trusted them both. He had never really had a friend apart from Lily and he was very content with Stan. As the trio walked the corridors of the hotel towards the stateroom, the event venue, Stan filled them in on the guests to expect.

"Big money," said Stan, "Europe's wealthiest will be here tonight." Stan thought about what Henry told him earlier and considered it a smart motivational tactic to inform him of some of the atrocities these guests had done in acquiring their wealth. It was probably true to some degree, reasoned Stan. Henry was appalled to hear of the sweatshops in some of the poorest countries. He hated the idea of these people being oppressed. Henry was a little confused really as a lot of capitalism went against his ethos. After wasting his childhood thinking people were all terrible, he had grown to believe that everyone in life should have an equal chance. The same chance. Workers of the world, unite. Some of the things Henry said may make a stranger think he was a commie. But try telling Henry that.

"Let's take them for so much more then," snapped Henry, "if they are so rich."

"Stick to the plan Henry, I was just joking," said a suddenly anxious Stan. It wasn't so much the thought of taking more, that was never going to be an issue, it was the attention that would come with it. Added scrutiny. They had a system and it worked. There was no reason to rock the boat. Stan regretted what he told Henry and, by the time they reached the event, he was not confident Henry wouldn't go rogue again.

"Henry, I was only joking," reiterated Stan.

"I don't believe you," said Henry as he marched into the room.

Stan watched on as beads of sweat slowly congregated around his forehead. He was trying to act aloof whilst casually conversing with other investors but was failing. Constantly claiming the room was a little too hot though nobody else seemed to feel it. With his eyes continually checking on Henry, his company would become insulted by this man who seemed to be looking for someone better to talk to and soon depart. Though this was not how Stan liked to come across as it broke his appearance of being self-assured. An appearance that was used to great effect in encouraging investors to listen to the random couple who seemed to know so much about the opportunity.

Henry was not doing much to reassure Stan either. This work had changed Henry. Before, reckless Lily would have been the risk in this situation but she was following the plan to a T. She knew it worked and enjoyed the performance. Henry seemed to have a personal vendetta against these guests and was trying to fleece them for everything. The returns on offer were becoming ridiculous. It was not a get in early for great returns offer so often available to those with vast means, it was over the top. Two thousand percent returns in one year. Three thousand percent returns in six months. Double your investment by the time you wake up tomorrow morning.

He was losing them. He was risking the whole event and in doing so risking the whole operation. Something that would not go down well with the Organisation. The damned arrogant fool could not see he was risking all their lives. Jeers of laughter erupted from Henry's congregation which was by now most of the room. Groups of Saudi representatives, investment bankers, gold dealers, arms dealers, and a Russian General all walked off in amusement or feigned amusement masking suspicion and cynicism. The event was a bust.

"Henry, what the hell was that?" asked Stan.

"I know. Idiots missed an opportunity there," said Henry as he left for his room. Stan could not believe the arrogance of the man. He thought he was the one in the right. Stan wasn't going to get any sense out of Henry in the mood he was in and felt somewhat responsible for riling Henry before the event. He would wait until tomorrow to let Henry know that if Stan couldn't iron this out, they were all going on the run. Henry and Lily wouldn't just be wanted by the legitimate law but also hunted by the organisation.

It was about 03:00 hours when Henry and Lily were awoken by frantic knocking on their hotel room door. Henry slowly woke as the knocking got louder and faster.

"All right, I'm coming," shouted Henry, waking Lily. Lily was not a morning person or someone who liked being woken at any time. Henry opened the door to find a fully dressed and frantic Stan. He did not have his usual cool reserve about him and there was a sense of foreboding in his demeanour.

"We have got an impromptu job," said Stan.

"Now, it is the middle of the night?"

"Now. It is a private gig for some VIPS aboard a jet to London. We have thirty minutes until our car arrives. Get ready."

"Can they not wait until tomorrow? Make them want it more."

"Henry, you don't get it. That little stunt you pulled last night has put us all at risk. This could be the opportunity to redeem ourselves. If we don't then we are dead for sure. This is the organisation testing us. We must pass."

"Lily rushed past Henry into the bathroom and was washed and dressing before Henry had finished his brief chat with Stan. She knew the importance; she had understood the seriousness of the situation they were in. She wanted this life to continue forever and would do anything to make sure it did.

"Henry, get dressed," she said as she threw his shirt at him.

It was 04:00 when the plane commenced take off. They were all to stay at a luxury flat in Mayfair and this motivated them through their fatigue. The event was to take place in the first-class cabin and the trio were preparing themselves in the staff area. Henry and Lily were desperately trying to learn their characters for this event and Stan was desperately trying to create the characters. He normally had a little more time to create complete people from scratch. They had to go with the bare basics on this one. Names, nationality, accents, relationship and a little professional background. Enough to get by and the rest would have to be improvised.

On the journey to the plane, it had finally clicked with Henry how important the success of this event was after the last debacle. It had taken a lot of explanation from Stan and affirmation from Lily but Henry had eventually backed down from his argument as he realised, they were in a position that talking may not get them out of. He would be at a loss. The trio were all nervous and were still struggling to hide it when the time came for Stan to introduce the presentation.

It was not to be a mingle event as usual as the plane lacked the space. The couple were to offer a presentation to a small group of dignitaries who would hopefully then invest vast amounts. Enough to cover the last events losses was the ultimate goal and they all knew it. Stan could feel his face burning red as he stumbled over his words whilst introducing Nigel and Philippa Dimbleby from London. He was relieved to retreat to the back, as soon as he could, where he could be out of sight and ignored.

"The greatest thing about an event at thirty thousand feet was that, even if people got bored, there is no escape," said Lily. They had all agreed to start with a joke and hopefully, it might help them to relax. There was a slight murmur of laughter but it was a mere moment offering no rest for the presenters. Nigel and Philippa started to go into their spiel. Speaking of lack of space in their current confines much like the ever-increasing lack of space in London. What was on offer was escape. Freedom. Space. They were not speaking of outer space but the space about one hundred feet above.

"Towers?" enquired one of the investors, "what is so new about that? Have you seen Manhattan?"

"We wouldn't suggest towers for a gentleman like you. This is so different. A gentleman like you needs luxury," flirted Lily, "You want to mix with your own class and escape the masses below."

"Save your silver tongue charm. I am not the investor but his representative. I am probably from the class you wish to escape your Highness."

"Well, what would your employer want?" asked Lily.

"Probably that," the representative laughed, "So I am guessing you are building up in some way?"

"Directly above." Henry handed out the promotional images for the concept being offered. The group of investors all studied the information in front of them with complete confusion and utter cynicism. A floating city. Higher London. Henry went on to explain the plan to build a floating city above London that would be supported by large pillars in prominent places. Yes, there would be less space below but space was the luxury. Space was the commodity being sold and the lower classes could just live without or do better. Henry would hate Nigel Dimbleby if he existed but he portrayed him very well.

"Never need for anything. Never see anything undesirable. It will all be below you and thus behind you. Don't look down because you have no need to." Henry had found his patter and the flow had returned to the group. The tension had eased and they could sense it was going well until a guest began to laugh.

"Apologies. It just took us all a bit by surprise. This is one hell of a big plan," said the representative.

"It is but it offers incredible returns for people who get in early," Lily responded.

"Within eight weeks the plans will pass through parliament and be accepted. Fully endorsed by other original investors who have already signed up. You will stand to make a ten thousand percent return within ten weeks of the proposal passing as people clamour to get onboard," said Henry, "when the city is built you will stand to make a percentage of every single piece of real estate available."

"Who are the other investors?" enquired one of the guests.

"Though we are not at full liberty to say yet I can disclose that there is royalty involved, Generals and high-ranking officials from a variety of nations, oil barons and a Rockefeller or two." With this revelation, the whole cabin erupted in laughter. There was no longer any possibility of stifling.

"Rockefellers? Kings? Ten thousand percent return, my word Nigel, it gets better and better, doesn't it?" jokes the investor, "should I sign up Philippa?"

The unexpected reaction completely threw the couple and, before they had a chance to respond, the representative continued.

"Or should I say Herr Volz and Madame Gavriete or Signor Ragenta and Fraulein Kreiner or simply Henry and Lily?" The trio turned white as ghosts. Stan had been right. It was the organisation and they had failed the test. Henry was about to start begging for their lives when the representative reached into his jacket. But he didn't produce a pistol, it was much worse, he produced a badge.

"Special Agent Croft, CIA. This is Agents Pearce and Wilkins," said the representative, "we have been following your activities for a while. How is the organisation?" The trio said nothing. They tried to think of anything, anything at all that may help them but nothing came to mind. They knew it was over.

"Very quiet for such skilled multilinguists. You should have stuck to just fleecing high society but you had to go and try and hoodwink a Russian General. Well, bravo, in the middle of the Cold War, two Americans try and scam the Russians. We are all working hard to try and find some peaceful resolution so all the citizens of our great nation don't have to go to sleep worrying they may not wake up and here are you two stirring the pot." Croft stared at the couple waiting to see if there was any response but he had got them and he knew it.

"Cuff these two and secure them in the staff cabin," Croft instructs his subordinates before turning to Stan, "and what shall we do with you, Stan?"

Stan didn't flinch. He didn't move a muscle and his eyes kept staring ahead. Another man entered the cabin and sat down next to Stan.

"Well, that is not my problem," continued Croft as the man took Stan's briefcase from him and cuffed them together. Stan slowly turned to find himself cuffed to a KGB field agent.

"Give my regards to Khrushchev, Stan."

WELCOME TO THE CIA

The room was dank. Dank and green. That puke colour of green often found as badly used contrast in government buildings. Either the original interior designer had an awful eye or they opted for colours that induced nausea. If it was the former then as soon as they realised it did the latter, they were going to stick to it. The room had no windows. It was an office but felt like a cell. It probably was someone's actual office. Someone who worked hard and studied all their life to achieve a good position in the CIA only to find themselves in this soul-destroying cell of an office. Maybe they got issued this office as a punishment. One dulled lamp with no shade hung from a dusty cord in the centre of the room flickering every few moments. There was a large mirror across one side of the room and to the left hung the pledge of allegiance. In the centre was a heavy steel table and chair bolted to the ground.

Henry sat at the table with his hands cuffed to its brackets. He had no idea how long he had been in that room. It could be days, it could be weeks, it could be years, it all felt the same. The room was designed to have that effect. It disorientates people very quickly. The truth was it had only been a few minutes but waking up in there had messed with his senses. He looked around the barren room and his eyes settled on the only thing to settle on. The pledge of allegiance hanging from the wall. Henry knew the pledge by heart.

He had taken great pride in reciting it at school. He had always tried to be loudest and most committed in the hope it may make people think differently of his family. It didn't. They all felt he tried too hard and it made them think he was a commie all the more. Natural impulse took over Henry and he began reciting.

"I pledge allegiance to the flag of the United States of America and to the republic for which it stands. One nation under God indivisible with liberty and justice for all. I pledge allegiance to the flag…"

Croft watched on through the two-way mirror as Henry continued to repeat the pledge.

"…of the United States of America and to the republic for which it stands. One nation under God indivisible with liberty and justice for all."

Croft entered the room and Henry silenced at once. His head dropped and he stared at the table. Thoughts rushed through his imagination of what may become of him. He had absolutely no control and that kind of situation panicked him.

"A patriot?" asked Croft.

"Yes Sir," mumbled Henry.

Croft stared at Henry as if weighing him up. Henry could not and did not lift his head. His eyes transfixed on one scratch on the steel table as if it would all disappear if he concentrated hard enough.

"Well let's do it together. I pledge allegiance to the flag of the United States of America… that was your cue to join in. Let's try it again but you start."

Henry began reciting through a mumble. Still not lifting his head. Focussed on the table as the words were firmly stored in his memory.

"I pledge allegiance—"

"Come on Henry, put some oomph into it."

"And to the republic for which it stands," Henry pushed it a little louder.

"Volume Henry, volume," directed Croft.

"One nation under God indivisible with liberty and justice for all—"

"What for all Henry?" snapped Croft.

"Liberty and justice for all," repeated Henry.

"From the top Henry and with some heart this time," commanded Croft as Henry became flustered and anxious at all the commands.

"I pledge allegiance—"

"What do you pledge Henry?"

"I pledge allegiance to the flag—"

"What flag Henry?"

"Of the United States of America."

"Yes, Henry. Let me add a beat." Croft stood directly in front of Henry and thrust his fists down on the table. Again and again, in rhythm. Eyeballing Henry throughout. The table bolts were slightly loose which made the noise of each hit echo throughout the room and Henry's cuffs jolt against his wrist bone.

Resulting in a deafening acoustic and threatening atmosphere. Smash, smash, smash…

"From the top Henry. I pledge allegiance."

"I pledge allegiance to the flag of the United States of America," Henry cried out, "and to the republic for which it stands."

Croft picked up the pace of his beat. Each smash forced Henry along as he struggled to keep up. He had never stumbled over these words before but he had never been in such a situation.

"You do the beat now Henry. I am going to march around this room with it."

Henry began to mimic the beat Croft had been doing at the pace Croft had been doing it, but with his hands cuffed to the table it forced even more tension on his wrists. He was starting to bleed. Croft was marching around the room to the beat.

"From the top Henry, from the top."

"I pledge allegiance to the flag of the United States of America—"

"Oh beautiful, for spacious skies, for amber waves of grain," Croft began to sing over the top of Henry, "louder Henry, I can't hear you."

"And to the republic for which it stands," yelled Henry as he tried to hear himself against the echoes of the beat, the marching and Croft singing.

"For purple mounted majesties above thy fruited plain," Croft got louder.

"One nation under God indivisible," Henry matched Croft for volume. The stress of the situation had got to him but determination would not let him be beaten. He was fresh out of cares.

"America, America, God mend thine every flaw. Join me, Henry. Let's do it together."

They both started singing America the Beautiful. It was now clearly a contest. Henry would not break. That is what Croft wanted and Henry would resist. He could sing louder than Croft and he could yell louder than Croft and Croft could do nothing about it. Henry was fooling himself. Mid harmony Croft stormed up to the desk and smashed his fists down hard, missing Henry's blooded hands by mere inches.

"One nation under God—"

"Do you believe in liberty?" he screamed in Henry's face.

"Yes Sir," whimpered Henry.

"Do you believe in law Henry?"

"Yes Sir," whispered Henry as his fight deserted him.

"Are you a patriot Henry?"

"Yes, I am," shouted Henry with renewed vigour.

"You sure?"

"Yes, I am." Henry erupted out of his seat to meet Croft at eye level. The strain on his wrists must have been agony. Croft knew he had him.

"Then why do you work for the Organisation?"

Henry slumped back down in his seat. He knew this was rhetorical. There was no good answer he could give.

"A man who believes in the law. Why?"

"I don't know."

"Come on Henry, we are both men of the world. Why?"

"For her."

Croft went to his briefcase and withdrew a file with Henry's name across the top and a stamp emblazoned across the cover reading 'Rejected – Communist Connections.' He sat on the edge of the table and opened the file to a specific page, the page titled 'William Miller – Traitor.'

"Well, that's not the whole story is it, Henry? You are in bed with them."

"I am not a commie," proclaimed Henry.

"No? This file says different."

"I am not a commie," screamed Henry.

"The perfect profile for them. The education and the family history. Easy pickings for the organisation."

"There was a mistake. My father fought on D-Day. He was a hero."

Croft returned to his briefcase and withdrew another file. A thick file entitled William Miller, emblazoned with a stamp that read 'Enemy of the State.' He laid it out in front of Henry and encouraged him to read. The sheer size of the file overwhelmed Henry. It was the first time he ever doubted anything he knew about his father. No, he must read it. His father was a hero but what if there was something Henry doesn't know? This was an extensive file and Henry was just a child. Henry shook as he found the courage to begin reading.

"This is all lies. My father was a hero. He was all American."

"Says who Henry?"

Henry sank into his chair the more he read. Had his mother been lying to him all along? Had his father died on D-Day? Was he even there? Had he been working for the commies all the time, was he still working for the commies? Were the people of Red Hill right all along? Croft brought him a glass of water and uncuffed him. Henry was no threat. The truth, like many before and many after, had broken him. This is what the CIA liked and Croft's performance was designed to achieve this. It always made it much easier when there was real intel to cause the demoralisation of a target, so nothing had to be concocted at short notice. It was always a sloppy job.

"It's lies," begged Henry.

"What reason would we have to lie? What difference would one Nebraskan farmer make? I'm sorry Henry."

"Well, what now?" asked Henry. He was despondent. He was lost.

Croft's demeanour had completely changed. He was much softer in his approach and knew that if he offered a fatherly feel then Henry would be completely submissive to him. Fill that father-shaped hole that this revelation had just created.

"Are you a patriot Henry?"

"Yes."

"I believe you. I felt it in our rendition."

"Can I go?"

"I am afraid not Henry. I believe you are not a commie but you are a criminal. You have to pay. You are valuable to us."

"How?"

"Over time a lot of criminals are successful because they are ahead of the game. Others are successful because nobody cares enough to chase them. Until they need something from them. We only came for you when we had something specific that suited your skill set. We could use a talented couple like yourselves."

"Where is Lil?"

Croft pressed a button under the desk and the lights in the room went off. Behind the mirror was a room now visible to Henry. Lily was there, bloodied and beaten. Tearful and ransacked. She was in cuffs and her clothes were torn and covered in filth. She stood there shaking with no control of her bladder. This was too much for Henry. It had all gone too far. He broke down.

"What do you want from us?" he whimpered, barely audible.

"I want you to make a choice. Either come and work with us and you can have that sweet little lady in your arms immediately or refuse and never see her again. Take your time."

Henry looked up at Croft. Trying to read anything from his face. There was a resurgence in him.

"I would have accepted anyway. Why all the intimidation?"

"That's what I told them. Henry hates the commies as much as any wholesome American. As much as you or me. Yes Sir," cheered Croft before moving right up in Henry's face. "But I sure as hell needed you to know that I won't stand for any shit and if, for even a moment, you think you are smarter than me then I won't hesitate, for even a moment, to shoot you in the fucking head...her too."

Croft opened the door and Lily came stumbling in as fast as she could. The couple wrapped as one with their eyes screwed shut. Perhaps it was all a nightmare. Perhaps if they held each other tight and kept their eyes shut it would all go away. They were just kids having some fun. Just a little adventure. How had it come to this? Neither could contain their shakes.

"Enjoy basic training. Berlin style," said Croft as he closed the door.

"Berlin?"

***

Four weeks was nowhere near enough time to train civilians into CIA field agents but that wasn't important. The skills required for the particular mission Croft had recruited the couple for, they already possessed to a greater standard than any CIA trainer. This mission was all about deception. Henry and Lily sat at a desk wearing long white coats with the names Dr Smolov and Dr Petrova tagged to their chests. Croft was scrutinising every little detail in their clothing. Nothing could be out of place or it would blow everything.

"So, training over. How are we both feeling?" asked Croft but Henry and Lily said nothing.

"And your intel is off-book? It needs to be. It is time to use your skills for the good guys. You do it right and hopefully, you won't have to use those side arms. You do have them, don't you?" They both nodded uncomfortably. Croft picked up the data file and read it aloud.

"Dr Bartosz Smolov, a nuclear physicist with access level four. He grew up in Leningrad. His parents were Reuben and Elena. He studied in Moscow and Berlin before joining the ranks of the Russian government. Dr Helene Petrova, nuclear physicist, access level two. Grew up in Kazan. Parents deceased and brought up by maternal grandmother. Her name was Rosalie Ektrina. Also studied in Moscow and Berlin." Henry and Lily nodded.

"Christ's sake, have you learnt a damn thing?" Croft erupted, "Smolov grew up in Krasnodar and Petrova was brought up by her paternal grandmother. It is lack of attention to detail that will get you killed. What is wrong with you people? You learn each and every tiny detail when you are defrauding someone but when it comes to your country, you are half-assed."

"We don't want to do this. We can't. We just want to go home," cried Lily. The spirit she had an abundance of had been taken from her. Her reckless nature was the reason they were where they were and she was distraught. She knew Henry would never blame her, but she would blame herself.

"We are sorry for what we did."

"No shit."

"Just let us get this down perfectly," pleaded Henry.

"What difference does it make? You had four weeks to learn this information and haven't got it down. I bet you didn't have that long in your previous work. I don't believe you don't have it down. This is all an act. A good one but an act all the same. You know all the info and you are as ready as you ever will be. Your lives are in your hands so get your game faces on, get in the car and get to the East. Hell, even I don't know what to believe when it comes to you pair."

THE MISSION

A black KGB GAZ-24 quietly pulled up to a sentry station at just after 22:00 hours. A Soviet guard approached the window requesting identification and was obliged with three standard military ID cards. One for the private who drove the car and two for the development department science attaché seated behind. Dr Bartosz Smolov and Dr Helene Petrova. The barrier was raised and the car drove down the lengthy main drive to the military outpost. The surrounding area was a thick wood which was covered in layers of snow at that time of year making the outpost feel even more isolated.

At the end of the drive awaited the most senior ranking official currently on site. Base Facilitator Panchev. He was a portly man who took little care of himself and even less for others. Everything was always just too much for him at his best moments but dragging him away from his drink at 22:00 would never win him over. If someone was lower rank than him or he cottoned on you were pulling the wool over his eyes he could be quite the sadistic bully. However, in his current half-cut state, it would take the worst of amateur dramatists to be rumbled by him.

The car pulled up beside Panchev and he made no attempt to move out of the way or assist with a door. He stood staring at the back windows waiting to see who was going to get out and whether he would be able to berate them or not. Before the car had even fully stopped, a rear door opened and a shiny leather boot protruded through, crunching down on the snowy gravel. It was soon followed by the frame of Dr Bartosz Smolov. Panchev could tell by the quality and condition of the footwear this man had authority. He looked at his dishevelled footwear, in desperate need of repair, and accepted it was an authority that exceeded his own. Smolov thrust the required documentation into the hands of Panchev and curtly instructed him to read and obey. He was to take them to the third-floor office and file safes at once. Henry knew the best way to play Dr Smolov was to say as little as required. Less chance of any slip on custom or intonation. Though they were highly educated and thoroughly fluent, mistakes could be made, and when your life depended on it that simply could not happen.

Panchev read the documents and there was nothing to suggest anything was untoward. Anyway, the quicker he followed through with his orders, the quicker he could return to his drink. He led the scientists through the corridors of the facility. Considering it was isolated and supposedly operated under the radar it was quite a monstrous place. Though also quite abandoned. They didn't pass another soul on their way through. Lily presumed others were in their quarters as it was quite late. Henry put it down to communism and the socialist system not having enough workers of the right access level. They arrived at the office door and once Panchev unlocked it he asked Dr Petrova what they wanted from the file safe. Lily froze. She hadn't said a word so far and, though she tried to hide it, her nerves were struggling. She was flustered.

"Why do you ask her and not me Base Facilitator?" interrupted Henry, "I outrank her and so will be addressed with any questions, however, I outrank you also and so will not be questioned. Is that clear?"

"Yes Sir," muttered Panchev as he led them to the file safes. Once they were all unlocked, Henry gestured towards the door and Panchev skulked out and back to his drink. The door closed and Lily had a panic attack, collapsing in the corner. Henry rushed to her aid and lifted her head. There was nothing more that could be done than offer reassurance and hope it would calm her. She needed to find her control or they were both doomed. Henry knew Lily well and so sat down next to her gently laying his arm over her shoulder and drawing her into his nook. Her cheek rested against his chest as it so often did. This was Lily's happy place and had the desired results. She found her calm and regained her control when Henry promised he would do anything and everything to make sure they both got out of there alive. She was always his number one priority. She knew this.

"Why did you get him to leave Henry? He will suspect something."

"He already does but he can't question a superior. It just dawned on me that there are a lot of files here. A lot of information that could benefit our side. Maybe what helps them will also help us." Henry got back to his feet and went to the file safes.

"Careful Henry, we are playing with fire here."

Henry opened the safes but they were mostly empty. Safe after safe was barren but for one. One safe housing one file. File #013K-OP-MAO. The office door suddenly reopened and Panchev stood there with armed guards on either side of him.

"What is the meaning of this outrage?" yelled Henry as Panchev offered nothing more than the smug grin of a schoolyard snitch as General Casztov stormed past him and straight up to Dr Bartosz Smolov. Demanding to see their papers for himself. He snatched the documents from Henry and made a phone call across the room. Henry and Lily were sweating. This was not in the plan. They were used to having an exit strategy in place should things go wrong in events but they hadn't been able to see the venue prior and they didn't have Stan to advise them. They were trapped and the only way out would be convincing this general they belonged, but whoever he was calling would need to vouch for them. They could only hope Croft had considered this eventuality and whoever was on the other end of the line was placed there to validate the scientists. Casztov ended his call, refolded the papers and handed them back to Henry. He thanked him and made to leave. As he exited, he called back.

"Arrest them."

"I am Dr Bartosz Smolov and this is Dr Helene Petrova working on behalf of the KGB and I demand to know what is happening here," commanded Henry as the heavy-handed guards marched him and Lily behind Casztov. But the General ignored him.

"I am Dr Bartosz Smolov and this is Dr Helene Petrova working on behalf of the KGB and I demand to know what is happening here," Henry tried again and, this time, Casztov stopped, turned and walked straight up to Henry.

"What was it you told Base Facilitator Panchev here in your very impressive Russian? You are not to be questioned by someone of a lower rank. Well, in the spirit of fair play, please count the pips on my shoulder. I speak impressive English, no?"

The guards opened a door leading from the corridors straight into a courtyard at the centre of the facility. Henry and Lily were dragged out and thrust against a wall. The armed guards stood at a distance of twenty-five feet with their rifles trailed directly at the hearts of the couple.

"It is late and I have no time for this so I am going to make it very simple. I am going to ask you what you are doing here only once and you will answer fully. You will explain without hesitation or omission of any information and then I will release you to the safety of West Berlin," said Casztov.

Henry looked at Lily. This was all too much for her. His poor Lil. Tears were streaming down her face; her breath was rampant but she had stopped shaking. She looked done in every way, as though she had accepted the inevitable. Henry hadn't. Not just for him but for her. She was his priority. First and foremost, always Lily. He would always do whatever he could to keep her safe. Henry turned back to Casztov to give him everything he had asked for.

"Henry don't," whispered Lily as if resigned to these being her last words, "you can't put me first. Not here, not now."

Casztov gave it a moment to see if he would obtain the information he wanted and discover what the intruders were after and, more importantly, what the

Americans already knew. Henry stared at Casztov with renewed vigour. He had been instructed by his Lil and that was the highest authority Henry knew. The information was not forthcoming, so Casztov gestured to his firing squad to ready their weapons.

"Last chance," said Casztov.

Henry and Lily looked at one another, lost in each other's eyes. They found their comfort and warmth within one another. Lily mouthed 'I love you' to Henry as Casztov commanded his squad to take aim. Henry stared at Lily and shook his head. This can't be their end. They are too young. His breathing sped up and his eyes began to well. He mouthed the words back to Lily 'I love you' then hastily turned back to Casztov.

"I will talk, I will tell you everything," surrendered Henry.

"Fire," commanded Casztov.

The guards fired off a couple of rounds at both targets but when the smoke subsided, Henry and Lily stood there still alive. Shaken, scared, confused, but still alive. The door crashed open and Croft stormed into the courtyard and straight up to Henry.

"Traitor."

***

Croft threw Henry across the cell floor crashing him against the hard brick wall. Nearby, Lily was dragged by her hair to an adjacent cell. Croft wanted them to be near each other without being close. He wanted to be sure they could hear the anguish and screams each other released in vain. Henry could hear and it was killing him. Lily's agony was evident for all to hear and he could only imagine what they had planned. It was heartbreaking for him to know something was happening that he could do nothing about. But that was why they were placed in adjacent cells. That was how Croft would make sure the failure never repeated itself. Henry was about to get an education he never wanted.

The cell door opened and a guard entered with a child's inflatable paddling pool and a small metal stool. The pool was inflated, filled with water and the stool was placed in the centre of it. A battered, bruised and naked Henry was strapped onto the metal seat with his feet submerged. Another guard entered pushing a trolley carrying a small electricity generator connected to two cables, leading to large rubber-insulated crocodile clips. Though the muscles of his eyelids were bruised and weakened, Henry could make out the shape of the trolley and through his haze, he recognised the crocodile clips as they were presented inches from his eyes.

The toying had begun. Croft was overseeing it. He seemed to be very accustomed to this procedure like an old dog. Croft had not gotten to his position without getting his hands dirty so he was perfectly experienced to make sure his subordinates followed due process correctly to elicit desired results. The first step was always to make sure the victim's ears were not blocked by anything. He needed to hear perfectly which is why maintaining silence was expected in the area except for pre-determined sounds. Sounds like the screams piercing through the wall from the next cell. Was it even Lily in there? Henry couldn't be sure. He could only go with what he had been told as he no longer seemed to possess the ability for logical thought. He had to believe it was Lily because, if he could hear her, even though the situation was desperate, it wasn't the unthinkable. This was his only glimmer of hope and yet it was this choice causing him the most pain in their predicament.

With each piercing through the cell walls, Henry would react with the same anguished cries. He wanted to save her with every bit of strength in his body but he had next to none. He had been drained and wiped with every method going. He was sleep-deprived, food-deprived and beaten. This inability to physically act in any way had heightened his senses. He could hear a pin drop like an explosion and he could smell the chemicals added to his water. The generator was slowly powered up as guards cruelly played with Henry.

However, this was no game. This was due process. Each sound heightened so Henry could hear the pitch of the hum and knew the charge was increased. He could hear the crackles and snaps of electrical current jumping from crocodile clip to crocodile clip like a Tesla coil. The sounds got louder as the clips grew closer and Henry now saw the blue jagged glows jump back and forth like deadly imps. The guard moved the two clips suggestively around his head so his ears could really hear the impending torture. The anticipation of when he would strike was part of the act. From ear to eye and eye to ear. Each time the sound or sight was at its clearest Henry would scream out and his cries would be echoed from the cell next door.

The moment that petrified Henry came as the clips drifted down and out of his line of vision. His body was numb. It was numb from the lack of energy.

It was numb from the beating. It was numb as a defence mechanism preparing for the worst. He only knew the burning of flesh had occurred when his nose could smell the stench rising. He could not move and he could not feel. He was defeated as a new thought tortured his mind. He would now never be able to give Lily children. If they ever got out of here.

"You will do exactly what I say from now on, there are much bigger things in the world than you and your girlfriend," said Croft as Henry passed out.

When he awoke, he was alone in the corner of the cell and the paddling pool, stool and trolley had all departed. Silence surrounded him and he hoped that was a positive but hope was all he had now. He gently checked out his wounds careful not to make them worse but something was off. He felt down but nothing was out of the ordinary. No singed hairs and no burnt skin. He was sure he would find himself disfigured to the point of never being a father but he was perfectly fine. He started to question his sanity. Had he dreamed it? Was he dreaming now? The only light that came into the cell was from above the door and it created a dull spotlight where it hit the floor. In the centre of the illumination sat two crocodile clips still clamped hard to a burned-out piece of pig skin. He had been played and it had worked. He would do exactly what Croft said now. He had to.

KEEP YOUR ENEMIES CLOSE

Croft was troubled. A message had arrived on his desk that had not come through the usual interdepartmental delivery process, meaning it had not been read by every department it passed through before being resealed. This message was for Croft and Croft alone. It had to have come from one of his closest allies within the service. The only allies Croft ever had were now distant memories and from the information enclosed in this message, this must be from a memory he would sooner have forgotten. He knew he was at risk of being exposed for improper conduct during the Korean War. Improper conduct was sugarcoating the fact he had dealt arms to the Soviets in the north whilst being stationed in the South. If this news got out, he would be on the first plane to the States, and if he was lucky spend the rest of his life in prison but more likely find himself strapped to the chair.

The potential whistle-blower was being held at Hohenschonhausen in the East, a prison that didn't exist. Well, not on paper. He had been there for the best part of ten years, refusing to talk and revealing nothing about his identity or affiliations, but he had finally exposed himself. Maybe he had found God or was simply ready to die and wanted to get it off his chest. Either way, you needed high-level clearance to obtain this information. Croft had it and needed to use it to his advantage. In Croft's role in the West, he had influence over the movement and use of political prisoners currently held and he was digging through files to find someone of stature. Someone who could hypothetically know things that would interest the Stasi. Possibilities that were much more intriguing or intel much greater than anything they could expect to extract from their current tenant. This is what Croft hoped they thought. If they knew for a moment the chaos the card they held could cause then Croft was done for. He needed to act fast.

A field agent who had operated under the code name Ali Baba suited him perfectly. He had been a Stasi agent who had been turned and handled by the British. His defection hadn't worked out well for him as he was currently languishing in an allied cell. Whether the Stasi knew his current whereabouts or whether they knew he had fallen out of favour with his new comrades was immaterial to Croft. He knew the intelligent thinking would be this former operative knows two things that would be of great interest to the Stasi, what he told the enemy and what they told him. He was worth ten of the has been anarchist they possessed.

A trade had been arranged for the early hours of the morning. A low mist was coming from the Spree, hanging across all roads and bridges it touched. It was the perfect weather for espionage and dirty deals between the counterparts of an intelligence war. Croft was no fool and had made a career out of sly deals, sneaky handshakes and false smiles so he was not going to agree to the Stasi's request of him to send over the field agent first and once they had confirmed it was him, they would send his target over. Croft didn't flinch at this request as he had expected it. So often in these situations, the Stasi would make such a request for the simple reason that with less experienced operators on the other side, it sometimes worked.

Croft was not wet behind the ears. Croft used his field glasses to confirm the identity of the trade and at exactly 01:15 two of his agents marched the defector back across towards the East and a very uncertain future and they took possession of a relic of rebellions gone by. A man in terrible condition with matted grey hair tangled and weaving into the grime and grip of his unkempt beard. His left arm was absent and he moved with the walk of a man begging for death. The agents had embraced their new man and taken him to the luxury vehicle brought to collect him. They had supplied him with a beer, a cigarette and a warm thick coat. Croft had told them how important this man was, but not who he was important to, or why.

The traded man stood in Croft's office still unsure as to who he was going to meet. He knew it was a good situation though. You don't get embraced by agents when you are being taken out of the game. You don't get to spend the next few days being pampered and cared for in a private hospital room. You don't get a barber sent in or supplied with a new suit. He stood there smelling of roses without a shred of evidence apparent to ever suggest he had been anywhere near a cell let alone spent so many years in solitary confinement. The man's optimism disappeared the moment Croft entered. He recognised him at once and it was not a warm reunion. They knew each other from the Korean War. The man worked in intelligence for the North and Croft worked for the CIA stationed in the South. Much like the events of a few nights earlier, often opposing factors would have to come together to make dirty deals that would have to be kept from public knowledge. They had both worked in this world.

"I hoped I would never see you again," said the man.

"I heard you were in a most difficult of situations and I wanted to help a dear friend," said Croft.

"Friend? Interesting choice of words. Then again maybe you mean it. I don't know what you currently think but I know what higher purpose you serve so maybe at the moment friend is quite apt."

The atmosphere in the room was palpable. It was a toxic mix of distrust and murderous capabilities masked by a phoney grin on Croft's face but the man hid nothing. He was scrutinising Croft. Trying to work out exactly where he stood with him and what he wanted. All he knew was it wasn't going to be the picnic he had been led to believe when he was collected.

The man was soon wearing the uniform of the base guards and had been put to work in the facility. Though he wore the low-level insignia of a guard his work involved being more of a personal assistant to Croft. Wherever Croft would go, so would the man. He had been allocated quarters next to Croft's which had a suspiciously large mirror on the wall. The man would often keep the lights out in his quarters. He was happier in the dark than being spied on. He had quickly reasoned why he was here and the constant close proximity of Croft had confirmed his suspicions. He was being watched.

From a prison that used countless tactics to cause mental anguish to one that pretended to be something else. He had gone through every possibility of what could be gained by having him here and he knew the answer was simply to keep him quiet. He had spent a lifetime trading in knowledge and secrets and what he had on Croft was why he was here. But for how long? He knew that he would never be allowed to walk out a free man. There was too much at stake for Croft.

Word had come file #013K-OP-MAO was to be moved to the outpost in the coming weeks. The mission Henry and Lily failed in a simulation was soon to become a reality. But they were not ready. Croft had left them shaking in their cells when he last saw them but he had no other agents available to complete this mission. The unique skill set made it a narrow pool and to have a pair that he could entirely control with the threat of death gave him great satisfaction. He knew they took him and the situation they were in seriously now, but they needed to regain composure to be able to play the roles truthfully. Anything hammy or wooden and it would be curtains.

Henry was leaning back against the wall of his cell as he sat on the cold floor. He was not the same man who had been dragged into the cell at some time unknown but he was not a shell. He had nobody to talk to but that was fine by him as he had grown accustomed to that most of his childhood. He was reflecting daily. The choices he had made and the choices Lily had made. Would he change her choices? Yes, if he could, but nobody could control her like that and he certainly would not want to. Would he change his choices? No, she is the only true happiness he had ever known and he would follow her to the ends of the earth.

With each day that passed he began to feel less sorry for himself and more amused by the situation he was in. He did not deal with isolation as well as he thought and was losing the ability to gauge severity. This would not serve him or Croft well and so Croft gave him some company. Someone to talk to, to keep his mind active. Someone who also had strong views on political ideals and felt opposing opinion was the hated enemy. Someone who could reignite his fire.

Henry woke to find a one-armed guard staring at him from across the cell. He was completely oblivious to when he had entered, how long he had been there or whether he was imagining him. The mind plays tricks on you in such situations and this may just be a reaction to circumstance.

"Please don't be alarmed," said the man, "they think some company may be good for you."

"You're real?" asked Henry.

The man smiled and confirmed he was. He was not taken aback by such a question. He could relate. After nearly a decade in The Submarine, as Hohenschonhausen was known, enduring various mental and physical torture practises he knew the feeling of uncertainty to certainties you had always taken for granted.

"Do they care about what is good for me?" asked Henry, "it is difficult to tell from one minute to the next."

"It seems that way to me but you can never be sure. Best to always keep your wits about you I find."

"What do we talk about?" asked Henry.

"Anything you like or we can just sit here. It's up to you."

Henry sat for a while trying to look at anything but the man. There was nothing but the dank, dark walls he saw every day and the flickering light outside his cell door. Visible enough to always be in his peripherals and getting more and more irritating with every flicker. By design no doubt. He kept trying to look elsewhere but his eyes were naturally drawn to the abnormality in front of him. The obvious curiosity that he felt it rude to enquire about. The man knew this look.

"You want to ask about my arm, don't you?" said the man.

Henry was glad he had said it and felt reassured that this conversation was perfectly fine by the manner of the man. The man went on to tell Henry how he had found himself in Normandy in 1944 and forced into a service he did not want to be in resulting in him having to fight on D-Day.

"I never fired a shot that day," said the man, "I don't know why I told you that but I feel I want you to know."

"You let your brothers die?" asked Henry. Suddenly he was feeling a little of that old anger. A fire was brewing in him.

"I wasn't fighting for the allies," said the man.

Henry was confused. The man was a Nazi. Wasn't he? He did say he didn't want to be in that service and said he didn't fire a shot. So where had he been until then? Had he not fired shots before in the name of Hitler? Who was he?

"I was a prisoner. I have been most of my life in one way or another. Forced by the Germans to fight on the front line as the only alternative to death when my unit was captured in May 1944. Then captured by the allies at the end of the battle on the beaches."

"You're Russian," exclaimed Henry.

Henry studied the man in front of him and the man sat quietly permitting this. He knew the way to get into Henry's mind was to first make him feel comfortable in his presence.

"You're old Russian," said Henry, "when we were allies?"

"Yes," confirmed the man.

"My father died on D-Day," said Henry, "well I used to think he had but now I'm not too sure." Henry was feeling a comfort in this man. Something about the way he held himself, the warmth in his eyes and the truth in the corners of his smile told Henry he could open up to him. Maybe even trust him.

"Are you a commie?" snapped Henry.

"Used to be," said the man, "for a long time."

"What changed?"

"I had fought for it for years. For various preachers of the greater good and their ideals but all I saw was the tragedy of life living under these regimes. I was in Hungary to help suppress the uprising, I was in North Korea, all across the Soviet Union and then finally here in Berlin. Do you know what you truly see when you look across the wall from East to West? Smiles."

"So why are you here now?"

"I honestly don't know for sure but I am trying to work it out," said the man.

"Are you real," said Henry doubting his sanity again, "what's your name?"

"I'm Karl."

For the past few days, Karl visited Henry regularly and they had become very chatty. They really got on well and, in other circumstances, may have been drinking buddies putting the world to rights in a Paris bar whilst the owner tries to close up around them. This was what Croft wanted to hear. Croft had never desired to spend much time with Karl, but he knew how strong his communist convictions always were and believed he must be pushing all Henry's buttons. Croft thought himself very smart and knew Henry's spirits were up. He had renewed passion. Croft believed this to be the effects of a communist preaching what Henry despised, when in fact it was the tales Karl was telling. Stories of his post-communist days and all the places in Europe he had seen. Monte Carlo, Vienna, Paris, Barcelona, Brussels. They all brought back memories to Henry and offered the amusement and warmth nostalgia so often does.

"I am glad to hear things are going well," said Croft, "here, take a look at this. See if anything could be helpful."

Croft passed Henry's file across. Karl read through all the information on Henry's work with the organisation and was surprised to read about Lily. Henry's girl was also in a cell here and Henry hadn't mentioned it once. Surely, he would have wanted to know how she was. Karl thought it very peculiar to imprison a couple in the same facility, but he felt everything he knew so far was peculiar. Why would you get prisoners to complete missions instead of trained operatives?

Karl continued reading about Henry's education, his background and his application to the CIA. He read the reasons why Henry was rejected by the CIA and saw the attached family file for his father. William Miller. Karl was shocked. He read on about what happened to William Miller after the war. Held as an enemy of the state under the supervision of the CIA for a brief time until he died under suspicious circumstances. William Miller. It had been a long time but that name was always fresh in Karl's mind. William Miller. No matter where Karl had been, what he had seen, endured or committed the one name that was always remembered greater than any other valuable intelligence was the name of Sergeant William Miller from D-Day. He flicked back to the section on Henry's childhood and read about his hometown. There he saw written the second name that was always at the forefront of Karl's memory. Red Hill.

WHOSE MAN ARE YOU?

K arl knew his long game had changed. He still needed to work out all the peculiar activities surrounding the situation around Croft, but he had a much more important role to play now. He was going to help this couple. He was going to get them out of here. He was going to repay his debt. The breath of a guard standing outside the cell door was often the only sound a prisoner would hear in the dead of night. The isolation amplified the monotonous release and it almost became white noise to a prisoner. Something they relied on to sleep. They would rarely be standing guard if you had another guard in with you as it made no sense to have two people do the same job. They didn't have the resources for that kind of luxury. Yet when Karl sat in with Henry, guards would often appear at the door, hang around for a few minutes and then leave again.

"They are assessing conversation. Subject, context." explained Karl as footsteps could be heard approaching on the hard cement corridor beyond the door.

"Watch for the shadow over the peephole. It will appear as soon as either of us says one of many words." Karl waited a few moments so the guard was in position and more importantly in earshot.

"And then the revolution will begin," blurted out Karl as though a whole plan had preceded it. A dark ring immediately appeared around the peephole and shrunk as the guard closed in and blocked the light. Karl waved to the door, a curse was uttered outside and Henry laughed. Karl was absolutely correct.

"So, you were going to explain your process on how best to make Chrysanthemums thrive in a drier landscape," said Karl.

Henry realised this was some rouse to bore the guard outside to leave them alone but had no real idea about flowers. He had never looked into it.

"Lots of water is key," said Henry and finished there.

This was not enough and Karl nodded to request elaboration. Something about Karl made Henry trust him, even though he was the enemy. Also, it was clear he had something to say to Henry and anything could improve his current situation.

"The Chrysanthemum is from the renegal-hopata-mocrial family and therefore will always be able to thrive with the correct balance of heat and moisture." Henry was making it up as he went. "The interesting thing with the fauna and flora most associated with the renegal-hopata-mocrial family is—"

A deep sigh of boredom was heard from the other side of the door and footsteps began to clump away down the corridor. Karl held a finger up to instruct a pause until he could ascertain for certain they were safe from the earshot of the guard. The moment had come and his smile dropped in an instant. Henry could sense a revelation coming but why would this guard care about him?

"William Miller," whispered Karl, "Red Hill, Nebraska."

Henry's jaw dropped. Of all the words that may have come out of Karls's mouth, they were the last ones he would ever have expected. Karl allowed a moment for the gravity of his words to sink in.

"So, he was a commie," muttered Henry.

"A commie?" questioned Karl.

"You, a Russian communist who was at D-Day, fighting for the Nazis, know not just the name of my father but also his hometown. You don't get that from a dog tag. It's all so very clear."

"I don't understand," said Karl, "I say your father's name and town and you think commie because I am Russian. He wasn't."

Henry could not comprehend for a moment that Karl would be able to understand the horrific nature of his childhood due to being branded a commie. How could he? Where he comes from this is normal and nothing to be repulsed by. Commies are cold by nature anyway, he thought, but what else was there to talk about? Things looked bleak and perhaps understanding why his father had defected and what events led him to do so could offer some comfort and closure to it all. Perhaps it could be the final chapter of his childhood.

Something about Karl put people at ease. Perhaps his missing limb made him look incomplete and unthreatening or something in his eyes that encouraged you to open to him. This could be a skill he had perfected over many years of work but it also could be he was just a decent person. He couldn't be though, he was a commie, thought Henry, but he wasn't anymore. Henry told Karl his story from his earliest memory to the moment he left Red Hill and everything in between.

"Not many people were there that day by choice. Yes, there were some fanatics in the German ranks but not all. Many didn't understand what was going on and why, and the allies were only there in reaction to the Third Reich."

"So how did you end up there? Weren't you fighting against them?"

"I was caught up in the wrong front. My comrades were all based in the east and I was with a few remaining soldiers who had been forced off course a few years earlier and passed along again and again as prisoners. In war, it is amazing how far a small detour can end up taking you. Eventually, the choice was fight for us or nothing and I didn't see how my death would help anything."

"So, you were a communist, who became a Nazi, then returned to communism and has since denounced that. How can anyone trust someone who can't commit to their ideals?"

"Don't be absurd man. I was never a Nazi. You do what you must do in life to survive. I never helped their cause in any way and often sabotaged from within. If anything, I was a spy. Just without an affiliating government to report to."

Henry went white as a ghost. He sat on the edge of his bunk and his lips trembled. His focus was so far away that it would take an air raid to return him to the present. Karl had spent the last seventeen years since the war ended working for governments in different locations offering certain skills. This included intelligence gathering which was a polite term used for waterboarding. Karl was not your standard KGB agent though. His heart was not in the violent or torturous methods to break a man. Karl was an intellectual and knew that if he listened to the man in front of him, really listened, then he would tell him everything. Maybe from a misplaced twitch, a flick of the eyes or a bite of the lip that tried in vain to prevent the mouth from opening and secrets flooding out. They always talked in the end, even without speaking.

"He wasn't a Nazi either," said Karl.

This statement seemed so loud and bold that in that moment it was more deafening than an air raid. It came crashing down on Henry, returning his focus.

"He wasn't a commie," added Karl, "he was a human being."

Karl told Henry the truth of his experiences of D-Day and how William Miller was no more a communist than Roosevelt himself.

"In truth, I know very little of the man but from the actions I saw on that day, he was a decent man who cared for all human life. I was just a young boy at the time who he saved. Had I been any other nationality then he would never have been considered a communist back home."

"I want to believe you but you are just one man and this could all be lies. Some trick," said Henry.

Karl walked over to where Henry was sitting and dropped to his knees. He removed his shirt revealing raw wounds on his back. Clear evidence of recent torture. Henry knew that regardless of which side you were on, nobody did this to their own team.

"Croft is not my man," said Karl.

"Who is your man?" asked Henry.

"All my life I have felt immense gratitude to William Miller of Red Hill. A gratitude I could never return. When you carry such gratitude, it becomes a debt and that debt becomes a burden. Your childhood was my fault so my debt is with you and now I can repay it."

"If you are not Croft's man then you are the other side?"

"It is not as black and white as you think. Your father never asked who I was or whose side I was on. He just saw a person needing help. I don't care what your beliefs are as I just see the same. Affiliation and ideals mean nothing. We are all people. Let me repay my debt."

Though logic would scream to Henry this doesn't make sense, he had a feeling towards Karl that was very rare. Henry's isolated childhood made certain thoughts and feelings difficult to understand and this was very much one of them. He felt the same as he had towards Stan before they were arrested. It was feelings of friendship. He liked him.

"Let's do this Karl but you must know one thing. I am not here alone," said Henry, "my girl is with me. Somewhere here. I don't know where but I am not going anywhere without her.'

"The only reason I can help you is because they put me in to talk with you. I can't access anyone else."

"Well without her you will keep your burden of debt."

***

Croft walked Karl to the far east wing where the medical centre was housed. This situation worked in his favour as he would not be seen as the enemy and not considered to be lying. Henry would be gunning for Karl and Croft could add fuel to that fire so Henry would be ready to die for the cause. They stopped at the end of the corridor and Croft raised his finger to his lips.

"We can't make any sudden noises. You don't want to startle this girl."

Croft gently slid the peephole cover aside so Karl could witness the trauma within. The smell of human filth erupted through the small gap causing Karl to stagger back, retching as he went. He withdrew his handkerchief, covered his nose and composed himself. His eyes were watering as he stared through the hole to see a poor wretched soul, curled against the corner, mumbling to herself, surrounded by clumps of blood-crusted matted blonde hair. The dank, dark room, along with the situation, had taken its toll and there was no coming back from this.

"It is such a shame."

"Why did you let this happen to that young girl?"

"Oh, it wasn't us Karl, it was your lot, it was a nerve agent. They got it in somehow and I am sure you know their ways better than I do. This was your doing. Embrace your work."

"What do I tell him?"

"You have one job, make him mission ready. Tell him whatever you like to make sure that happens."

***

Karl twitched uneasily as he sat opposite Henry. He kept looking at his watch whilst listening out for the footsteps outside. Waiting for the perfect moment. Henry tried to keep calm and have faith in his rescuer. He kept telling himself that Karl knew what he was doing, he was a seasoned pro and Cold War operative and he would know the schematics of the base down to the last water pipe or cesspit. Henry kept telling himself all this because the beads of sweat running from Karl's brow and his forever darting eyes made Henry nervous. This seemed almost opportune and since Karl was just desperate to redeem his soul and pay off this debt, perhaps he had rushed this plan so as not to lose the opportunity.

The footsteps got louder until they were on top of the cell. The guard looked through the peephole, casting a shadow on the ground before a shallow thud momentarily rang out and the guard collapsed to the floor. The door swung open and one of Karl's brotherhood greeted him. Karl tapped on his watch the very second the thud was heard. Maybe there was more to this escape plan than Henry originally thought. Maybe there is more to Karl than it appears and maybe he is someone to listen to.

The trio trod lightly as they made their way down the lower corridors of the base. The concept of this escape was quite simple really. Karl got his comrades in, they disabled the unexpected guards and all that remained was a calm but speedy extraction. The brotherhood dressed in the uniform of the base guards so as not to draw unwanted attention on the screens of the surveillance system. Each camera would capture a small section of the base corridors where guards would stand. They were to make their rounds at exactly fifteen-minute intervals and the rounds should take them five minutes. Which meant every five minutes someone had to be posing as a guard for the cameras. There were eight cameras on the chosen escape route and only six of the brotherhood.

Karl held position at the corner of corridor three which led to exit 3W His timing had to be perfect and he was totally focused on his watch. This was all about communication and the team had to be in sync. The second hand closed in on twelve and the minute hand moved to the quarter-past position. With a flick of the hand, the signal was sent along the line and as one they ran. Karl took the lead and in doing so was responsible for taking out the final guard. Charging footsteps with thirty-second delayed echoes were not subtle and the guard was well aware something was up as Karl turned the corner closely followed by Henry.

For a man missing a limb, he was not to be underestimated. He knew how to make up for his shortcomings and wasn't about to give the guard any chance of the upper hand. At full speed, Karl dipped his right shoulder and charged the guard like a rhino. Henry, who was on his heels came colliding in and took out Karl. The three of them lay on the ground as the first member of the brotherhood turned the corner and suddenly stopped at the scene. Thirty seconds later, the second member of the brotherhood turned the corner and suddenly halted as he saw the guard detaining the three other men at gunpoint.

The guard had started to sweat. His arm was shaking. He couldn't maintain aim as the gun felt very heavy as another man rounded the corner. It had been one and a half minutes since the final run began and they could not afford to be held up. Two minutes struck as another member of the brotherhood crashed onto the scene panicking the guard fired off a round. But nothing happened. The sound, the spark and the damage didn't occur. Nothing. The click of an empty chamber sparked Karl back into action as he leapt onto the guard and knocked him to the ground. With a heavy boot from one of his comrades, the guard was out cold.

The group sprinted towards the west gate where their transport waited. Time was ticking and the deadline getting ever closer as the group caught sight of the gate. The west gate, which was always open, was firmly shut and the area was deserted. There was no transport waiting and there were no other people.

"You said she would be here. You lied to me."

"Henry, I have no time to explain. I am trying to get you out of here and I couldn't tell you the truth as you would never have come. Lily is…dead."

Henry studied Karl's expression as Karl showed impatience and panic.

"No, she isn't Karl. Where is she?"

The scream of the base alarms interrupted the conversation as searchlights began to frantically pan the perimeters. The brotherhood searched for an alternative exit from the yard but the direction they had come from was blocked by approaching guards. Their only choices were to attempt to scale the electric gate or beg for mercy which would never come. On the other side of the gate, the unmistakable silhouette of a Barka B100 slowly pulls up across the road.

"You are a commie still!"

"Put ideals aside. Am I a human?"

'You lied to me, Karl.'

The guards were closing in with Croft at the front. They did not run or rush or yell. They were composed and confident. They had the rats in the trap. Suddenly the lights on the top of the gate began to flash and the motor whirred as the gates began to part. A malfunction surely.

"Come with us Henry, I promise you, I will do right by you. We will come back for Lily."

"I can't do that. I can't leave her. Ever."

"My debt is not paid. We will be back for both of you."

Karl and the brotherhood escaped the base as Croft and the guards reached the gate. There was still no urgency in the prevention of the escape. Karl, who Croft had worked so hard to arrange a swap deal with the Stasi was being allowed to walk out the main gates in the possession of his brotherhood. A Soviet insurgent cell had been allowed back into operation by a man responsible for preventing such things. Why, thought Henry.

"Never believe in that man Henry. You can see, he is one of them. Forget anything he ever said to you. Trust me. I have your interests at heart as we share the same goal. We are patriots."

"But you let him go?"

"Did I?" said Croft as the Barkas B100 van turned the corner at the end of the road and was out of sight.

Smoke billowed upwards from behind the row of houses on the horizon as the sound of the explosion still rang in the ears of those nearby. The chemicals used for the bomb were so powerful it had ripped the rear end straight off and sent it back down from where it came. Nobody could possibly survive such an explosion and nobody did. In the middle of the junction, at the end of the road that led from the West Gate of the base lay the final resting place of a battered, burnt and crumpled blue b cross of the Barkas van.

TAKE MY HAND

The door to Henry's cell creaked open and natural light swarmed in. It had been something he had been missing without realising it. Whenever Karl had visited, the door was opened but there was no natural light. Either there was another door closed on the outside or Karl was only permitted to come at night. In a cell, alone, without a watch, you soon lose track of time. It could have been the middle of the day when Karl would visit. Henry pondered on this. Why would it have been the middle of the night if he was being sent here? Was Karl anything to do with Croft at all? Was he just infiltrating the base at night and breaking people out of the cells? But why all the talk?

Henry considered the idea that all the nights of conversation before the failed escape attempt might have been to butter him up. Maybe the KGB had got hold of the files of the detainees and worked out personal plans to get them all onside. Maybe show Henry that not all communists are bad. Show him a side to a person that he could really get on with. Maybe concoct some story of being at D-Day and being saved by Henry's father. Would they go to such lengths for him? It was just a small story that could easily be devised and improvised in the situation. What hurt Henry more than any of this possible manipulation was that he had liked Karl. He actually liked him. They say the devil comes in a pleasing form.

The natural light was not the only pleasantry Henry received that morning. He was escorted from his cell, through the grey corridors of the base, across the courtyard and into the private quarters of the base commander. The subtle warmth of the closest resemblance to an actual home was amplified when coming straight from a cell, and this modestly furnished apartment with its tablecloth and coasters looked like paradise to Henry.

"Do you take milk with your tea Henry?" asked Croft, removing a cosy from a teapot sat in the middle of the table surrounded by various biscuits.

Henry didn't respond as he didn't quite know how. Everything was a little confusing and he was trying to process it all. A powerful man, who had kept Henry in a cell for an unknown time, who could end his life with a click of his fingers, who had possibly just arranged the murder of six people in a car bombing, who held the power of attorney over whether Henry and Lily lived or died, was gently laying down a tea cosy and offering Henry one lump or two. It just didn't add up but it had been a long time since anything did.

Stan, Karl, Croft, it seemed nobody ever stayed the same. Just when you thought you had their character pegged, they would change. Most people would learn to understand that humans are not so black and white and the shades of grey between are vast. They would learn this in childhood. But most people aren't banished by society. Henry was learning late.

"Try it with a bit of lemon, it can be very refreshing."

Croft glided the teacup on its patterned saucer with a couple of biscuits on the side. Henry studied Croft wondering whether he was about to digest poison or some mind-control drug. He soon put this out of his mind as they could have poisoned or drugged him at any opportunity. It had been so long since he enjoyed any pleasure the sugary treats and lemon sweet tea were like a king's banquet to him. The slight moan of pleasure Henry released when biting into that first baked treat was enough to let anyone know his defences were now down.

"They were hand-made by a local baker. Good, aren't they?"

Henry let out another small moan but hadn't really listened to a thing said to him. He was in a trance. His body had received this small hit of sugar after such a long time of deprival and he was temporarily away with the fairies. Anything anyone said right now would not be listened to but would be heard. That is how Croft wanted it.

"I'm sorry about Karl," said Croft, "I know he has been filling your head with fantasies. It was unfair of him." Croft picked up the teapot, walked to where Henry was sitting and refilled his cup. He placed another couple of biscuits on the side of the saucer with a wink and sat back in his seat.

"Thank you," said Henry between mouthfuls.

"I wanted to use Karl to help prepare you for the mission. I wanted him to get to you and reignite the passion and hatred towards the East. We must stop them, Henry. It is for the good of mankind. They are smarter than we thought as Karl showed by trying to hide his roots and make up stories to befriend you."

"Who was he then?" asked Henry.

"Just a terrorist whose fanaticism I thought could help you. I needed you to understand the importance of listening to me and doing exactly what I told you. I now realise that the use of the cell and the fanatic were not the way to go about this. I am sorry Henry. Field agents don't get a manual for everything and must think on their feet. I came up with an idea and it was wrong. I'm sorry."

Henry left the last biscuit on the side of his saucer, the remaining tea in the cup and pushed it away.

"I'm ready but I need her," said Henry.

"That can be arranged."

"How is she?"

"She was struggling, I'm not gonna lie to you. But we have been working with her and she has been indulging in a lot of tea and biscuits. She is good."

***

Henry and Lily reunited to complete the mission as per the same MO as before. This was not a simulator and Croft made sure they were entirely acceptant of that and entirely ready. For the last few weeks, they had been living together comfortably in an apartment near the commander's quarters. The memories of the time spent in isolation seemed to dissipate as comfort and companionship were shared. They were so happy to be back in each other's arms. They had continued where they left off with their training and embraced it with new vigour. It was as though they had been offered a second chance at existing and they were not going to let the opportunity pass them by. Their backstories were perfectly down, their accents were acutely accurate and even their weapon training had resulted in high marks. Croft's plan had worked perfectly and the chameleon couple were sharp and ready to complete this mission for the CIA, for America and for the greater good.

"This office is quite high up," said Lily.

"Open the window and breathe in some of the air. Doesn't that feel better?" said Henry.

The couple had managed to infiltrate the enemy base using the credentials and personas of Smolov and Petrova and had reached the file safe as advised.

"Just the one we came for this time Henry. Promise me."

"Just the one." Henry unlocked the safe and found this choice was no longer his as the only file it contained was #013K-OP-MAO, the only file they had come for. It was during moments like this they truly understood the espionage world and how certain items, documents, objects or deals could be the holy grail to one government or another. It seemed this file could contain intel that would change the course of the war and the world.

The door handle twisted over and over as someone aggressively tried to enter.

"Open this door immediately."

"They are speaking English," said Lily.

"This is General Coltrane of the United States Army and I am ordering you to open this door."

"They know, Henry, it's a trap."

Henry grabbed the file from the safe and secured it in Lily's coat. Lily took him by the arms and held his gaze firmly with hers.

"Please don't talk this time, Henry. Whatever happens, don't give them anything. I don't think I could look at you the same."

"We are not caught yet Lil," said Henry and withdrew his sidearm from his holster.

"We are Russian scientists and will not be opening this door to anyone. Particularly phoney American generals."

"This is not a phoney American general son, open the door," demanded General Coltrane.

Henry raised his sidearm up to the left and fired off two rounds. A scuffle was heard from outside the door and the muffled command of 'Push back.'

"Now's our chance Lil. Open the window."

As Lily heard these words, she realised what Henry had in mind. The height she had considered lofty before suddenly felt impossible. Lily scurried into the corner and her body shook. Her breathing was fast, short and sharp. Her eyes were wide and water began to well up at the edges.

Lil, we need to do this. It is the only way out,'

"I can't Henry, it is too high."

"It is one floor up; it just seems higher. You will be fine I promise you."

"Oh Henry, I can't. You go without me."

Behind the door the sounds of body armour and shields being fitted and the assembly of a battering ram meant time was running out.

"Lil, we have to go now. We have what we need and our exit is right there. We can get a head start on them and we can get out of all of this. We are free after this."

"Even from the CIA?" asked Lily.

"Even them. Croft promised me." This was the first time Henry had ever lied to Lily but he felt it was excusable given the circumstances.

"Take my hand. I am here with you. We can jump together. I've got you."

"I don't want to play this game anymore," said Lily, "I don't like the cold."

"Take my hand."

"Everything always seems easier when you're with me. Like ripping off a band-aid," said Lily as she leapt up, ran forward and jumped through the window, rolling down the hilly ground below. Henry was impressed but not surprised. Lily always had it in her to overcome any fears or phobias as she had shown night on the Ferris wheel, which seemed a lifetime ago. Henry jumped through behind with more control, picked her up and by the time the battering ram was assembled, the guards wore their armour and the door to the office was smashed open, Dr Smolov and Dr Petrova were nowhere to be seen.

DOUBLE CROSSED

The weather in Berlin had been expectedly awful. It was late in the year and in the throes of winter. The snow on the ground had created an easy path for anyone chasing the two thieves to follow but also made it difficult for vehicles to pick up speed. The snow had also given their leap from the first-floor window a more comfortable landing.

"As per my design," boasted Croft.

Understanding weather and keeping abreast of meteorological reports can be greatly beneficial to many people in conflict situations. The snow has a habit of preventing vehicles from moving with ease and so causes backlogs of duty and communication such as the transportation of classified files. So, they have to stay locked up within their location until such time they can be moved quickly, efficiently and at no risk of interception.

"Well, little risk," smirked Croft.

Giving others time to perfectly plan a raid with the highest likelihood of success. It is all well and good knowing what direction someone left in but if you aren't fast enough then you won't catch them.

"Well, I hope from those grinning faces you have something for me?"

Henry and Lily had got back in one piece with the aid of an elderly couple in a Citroen 2CV with Swiss number plates. Nobody ever suspects the 2CV driver and particularly not ones that look like one foot is firmly in the cemetery. Don't judge a book by its cover, Henry had thought, as he had been covered in a blanket on the back seat. He had always known his kind of intelligence was suited to this line of work and now he had shown it. Something about it all made him feel alive. Something had woken and he hoped this success might reopen a door into the CIA.

"I want more work with the CIA," said Henry.

"Henry. Do you not think this is something we should discuss?" argued Lily.

"Whoa there. Let's take one step at a time. The file please?"

The look on Lily's face was thunder as arrows shot from her eyes in Henry's direction. Her stare did not soften or move from Henry for even a second as she undid her coat, removed file #013K-OP-MAO and handed it to Croft. Henry was a little scared to look over and catch Lily's glare. Though he had always followed her in what she wanted and where she wanted to go, she would always ask him first. It may have always seemed to him there was only ever one correct answer but at least she had performed the pretence. All he could do at this moment was wait for Croft to review their spoils and say something. Say something soon.

"Good. This is more than good. If these plans had fallen into the wrong hands... my God, I must call this in with my superiors," said Croft.

He walked across the office, past the telephone, and locked the door. He came back, passing the telephone again, and went to his filing cabinet. He withdrew a small set of keys, unlocked the cabinet and pulled out the bottom drawer. It was totally empty. Croft pulled the handle slightly to the left which initiated a new path for the mechanism. The drawer front now moved vertically and back to reveal a false bottom. A small wooden case sat hidden in the shadows. Croft pulled it out, placed it on the desk and chose a further key from his ring of many and opened the box. Henry and Lily were confused. A field radio was revealed to be housed in the box. The confusion was soon replaced by fear as Croft called in the success to his superiors.

The couple expected Croft to call the Pentagon or perhaps a general responsible for this area of Berlin, but this was definitely neither.

"Blackbird calling, Blackbird calling," said Croft in Russian, "we have recovered file #013K-OP-MAO from the Americans and they will be forwarded to their final destination. Operation Mau can commence Comrade. For the party."

"What the hell was that?" said Henry, "all that blackbird and comrade stuff?"

"Informing my superiors of the mission success," said Croft.

"Your superiors? I thought you were a patriot?"

"I am," said Croft, "just to a different nation."

"You betrayed your country," said Lily, "but why?"

"I don't care about nations and all that. I am a worker and will work for whoever offers the greatest salary."

"You are a mercenary," balked Henry.

"What actually happened today," cried Lily, "I am finding it hard to follow."

"You stole from your own government. You are traitors. Did you never think to question why, out of all the resources and personnel available to the US military, you two criminals were chosen for this mission? Very arrogant Henry."

"They don't even know about us, do they?" said Henry.

"Of course not. You are nothing to them; or were. Now you are a couple of traitors who stole classified information and handed it to the enemy. Oh, they will know you now."

"I still don't get it," cried Lily, "we stole from the Russians?"

"We stole from the Americans Lil. General Coltrane's accent wasn't just particularly good, it was native."

"Texan, I think," said Croft.

"You used us," said Lily.

"The thing you are really going to find funny is they had completed the mission. The documents had already been taken by the Americans and were soon to be shipped out. My position is handy for information.

You just reversed the mission and gave the file back to Mother Russia. She salutes you."

Henry erupted at the tone of Croft's voice. Not only had he been lying to them from the start, but he had also tricked them into committing treason and now he was mocking them. Henry had never known such anger directed at one person. As though a lifelong hatred of communism had been compounded in one tiny bullet and fired at Croft. He embodied everything Henry believed he understood and his blood was boiling. He lunged across the table at Croft, knocking the field radio to the floor and scattering the file. He stood, with his jaw clenched and body shaking but then froze. He had always been a pacifist and even in such dire circumstances his natural instincts kicked in. Croft took advantage and grabbed Henry by the throat.

"You want to play Henry? I love the spirit. I always knew it was in there somewhere. I was kind of hoping you would join me. You know, the apple doesn't fall far from the tree and all that."

"I know you now. I don't believe a word you say. Karl was right."

Croft squeeze Henry's neck harder and soon they were down on the ground.

"What did Karl tell you then? That I was an arms trader in the Korean War? That I sold to both sides? That I just look out for myself? Oh well, boo-hoo."

"No, he told me that my father was not a commie and he told me not to trust you. He was right. That last thing you said is the first thing I believe."

"Well, isn't that sweet? Your last words"

"I know something," whispered Henry as he gasped for air, "other files at the US base. I saw them. I read them."

Croft released his grip on Henry's neck.

"God damn you, Henry. I was quite enjoying this game but you go and say something like that. I don't know whether to believe you or not but I gotta find out. Remember the fun we had with the paddling pool, well you are about to be in a heap more trouble than that. What did you read at the base Henry?"

Suddenly, the hard wooden box that housed the field radio came crashing down on Croft's head and he collapsed to the floor. Lily stood there breathing deeply.

"Now what?" asked Henry.

Lily scoured the room, formulating an exit strategy. They were not going to be able to just walk out of the base. Croft is no fool. He would have given clear instructions to all base personnel that the couple were not permitted to leave without his presence or direct authorisation. When the guards find Croft on the floor, having been attacked, they would surely be immediately arrested. Who would believe them over Croft? It would just seem like another act of treason on the part of the couple. Lily looked at the desk telephone wired to the wall. She noticed the desk lamp also plugged in and a radio on the other side of the room.

"Put him in the chair, Henry, I know how we can get out of here."

Two guards stood directly outside Croft's office as special detail for his current guests. Lily was right to consider everything Croft would have prepared including guards instructed to use all means necessary if anything were out of the ordinary. The handle turned and the lock clicked, sending the two guards into a prone position with their guns aimed directly at the opening door. They had no idea who or what situation was about to approach but they knew their orders and, unless Croft exited with the couple, they were authorised to use deadly force to prevent any escape. A moment's relief was shared by the guards as Croft came through the door with Lily sitting on his lap. They relaxed believing him to be using some field agent trick to manipulate the couple but that relaxation soon disappeared once they saw his hands tied to the chair with wires. He was unconscious and Lily held a gun underneath his chin.

"Excuse us gentlemen," said Lily.

"This is treason. You will be shot."

"We will be heroes," retorted Henry, who pushed the chair along.

With a loaded pistol pushed hard against the underside of Croft's neck it made exiting the building relatively straightforward. Henry pushed the chair holding Croft and Lily down the corridors, past the offices, down the entrance ramp and to the nearest available car. With each few steps they took, new attention was directed their way and by the time they had reached the vehicle they had at least ten gun sights trailing them. But with one gun trailing Croft, there was nothing the guards could do. With Lily and Croft loaded into the back seat, Henry drove off down the drive as the guards sent instructions to the sentries to not permit the vehicle to pass. The moment the barrier lowered the sentry ran back into the box.

"I must call this in sir," said the sentry as he picked up the telephone and dialled frantically. Before he got halfway. his finger slid off the phone as his body fell right and collapsed to the floor. His superior officer placed his still-smoking silenced pistol down on the table, cancelled the call and replaced it with one of his own.

"They have escaped with Comrade Blackbird and the documents. Heading east in a black vehicle with American plates. Intercept them." The senior sentry then strolled back to the barrier and raised it. Saluting the couple as they left. Did he just help us? wondered Henry.

The road was dark and visibility near non-existent. The car rushed down the rural road overshadowed by trees on either side. It was not an ideal route for any night-time driving so an escape took a great deal of skill. It had been a few years since any road maintenance had been done on this stretch and it was always left unfinished. Resources were spent maintaining the parts of Berlin on show, and not the unseen back roads. The car hit a pothole and bounced forward a metre. The sudden jolt stirred Croft who sat in the backseat with Lily. His hands were tied together with wires and cables, but they would not hold him for too long.

"He's waking up," said Lily.

"Can you knock him out again?"

"How?"

"We can't let him interfere."

"We could just dump him."

"He is our collateral."

"Henry, we don't need him. We hand the file to the Americans and we are free."

The car pulled over to the side of the road. Henry dragged Croft from the back seat, leaned him up against a tree and returned to the vehicle. The car was less than ten metres further down the road when Henry felt eyes in the back of his head. He glanced to the rear-view mirror and the look on Lily's face was familiar to him. Her caring nature was always going to be something he loved about her but he wished she would pick her moments better.

"Really? Even him?" asked Henry.

Henry reversed the car back and pulled up beside where Croft had been dumped. Henry muttered to himself and blew into his cupped hands. He removed his coat and wrapped it around Croft's shoulders. It would keep him warmer but it was not offering great coverage. Henry went back to the car to see if he could find anything else. More to appease Lily, than to save Croft. He found a blanket in the boot of the car and wrapped Croft with that and his coat. This was the best he could do. He returned to the car, shivering and pumped up the heating. It was going to be a while before the temperature raised and he would simply have to take his mind off it by driving. Shivering does not make getaway driving easy.

"Happy now?" asked Henry as he looked back at Lily again.

She confirmed she was satisfied with a smile and then turned to the file laying on the seat beside her. Emblazoned across the front were the words 'Top Secret' and 'Classified.' It had a seal holding the opening that once opened could never be closed again. She continued to stare at the file. Suppose the Russians opened them. That would make sense as they would want to make sure they retrieved all information stolen from them. They could say they found it that way and had not read it. What if they did not believe the couple had shown such discretion? or trusted they would show discretion going forward? Lily could not take her eyes off the document. Just a flick of the finger and it would open, almost by accident. So many reasons telling her not to do so, but Lily was reckless.

"Go for it. After all this we have to know," said Henry watching in the mirror.

Henry had grown to be reckless too. Lily flicked the seal and pulled out the documents inside. There was an attempted translated version first but it was incomplete. Resting underneath was the original written in Russian. Lily read and as she did, she gasped.

"What is it?" asked Henry.

"It's reprehensible, it's barbaric," exclaimed Lily.

"What is, Lil?"

"The Russians are going to fire missiles. Missiles that will kill millions of innocent people."

"Where's the target?" asked Henry.

"Beijing."

"China? But they're communists too," said Henry.

"They aren't planning on using their own ones," said Lily, "they have US ones."

"Where the hell would they get them?"

"I don't know, but I think we just dropped off someone who would."

"So, they plan to send US missiles into Beijing. Jesus, the repercussions would be global. Russian missiles can't reach the US but Chinese ones can. They would obliterate each other leaving one superpower. The Soviet Union."

"Looks like the Cuban missile crisis might just have been a distraction whilst they worked on this operation," said Lily, "there is never going to be peace in our time is there?"

"We can only hope," said Henry, "let's get these back to General Coltrane. This must be exposed."

Headlights came screaming around the bend illuminating the inside of the vehicle and blinding Henry. A smash was felt from the rear wing as something powerful crashed into them at high speed. Henry had no hope of control and no chance of preventing the inevitable. The car span off the side of the road and crashed into the trees. There it sat, silent and smoky. Nobody moved.

THE KOMITET

It was pitch black and a rancid stench of blood, death and suffering attacked relentlessly. With the eyes blinded, the other senses heightened. The smells could almost be apportioned to each and every poor soul who had ever had the misfortune to find themselves in this hell. The poor soul currently occupying this habitat happened to be Henry, and he was alert. As his eyes slowly adjusted to the dark, he could start to make out corners, cracks, and shadows slinking through the edges of the door. As his nose came acclimatised to the surroundings, it slowly closed off and he could almost block out the odours. Almost. Touch was not a sense he had the luxury of as his hands were tied firmly behind his back as he sat on a chair. That is about all he could be sure of, he was sat in a chair, his hands were tied and wherever he was, was a place nobody would ever want to stay.

His ears were his eyes right now. The one sense heightened above the rest and he listened intently for anything and everything. Southeast of him, about two metres away, water slinked down the wall. He could hear it weave through, across and over uneven cement, broken brickwork and decades of built-up dirt. He hoped it was built-up dirt, but something inside him suggested a much more sinister substance. For every person, whose last earthly visit was this devil's lair, whatever happened to them whilst in this room, there had to be some remains. Whether it was blood bursting out of a fresh wound, chipped bone from blunt attacks or projectile vomit from poison taking hold of a digestive system.

On the ceiling, he could make out the obvious shape of ventilation shafts. Three, each one metre apart. Perfectly placed to easily seal and feed in mustard gas or Zyklon B. There was no chance he was anywhere near any former World War II camps, but this room seemed akin to something you might find at Auschwitz. There was a buzzing coming from the northwest of him. About three metres across and about two metres up. As though it was floating. It wasn't an insect; it was too consistent. It sounded more like a hum with a charge. Perhaps something electrical. A TV maybe, Henry couldn't quite put his finger on it but he had been out cold for twenty-four hours. It may have even been a constant zap. He tried to put it out of his mind as the unknowing always frustrated him the most. He could hear his fingers cracking as he stretched and wiggled them around. Trying to get some blood pumping through his veins. A stretch of his toes and a shuffle in his chair was about all he could manage before the loud clunk of a key slamming into a lock echoed throughout the room.

The click of each pin shifting in the cylinder was amplified, sounding like a revolver loading. The handle came down slowly and it was clear this was a heavy door. It had been put in place to serve one purpose; to prevent anyone coming through it who wasn't meant to or wasn't welcome. The side Henry sat on was the side without the power. The door slid open, but no light flooded in. It was as dark outside as it was in. However, Henry's adjusted eyes could make out the form of a large man standing in the doorway. With a flick of a switch, the room was awash with artificial light, temporarily blinding Henry. Once his eyes readjusted, he could see he had been right in his assumptions. Right about everything. The vents in the roof were clearly used for dropping in unwanted gifts. The obstacles on the wall blocking the winding water were congealed human remains, the buzzing was an electrical hum of a television set and in the doorway stood a very large man. A very large Russian man wearing the unmistakable GB-adorned shoulder boards of the KGB.

The man looked gruff. He obviously only possessed a blunt razor and didn't get much sleep. His eyes looked dead but for the laser-like focus targeted on Henry. Henry could feel it burning into his mind. He had no idea what the man wanted and couldn't fathom any reason the KGB would be interested in him. He no longer had the file and could sensibly reason they probably did. So, what did they want with him? Regardless, he knew this wasn't going to be a friendly meeting of minds.

The man approached Henry and stood directly in front of him for what seemed like an eternity. He took one deep breath and, in a flash, firmly slapped Henry across the cheek. Though only a slap, it threw Henry to the floor with the chair in tow. Before he could even spit out the floor dirt he was dragged back up and repositioned. The man smiled at Henry. Like a shark. Then slap, and he was down again. This time the man left him there. He switched on the TV, which turned out to be a monitor and left the room.

From his home on the floor, Henry could see the monitor perfectly. This position was planned. The monitor flickered and the snow slowly subsided leaving a pitch-black screen. The audio was clear and heavy breathing could be heard. Not rough, not intimidating, not sinister. It was panic. A door clanged open and the light revealed a frightened Lily also tied to a chair. Her eyes blinked furiously as she desperately tried to adapt to the sudden blinding light. The gruff man soon appeared on screen. He turned to the camera and smiled for Henry's benefit.

"Bastard," screamed Henry.

His anguish was irrelevant. Even if anyone could have heard him, nobody would have cared. He didn't have any friends here.

"Leave her," whimpered Henry.

The man walked up to Lily and stood in front of her for what seemed like an eternity. Henry closed his eyes, desperate not to witness his Lily in such peril. He had no means of blocking his ears and the familiar sounds of a slap and a chair crashing to the floor, followed by a scream of pain, were horrifyingly familiar.

"Leave her," whispered Henry, if only to himself.

The chair crashed over again, soon followed by his own door clunking back open. The monitor showed just Lily, laying on her chair on the cold floor of whatever room she was in. Blood seeped from her nose and her face was red. The gruff man stormed straight up to Henry and grabbed him back up.

"She see you too," said the man in broken English, "Talk. Files. Talk."

"I don't know what you want," said Henry.

"In Russian," the man commanded. Henry looked blank.

"Na Russkom," shouted the man. Henry shook his head.

"Na Russkom," the man was enraged. He kicked Henry in the chest throwing him backwards. Laying on the chair on his back the man pulled out a rag and covered Henry's face.

"No, please," cried Henry.

"Na Russkom," screamed the man.

"No Russian," cried Henry. The man pulled out a bottle of water and began to pour it over Henry's rag-covered face. Henry spluttered and coughed as the man waterboarded him.

"Na Russkom, Na Russkom, Na Russkom," until his bottle was dry.

"I will talk, please, I will talk," cried Henry, "anything you want, but no Russian." He removed the rag from Henry's face and could see little fight left in his prisoner. The man was no novice at interrogation. Knowing he had broken Henry, the man accepted he couldn't speak Russian and a new plan was needed.

"They tell me you talk Russian. Intel wrong. Like usual. My English no good."

The man stared at Henry as he lay on the floor. His face was a mix of thoughts as he tried to find a solution to his predicament. He seemed to arrive at an idea he was reluctant to go with but appeared to be all he had.

"We have English talker," he sighed in resignation, "he bloody soft though."

"Please, I will only talk if you pull the wires from that camera. I don't want her to see." This amused the man. A capitalist pig caring about his capitalist dog watching him squeal. But if it got results?

The man ripped the cables from the camera and the lens lowered to the floor. He stormed out of the room, slamming the door behind him.

Henry laid flat on his back; his hands crushed behind the chair by his own weight. Water still blurring his vision. Another pair of footsteps entered the room. They sounded different somehow. Less militant. They almost had a tentative melody to their slow rhythm. He recognised the sound of heavy metal being placed beside him and soft hands carefully lifting him upright. Through his blurry eyes, he could just make out a handkerchief slowly approaching his face and, gently, wiping the remaining water from his eyes. His vision was restored.

"Stan," gasped Henry, "what are you doing here?"

"I have been sent in as my English is fluent," replied Stan.

"Of course it is, you are a native, why are you working for the Russians, Stan?"

Stan sat down across from Henry and turned on the recording device beside them.

"You are a traitor, Stan," hissed Henry.

Stan let out a long sigh. Henry expected to hear some weak excuse involving saving one's skin. He had always known Stan was all about Stan.

"My name is Stanislav not Stanley as you presumed. I am Russian. I just found the British persona to be more effective in our line of work."

"So, this is your new line of work then?"

"Much like you, I was given a choice by my country, the alternative was the unthinkable. What was yours?"

"Death would have been the nobler choice," said Henry.

"You need to realise something Henry, we are not all Americans. We don't all think the same way and we don't all want to be a part of Uncle Sam's marching band."

"Yeah, but you do," replied Henry, "why are you here, in this room, right now?"

"Because of her." Stan gestured to the monitor. Lily was looking straight at the camera. Almost pleading with them.

"She will never be yours Stan, you need to let her go."

"I know that. I accepted that a long time ago but my superiors strongly believed you would talk, to save her."

"I talk in exchange for her life and then she spends her life disappointed in me," said Henry.

"I came in here hoping that I could find any small way of helping you two. Anything at all but for me to do that, you have to give me something. Tell me about the files."

"Such a hero! Liar. Pretending to hate communism. Such an act."

"We were all acting Henry," said Stan, "it was our job. Now please, tell me what other files you saw."

"I was acting too. I won't talk. I was just buying time."

"Henry, can you not understand the severity of the situation? These people don't play games."

"These people?"

Henry stared at Stan as though he was trying to burrow into his thoughts. Maybe hoping some telepathy would allow him to read Stan's mind. He studied every inch of Stan's face meticulously. His hair was a mess and his face weathered. Far removed from his usual perfectly groomed appearance. His brow was sweaty and getting worse by the second. His eyes darted frantically between Henry and the recording device and his head would jolt as he kept trying to keep an ear out for anyone outside the door. This was not a man in control of a situation, this was a man under duress. Stan was as much a prisoner as the couple was and probably in equal danger.

"I don't believe you, Stan," whispered Henry, "your sadness betrays you. You don't need to do this. We can still fight the commies."

Stan thrust his head closer to the microphone.

"I believe in our beloved leader, our wonderful nation and the manifesto, said Stan, panic-stricken, 'I am a brother with all my comrades and honoured to be a part of their brigades. Please the intel?"

"Come on, Stan, whispered Henry, 'there were no other files but the ones you have. I have nothing else to give and are of no use to you. We can still all get out. With the file. Have you read it? It is bad, Stan, world ending bad."

"I am sure there is a good reason behind them," said Stan unconvincingly.

"They are going to bomb China."

Stan's jaw dropped at the sudden revelation. It made no sense. China was an ally.

"They are going to attack China using US missiles. Mao will respond in kind. This could go nuclear and send the world back to the dark ages. Leaving one superpower above all. Guess who?"

Stan leant forward to the microphone again but this time covered it with his hand.

"Please Henry," begged Stan, "I can't do anything to help. I am stuck and have nowhere to turn but I cannot resort to becoming a traitor.

"For the greater good, Stan," said Henry.

"Do you know what they do to traitors in my town Henry?" asked Stan, "my people are Cossacks. We still get called Mazepists, two hundred and fifty years on. They will all suffer. Anyone even considered a risk is soon found in a shallow grave. A warning to all to never bring back the scorn of the nation. I will never be able to return and my family will suffer for my deeds for the rest of their short lives."

"Stan, you are a good man. I get this is tough and I understand your situation but, if this plan is executed, then there will be no rest of their lives for millions. Come on, Stan, Defect."

"I can't," said Stan weakly.

"You can and you must. For the future of humanity," said Henry, "for the good of mankind. Let's get this file back in the hands of the Americans. Defect. We will go to America. They will protect you. We will all be safe. Defect."

"How can you be so sure?" asked Stan.

"I can't but I know I cannot, in all decency, live in any kind of world where I have stood by and let evil take over. Please, Stanislav?"

Stan removed his hand from the microphone. He sat upright and looked at Henry. For the first time in a long while he looked calm. He looked like the Stan Henry had known before. The man with the plan. The one in control. Henry had him onside now, he was sure of it.

"I don't think it matters what the microphone records now since my superiors will soon know what I have done. We just have to make sure we succeed," said Stan.

"Yes, Stan. Talk to me. What is the plan?"

"I will not defect. I cannot and will not for my people. It is something I just can't do. However, if someone else were to take the fall for this, then the KGB can hunt them down."

"But who?" asked Henry.

"A ghost. A phantom. I have made a career of concocting new people, I can make a few more."

Stan smiled and stood up. He reached over and lugged the large recording device onto the seat he had just vacated. The two men nodded at each other. Both were well aware of what the plan was as they could see only one viable option.

"My gotovy," shouted Stan.' Which Henry knew meant we are ready. His Russian comprehension miraculously returned.

The key clunked into the heavy door and it creaked open again. The gruff man, with eyes like death, marched in with a smirk on his face.

"I knew I broke you," said the man.

He turned to Stan as a ruckus came from his right, turning back just in time to see Henry fly head-first into his stomach with the chair still attached to his back. For the first time, the man found himself in the unprecedented position he often left prisoners in. Laid flat on his back staring at the ceiling. Before he even had a moment to think about getting up, he saw a heavy metal Russian standard recording device come into view. It came crashing down with the force expected from such a weight crushing his skull in one blow. Which was very handy as Henry doubted there would be any chance of Stan lifting it again.

The two men had managed to put aside their natural pacifist tendencies. They accepted for this short period, and for the greater good, they may have to undertake certain acts that would normally repulse them.

The corpse of the gruff man was soon curled in the corner of the room and Henry looked very much the authentic KGB officer. His uniform was adorned with blue piping and GB was displayed prominently on his shoulder boards.

REUNIFICATION

Henry and Stan peered around the edges of the doorway. It was as dark outside the room as it was inside, but flickering artificial lights began illuminating the corridor. This was another of those crude by-design details. Making it appear as dark outside as it was inside would leave most prisoners with a feeling of utter hopelessness. The corridor was clear and they listened for any incoming. Nothing. Henry thought to himself he would rather have heard footsteps or mumbled voices so he could place the guards and know exactly where to avoid, but, instead, it was silence and this did not sit well with him.

"We need to act like we belong," said Stan, "remember what I always told you, confidence sells."

The two men began to walk down the corridors, slowly entering the slightly lighter areas under the flickering lamps. To most, it would still seem extremely dark but having spent so long in the conditions of the interrogation room, Henry had perfect vision.

"Do you know where they are keeping her?" asked Henry.

"Yes," replied Stan as he continued down the corridor.

As they reached the next adjoining corridor, Henry stopped to peer around before going any further.

"What are you doing?" asked Stan, "I said act like we belong," as he boldly strode forward on the route. The lights were solid in this corridor and the floors were much cleaner. A clear indication they were leaving the cell area.

"Lily?" said Henry.

"Yes. One thing first," replied Stan.

Moving towards them was a guard with eyes locked on the pair.

"This is it," said Henry.

"Shhhh, confidence," ordered Stan.

Henry pulled himself up and pushed his shoulders back. He had never seen a KGB man before today, but very much doubted they ever slouched. The guard got closer and closer, looking them up and down. Taking in every detail he could. His hand rested on his holster. Stan did not break stride for a moment and Henry mimicked him as best he could. The guard kept his hand on his holster and Henry replied in kind. He had absolutely no intention of firing the weapon but knew he must make the guard believe he would if indeed the guard suspected anything. The guard drew closer to the two phoney officers and then, with about two metres between them, he moved to the side clearing the path. As the men passed, the guard raised his hand to his forehead offering a salute. Henry looked at his epaulettes and realised he outranked him. With the first air of confidence, since he had woken in this hellhole, he returned a salute to the guard with an acknowledging nod and all three men walked on. Henry walked tall. He knew the right demeanour for this character and he had found his physicality.

"Just another role," he whispered.

"Such is life," replied Stan.

Having walked down multiple corridors, all looking similar apart from the cleanliness and upkeep that seemed to improve as they approached the administration areas, they reached a large wooden door. The wood was polished and a nameplate adorned it. Lt. Colonel Rasintov was the English translation. Stan reached into his back pocket, retrieving a large ring with what looked like, hundreds of keys attached.

"Where did you get them?" asked Henry.

"I swiped them from the previous owner of your costume, I thought they may make our life a little easier."

"Lil is in here?" asked Henry.

"File first," said Stan.

Stan quietly opened the door. Concern was written all over his face. Henry felt the anxiety too. This was extremely risky and the danger was greater than it had been when he previously stole the documents. He knew exactly what to expect from his dummy run and he knew the layout of the base. This was going in blind. What was behind this door? For all they know there could be a welcoming committee with weapons primed ready to unload the moment they enter their crosshairs. Stan's hand shook as he moved it towards the door handle. The sweat seeping from it had made his hand glisten and Henry wondered if he would even be able to grip. Henry's hands were the same, needing to continually wipe them on his borrowed KGB trousers.

The door opened quietly and they both held their breath, desperately hoping to make it through safely. Their hearts skipped a beat, their eyes darted around the office looking for any personnel in any direction. It was clear. With a sigh of relief, they closed the door behind them and secured it. Leaving the key in the lock made it more difficult for anyone to enter should they try to. Though they would have little chance of getting out if anyone did discover they were in there, little chance was better than no chance at all.

Stan headed straight to a filing cabinet on the far side of the room. He pulled out his carousel of keys and went through them one by one. Though it only took a matter of seconds to find the right one, to the two men, it felt like hours. As soon as Stan was in the filing cabinet he rifled through the multiple files until he came across the one marked #013K-OP-MAO.

"Here," said Stan, "this is what you wanted."

Henry took the file and tucked it into his coat, secured under his belt.

"Lil now," said Henry.

"One more thing," said Stan.

"Come on, we have to go."

Stan held his finger out to Henry as he turned towards a painting on the far side of the room. The command was clear, wait. Stan approached the painting and, with little care, ripped it from its mounting, revealing a large safe. Finding the right key was easy this time as it was much larger than the others and had that old-fashioned shape and feel with teeth on both sides.

"What are you after?" asked Henry.

Stan opened the safe and removed only one item. A black leather executive briefcase. His black leather executive briefcase.

"What do you keep in there?" asked Henry.

"Freedom."

Stan unlocked the briefcase and turned it to Henry. All he could see were some traveller's cheques and documents belonging to Stanislav Orel.

"What does it mean?" asked Henry.

Stan gave him one hell of a smug grin. The kind of grin a person gives when asked if they were proud of something they probably shouldn't have done but in reality, yes, they were very proud. He rotated the combination locks on the front to a different number, pulled the openers aside and the bottom of the briefcase lifted to reveal a hidden chamber. A chamber that was in no way empty, and the contents no way sparse. Besides a few thousand US dollars in tight rolls, it was brimming with various ID cards, passports from all over the world, birth certificates, bank details and driving licenses Any documentation needed to make a made-up person appear legit was there. They all displayed Stan's photo but with different names.

"I can be whoever I want to be," said Stan, "that is freedom."

Stan rummaged through to the bottom where he pulled out two recognisable blue passports.

"And so can you."

Henry took the passports from Stan, grateful to know they had never actually been sent to the authorities in the US. He opened the passports and studied them like he had found a long-forgotten toy from his childhood.

"Why?" asked Henry.

"I always had them. They were our get-out-of-jail cards. If it ever all went wrong and came crashing down around us, I wasn't ever going to desert you. Use them to get any documents you need."

Henry put the two passports safely in his pocket and hugged Stan.

"I always knew you were decent," said Henry.

"We aren't free yet," said Stan as he passed Henry a roll of cash, "in case we get split up."

Stan closed his briefcase, quietly turned the key to the door and peered into the corridor.

"Act as we belong?" asked Henry.

"There is no good reason for us ever being in this office," replied Stan.

The corridor outside was empty. It reassured Henry as he thought to himself how undermanned this place was. Complacency was kicking in and he knew he needed to shake that feeling as it could be the death of them.

"Now let's get Lil," said Stan.

Stan and Henry inched along the walls of the corridor just outside the cell holding Lily.

"We need to move," said Henry but before he could get his words out Stan had thrust his palm over his mouth. He pulled his finger up to his lips and stared at Henry. Once he knew he had his complete attention, he raised his finger to signal 'One,' then returned it to his lips. Stan quietly looked through the slot of the cell door and gestured for Henry to do the same. Lily sat on a chair with her back to them, her hands cuffed behind her. By the door stood one guard and Henry understood Stan's communication. Stan looked down at the holster on Henry's belt and gestured for him to hand over the pistol. Henry's face went white with panic. Stan rolled his eyes before reassuring Henry with a calming gesture it was not going to come to that. Henry paused for a while before reluctantly nodding and passing the pistol to Stan.

"The man with the plan," whispered Henry.

Stan pushed Henry back against the wall to the side of the door, out of sight. He leant into the hatch and called through to the guard.

"Comrade," said Stan, beckoning the man to the door.

The guard approached, placing his head close to the hatch and before he knew what was happening, he found the barrel of a Makarov pistol pushed firmly against his forehead.

"Otkroy dver, medlenno," said Stan ordering the guard to open slowly.

The guard complied and unlocked the door. He slowly pulled it open without taking his eyes off Stan for an instant. Out of sight of Stan, the guard stealthily unclipped his holster. When the gap in the door was wide enough, the guard thrust his pistol through, pointing it straight at Stan.

"Stand-off," said the guard.

Before either man with a pistol in hand and another facing him had time to think of any possible move for a satisfactory resolution, Henry leapt into Stan and the door simultaneously. Stan flew to the floor in the corridor and the door smashed hard into the guard. His pistol crashed to the floor and was quickly retrieved by Henry. Stan jumped to his feet and the two men entered the cell where the unarmed guard agonisingly held up his busted arm. They closed the door behind them and shut the hatch.

Henry rushed to where Lily was tied to the chair. He gestured to the guard for the handcuff keys and for Stan to take the man's uniform. He freed Lily and helped her to her feet. He pulled her in for an embrace but it felt cold. Nothing like what he expected. Her arms remained by her sides and she seemed to only be a part of the embrace as she lacked any interest in fighting it.

Lily looked up at Henry, her face was cold and stern.

"You talked again," said Lily.

"No," said Henry.

"Don't lie to me," said Lily, "it was the last thing I saw on the monitor."

"No, it was a ruse. I was trying to buy time."

"You talked before to Croft and now to the KGB," said Lily, "I thought you were an idealist, not a traitor."

"Stop this. I didn't talk," said Henry, "I didn't have anything to say. You know this. There were no other files. I had nothing to give. I was just buying time."

"I don't think I can believe you," said Lily, "I think you would sell out your country to save me. Should I be grateful? No, it makes me complicit in the worst thing someone can do. How can I ever look at you the same way?"

"Lily."

Lily looked over to the shadows of the room having been unaware of anyone else's presence.

"Stan, what's going on?"

"There is no time for that right now but you must believe Henry, he did not talk and was in fact willing to sacrifice himself and also you for the good of his country."

"Really?" asked Lily.

"Really. There is one thing I know about this man above everything, he would do pretty much anything at all to keep you safe but selling out his country is a step too far."

"But he asked them to turn the monitors off?"

"If the worst came to it, then I didn't want your last memories of me to be my murder," said Henry.

"I hope one day I can find someone who loves me enough to lie to the enemy whilst being tortured in a dank, dark cell in God knows where just to protect me. Lily, he's a good man," said Stan.

Lily looked back up at Henry's face. His eyes were welling up and the anguish at the idea of losing Lily and even more so her faith in him was tearing him apart. She gently took his hands and her demeanour completely softened. Her eyes had brightened and she looked at him as she so often had before, as though she could see nothing else at all.

"He really is, isn't he," said Lily, "I think I am ready to be the wife of a boring professor now."

"Good, we need to get out of here," said Stan, before tossing the guard uniform to Lily. Lily looked at it bemused before she noticed Henry had been wearing one the whole time.

"What about the guards?" asked Lily, "they will notice I'm not a man."

"The place is pretty empty," said Henry.

"Walk like you belong and hopefully, nobody will look too closely."

The three desperate prisoners crept out of the cell, checking every direction for any incoming. In a close-knit group, the two men flanked Lily who looked like a little boy playing dress-up with their father's uniform. None of them really believed Lily looked convincing and none of them believed she would fool anyone who even glanced their way but nobody was going to mention it. All thought the other two were confident and didn't want to break their spirits.

Footsteps came from ahead. They grew louder as they approached the three making Henry and Lily freeze. Stan was unaffected.

"Play the role," said Stan.

The footsteps got louder and louder and suddenly picked up pace. Lily squeezed Henry's hand and he felt both their heartbeats rocket. The two hands clasped together, coated in sweat. Stan slapped his hand down on the couple separating them.

"KGB do not hold hands," snapped Stan.

The now running footsteps turned the corner of the corridor ahead of them and a soldier with a rifle over his shoulder came storming towards them. Stan reached into his jacket, his hand shaking and his breath short. Henry reached for his holster but could barely still his hand enough to unclip it. If ever they were complete underdogs in a situation where they outnumbered the opponent, this was it. Anyone who knew how to fire a weapon and had an ounce of composure could take them down with ease. The soldier grew closer, making a quick analysis of the three prisoner's apparel as he approached. He could determine Stan was a civilian consultant, Henry, his superior officer and then what looked like a soldier who had shrunk, though the shrunken soldier was obscured by the others. The three held their breath, ready to leap into action, should it be called for. For once in Stan's life, he had absolutely no plan. The soldier was mere feet away from them when he fully clocked Lily in her majorly oversized uniform. The unexpected spectacle before him made him lose his stride and he collided with Henry and stumbled over. The soldier's face went white with dread. He had barged into his superior officer. Fear of the repercussions was clear in his eyes. Henry stared at the man as he writhed on the floor trying to get back on his feet whilst desperate panic hindered him.

"Prodolzhat," shouted Henry, and with a clear command to carry on, the soldier gratefully did. The three could breathe again.

This moment of calm was short-lived. It was no time for complacency and within a few short minutes, more footsteps could be heard coming their way. These footsteps were not gathering speed, they were already coming at full pelt. It was not long before another armed soldier came running down the hallway. This one barely even glanced at the three walking by. Panic etched all over his face as he stormed past. Before he had even turned off from the corridor, another soldier appeared as fast and as panicked as the one before.

"I thought this base was empty?" asked Lily.

"These areas usually are," replied Stan.

The three stopped as a rumble could be heard ahead of them. A rumble that was growing. Voices could be heard. Not distinguishable but heard. Multiple voices all shouting over one another. The rumble soon became a thunderous roar as a whole platoon ran along the corridor, passing at breakneck speed. All their faces showed the same panic and dread seen on the earlier passers-by. The fear of men who doubted wherever they were headed, they would ever return. The three watched the men go by. Though a great benefit to know they were of no interest to the soldiers, something was going on. Something big. As the platoon filtered out, Henry grabbed the arm of one of the stragglers.

"Kuda ty idesh," Henry asked to find out where they were going.

"K stene," replied the soldier as he tried to wriggle free from Henry's grasp.

"Why would they be heading to the Wall, Stan?" asked Henry. Stan shrugged.

"Pochemu?" asked Stan

"Oni zastrelili Kennedi,'" replied the soldier who easily pulled out of Henry's clutches as he stood there shellshocked.

"They shot Kennedy," said Henry, "dear God."

THE HIGHEST BIDDER

Henry could barely stand upright as the news hit like a bullet to the heart. His thinking was fuzzy at best as emotions took control of him. A mix of rage and sadness ripped through his whole being. Henry believed in the US. Henry believed in capitalism and the Democrats. Henry believed in Kennedy. The great hope of ending the constant threat of nuclear attack that loomed since not long after the war.

"Who could have done this?" seethed Henry.

"It must have been a commie," replied Stan, "they are rushing to the Berlin Wall to prepare for repercussions. There will be bloodshed tonight."

Henry threw himself against the brickwork as a fit of rage possessed him. Punching repeatedly as he questioned the arrogance of it all. He clenched his fist around the sickle and hammer motif badge displayed on his chest and ripped it off as though removing a plaster. He reached again to his holster but this time his hand was deathly still. He withdrew his pistol. There was a look in his eyes that had never been there before. A look that scared the others.

"Henry?" whispered Lily, "what are you doing?"

"It's always the same, isn't it? It always has the same outcome all over the world," said Henry, almost to himself, "they all just take whatever they want. The Crimea, the Eastern Bloc, Kennedy's life. All with this. The power of life and death in the hands of every brainwashed fool."

"Henry, please can you calm down," said Lily, "breathe."

Henry raised the weapon held firmly in his hand and directed it straight down the corridor. If another soldier was to turn that corner, he would run right into the sights. The atmosphere was tense. Neither Stan nor Lily knew what to say or do and neither were equipped with the training or strength to wrestle the gun from Henry's grip. Henry continued to aim in the one direction, never wavering. He was like a statue. Footsteps approached the end of the corridor. Henry's gaze was steely and focused. His finger poised on the trigger. The footsteps were inches away from the turn. Henry's thumb twitched. A foot came into view soon followed by a uniformed skirt. Henry lowered the pistol at once. He realised this was not a soldier but an admin secretary and his moment of madness subsided as the secretary turned back on herself without even looking their way. Never knowing how close she had come to her end by a momentary grip of vengeful insanity.

Henry was shaking. Coming to his senses to find himself holding a pistol and harbouring thoughts of intent. It was not him. It was something he never wanted to be. He felt disgusted. He flicked his thumb over the chamber switch, dropping the magazine to the floor. He placed the weapon on a nearby windowsill and tentatively stepped back. Lily reached out and drew him to her chest. He looked up at her and his sorrow was evident. No words were spoken as no words were needed. Stan approached the weapon laying on the windowsill. He removed his pistol from inside his jacket, released the magazine and placed it alongside.

"I could never do it either," said Stan.

The three exited the main entrance onto a courtyard. Even here was deathly quiet. Any vehicles previously here had all left recently to head to the Wall.

"We have to go by foot, through the woods," said Stan, "it will only be military personnel on the roads tonight and there will be blocks at every junction."

"We are in uniform though?" said Lily.

"You look as though you stole someone else's uniform, he has ripped the sacred emblem from his jacket and I don't have an authorised pass,' said Stan, 'I don't fancy our chances."

The area was deserted. It looked like a ghost town where people all upped and left at short notice. The lights were still on in the buildings. The courtyard floodlights were bright and the drive lights lit. They could see the guardhouse at the driveway entrance was dark and empty and the gate sat raised. If they did have a vehicle and the roads were a viable option, then getting out of here would have been a doddle. With no reason for stealth and no apparent tail on them, urgency was felt by all and they started running towards the gate.

As the road exited the base grounds it took a sharp right, as directly opposite was the woods. The perfect route for an escape and even better if nobody was chasing you. It was only a matter of metres and they would be through that gate and hidden by the canopy of the trees. Out of the corner of his eye, Henry swore he saw a shadow through the window of the guardhouse but looked again and it was clear. His mind playing tricks on him he thought. A gloved hand reached up and grabbed the gate rope dragging it down and shut fast. The arm was soon followed into view by the sinister smile of a man who should never be trusted.

"Croft," hissed Henry.

As if the assassination of Kennedy wasn't enough to enrage Henry, he now stood twenty feet away from the mercenary who had played him. The man responsible for Lily being in this hellhole. To make matters worse the grin on Croft's face cut to the bone. The man showed no care, no remorse and was the embodiment of selfish desire. Like a spoiled child in a position of power.

"I like to think you are pleased to see me," said Croft.

"How can you do what you do," snapped Henry, "does nothing matter to you?"

"I see myself as a businessman," replied Croft, "I see an opportunity and I take it."

"By playing off an enemy against your own nation and questioning other's patriotism?" seethed Henry.

"I'm sorry my hypocrisy offends you so much," said Croft, "you'll live. Maybe."

"Don't think you have had any effect on my mood," said Henry, "they assassinated Kennedy."

"Yeah, well, too bad. You put yourself in that position and you make yourself a target," replied Croft, "though he was always too liberal for my liking."

The whole area was silent and besides these four people standing by the gate, the place seemed deserted. Henry weighed up the situation. Croft stood alone in front of them. He had no backup. He had nobody to call on since his comrades were all at the Wall and he wouldn't have any hope of any US personnel getting to this location presently. There were three of them and one of him. For once, they had the advantage.

"In case you are thinking of doing something dumb," said Croft, "I did bring a friend with me."

Croft pulled his hand out of his pocket, attached to his service pistol. His Russian service pistol. Stan and Henry looked at each other, sharing contemplation of the mistake they had made and how much they wished they hadn't discarded their pistols. If only to use them as a bluff.

"Who do you work for?" snapped Henry, "Really?"

Croft just chuckled to himself before raising his gun. He pointed it at Henry.

"Bang, you're dead."

Then he pointed it at Stan.

"Bang, dead."

Finally, he pointed it at Lily whilst smirking back at Henry.

"Bang, you're dead too. Three dead traitors. I will come out of this looking good," said Croft, "might even get me a medal."

"We are not traitors," cried Henry.

"Sure, you are. He is aiding the escape of two spies and you stole intel from your own nation and supplied it to the enemy."

"A traitor knowingly betrays their own country for personal gain," said Henry, "come on Croft, I can see it in your eyes."

"You got me. I am no idealist," said Croft, "and honestly, I couldn't give two hoots who comes out on top in all this so long as my pockets keep getting lined. I am fine and dandy. So, did you talk again?"

"No, he did not," said Stan.

"Not even to save that little lady?" asked Croft.'

"No, he did not," said Lily, "He has honour. He's twice the man you are."

"Well, I told them you wouldn't but they always think they know best. KGB methods never fail and all that," said Croft, "look, it is getting cold out here and you clearly don't know your next move so I will get the ball rolling. Make me an offer."

"Money?" balked Henry.

"Of course, that is what all wars are really about," replied Croft.

The three glanced at each other to see if any of them showed signs of being able to make any kind of financial offer that might appeal to Croft. Henry and Lily didn't have a penny and if they did then they certainly wouldn't have access to it here. Stan's eyes widened. The corner of his mouth twitched. The couple could see he wanted to say something but there was no chance Croft would not overhear. They took solace in this look. It was a look they had seen many times over the years. A look that said trust me, I have a plan.

A gunshot blasted through their ears and the gravel flew up as a bullet skimmed past their feet. They froze and stared at Croft and the smoking pistol in his hand.

"I'm losing patience," said Croft.

"Wait, wait," said Stan with his hands raised, one still holding the briefcase, "I can make an offer."

"Now we're talking," said Croft, "I knew a successful crew like you would have something somewhere. Especially him," he gestured towards Stan.

"So, Stanislav, what have you got?" asked Croft, "a nice little retirement fund? Sure, you do. The man with the plan."

"In here," Stan tapped on his briefcase.

"No, we've been through that," said Croft, "just some traveller's cheques. It will take more than that."

"If you think that, then you haven't really been through this," said Stan.

Stan nodded his head and Croft read it loud and clear.

"You sneaky son of a gun, have you got a secret compartment?" asked Croft, "of course you have and of course they missed it. What you got Stan?"

Stan crept towards Croft, who kept his pistol trailing Stan with every step.

"No funny business now," said Croft.

"I'm just showing you how to access it," replied Stan.

Stan stood two feet in front of Croft who now rested the tip of his pistol barrel on Stan's forehead. Stan calmly lowered the briefcase and lay it flat in his arms. He opened it as normal to access the standard compartment containing nothing of interest. Croft tilted his head at him. The look said it all. You are on thin ice. Stan turned the combination to the second code and pulled back the fasteners. The underside popped up and revealed to Croft the assortment of false documentation.

"About three thousand dollars and a load of forged passports. What the hell am I gonna do with a load of forged passports with your picture in them?" shouted Croft.

"Open them," said Stan.

Croft kept the gun resting on Stan's forehead as he used his free hand to retrieve one of the passports from the briefcase. He opened it to find the lamination unsealed and bank details relating to that identity.

"You can put your photo in every one of these," said Stan, "each account holds ten thousand dollars. There are thirty in total."

"You have been a busy boy," said Croft as his face lit up.

"Retirement fund," replied Stan.

Croft went to inspect more of the bounty contained by the briefcase but stopped suddenly as he was about to dive in.

"This thing doesn't have anything else secret about it now does it?" questioned Croft.

"Not a thing," replied Stan but Croft couldn't read him at all.

Croft looked back at the contents of the case and slowly lowered his gun from Stan's head to use as an extension of his hand. He moved it around inside the case, rummaging through his newly acquired treasure chest. He would flip a passport open, see the lamination unsealed, note the bank details and move on to the next.

"I may even retire myself," Croft said to himself.

"Well, maybe one more secret," said Stan.

He pushed on a hidden button and before Croft knew what hit him the briefcase slammed shut on his arm. He pushed it into Croft and manoeuvred to the side. Croft stumbled backwards, grabbing Stan's coat as he fell and dragging him down on top of him. Another gunshot rang out.

Absolute silence returned but for the echo of the gunshot floating into the distance. The two men lay still on the floor with the briefcase between them. There were passports, bank details, licenses and Identification documents littering the gravel drive whilst the traveller's cheques were being stolen by the wind. Quiet laughter began to grow from the ground. The sound of relief and personal victory in the face of such high stakes. The laughter grew louder and had a Russian twang to it. Stan rolled over with a smile on his face.

"Let's get out of here," said Stan, "quickly."

Henry and Lily rushed to help him to his feet.

"Let's go," said Henry.

"No, wait," said Stan as he stopped to collect up the spilt contents of his case.

"Come on man," said Henry, "we have to go."

Stan just raised a finger to gesture he would be quick.

"Stan," said Lily.

"Go on, I will be right behind you," said Stan.

Henry pulled on Lily's arm and the two began their final escape to the edge of the road and across into the woods and the cover of the canopy. They stopped just past the first row of trees, where they were out of sight, and looked back to see Stan right behind them when a further gunshot rang out. This was not the same sound as before. It was louder and the echo made it sound like it could be coming from anywhere. Stan stopped in his tracks to check himself and then looked to see if he could identify where the threat was coming from. Croft was down and all military personnel had left for the Wall. Stan looked back at where Croft was laying and the pistol was a few feet from him. After the near-fatal error in discarding their weapons earlier, Stan was not going to put themselves in peril again. He ran back and retrieved the pistol. Henry and Lily could only wait and hope he made it out. None of the three liked the idea of using weapons or taking human life but the severity of the situation they were in had finally hit home. They were fighting the enemy and the enemy wouldn't think twice.

Stan ran towards the wood with his briefcase in one hand and pistol in the other. A shot fired out hitting him straight on the back of his lower leg. Stan crashed to the floor with the briefcase and pistol flying out of his hands. Soon the contents of the briefcase, Stan's artistic creations, the bank details and his retirement fund were also stolen by the wind. Stan tried to scramble to his feet and desperately continue but after a few feet, he fell again. Blood ran down his shoes, leaving pools on the floor. He tried to fight on but collapsed down on the main road just outside the base gate. He could not go any further.

About thirty feet behind him a rustling of boots on gravel. Not marching but movement. From behind the trees Henry and Lily watched Croft slowly getting to his feet. One hand gripped against his torso and the other gestured back to the base. A flashlight signalled back to Croft and the sniper stood down.

"I will find you. You won't escape me. Where you gonna go?" shouted Croft so as to be heard in all directions, "they left you, Stan."

Stan looked up from his viewpoint on the floor towards the rows of trees in the darkened woods. He could make out the eyes of Henry and Lily. He could read their urgency to want to come to his aid but he shook his head. He knew he would not escape this time. Even if they got him out of there, his injury would slow them down and they would all soon be caught. Stan lifted his shaking hand and pointed towards the floor of the wood. A few feet from where the couple were masked by the foliage, lay the pistol. Lily crept towards the weapon, making sure not to be seen or heard by Croft. She lowered herself flat onto her stomach and reached out. Her hand edged towards the pistol but passed it by. She crawled out of the edge of the wood and onto the road. Keeping as low as she could and using Stan as cover. With one huge effort, she stretched as far as she possibly could and this was far enough to reach Stan's finger and clasp it. Thank you, she mouthed as she gave him the warmest embrace she possibly could in the circumstances.

"Lily," whispered Stan with all he had in him, "I can't be captured. I can't be a traitor. Henry knows."

"Stan?" asked Lily.

"Please, help me," whispered Stan.

Lily nodded in recognition though her eyes were teary. She slowly crawled back behind the trees, picking up the pistol as she went. She handed it to Henry. Henry shook his head defiantly. It was very clear what was being asked of him. He looked back to his friend, laying on the floor in the road. His eyes crying out for the relief only death could bring. Henry was lost in a battle with his own ethics.

"Please Henry," mouthed Stan.

Lily gently took hold of Henry's arm and raised it so the pistol was aimed at their friend.

"This is not wrong. This is mercy. You are saving him," reassured Lily.

Henry's arm was shaking and the aim kept wandering.

"This is the right thing," said Lily as she supported Henry's arm, "I am proud of you."

Henry began to calm. His arm went still and steady.

Stan nodded at Henry before he closed his eyes tightly.

"Thank you, Stan," whispered Henry, before firing the fatal mercy shot into Stan's forehead.

The loud sound of the pistol made Croft dive to the floor for cover whilst frantically gesturing back to the base for assistance. He was unsure of where the shot came from but had no intention of finding out. The dread felt by Stan and Henry when realising they shouldn't have discarded their weapons was now being endured by Croft. He couldn't believe he had dismissed the sniper prematurely. His only backup. Unarmed, he clambered up and started to shuffle towards the base. He soon stopped in his tracks as he heard footsteps walk about five paces and stop. He turned to see Lily standing on the edge of the wood pointing the pistol right at him. Croft grinned at her. The smug grin that says you haven't got the balls before it dropped to a grimace as lead flew into his head and out the other side. He collapsed to the floor with a look on his face that said I wasn't expecting that.

"For mercy?" Henry asked from behind the trees.

"For the greater good," replied Lily.

GEORGE AND EMILY

Daylight had broken through and birds sang their morning chorus. There was a cool, fresh, crisp bite in the air. Not something people run to shelter from but that November morning air that makes you feel alive. Especially common in this area of the world. A nondescript car with Czechoslovakian plates pulled up on a main road about fifty metres from the crest of a hill. A nondescript couple stepped out of the vehicle, thanked the driver and composed themselves.

"This is it," said Henry, "the most important thing we will ever do in our lives."

"At twenty-two," replied Lily, "What an adventure."

"You want to go again?" joked Henry as Lily shook her head.

Henry opened his jacket and dug out file #013K-OP-MAO from the safety of his belt. He flicked through it to make sure everything was intact and read through it one last time.

"My God, can you imagine if they had pulled this off?" said Henry, "life as we know it would end."

Lily moved in, closed the file in Henry's hands and gently took them from him.

"But they didn't," she replied, "let's get these back to General Coltrane."

The couple began walking over the crest of the hill. The sun was now high in the sky and beaming down on the road. It felt like a calling to Henry. Each step was a step into the light. In the distance, the guarded area of the US base came into view. It was a marvellous site. Though still in Berlin, Henry felt his feet firmly approaching US soil. Lily halted mid-step. One hand covering her mouth, the other grabbing Henry's arm.

"We can't take these back," said Lily.

"What do you mean? Why not?"

"Don't you see? If we walk in there and hand these to General Coltrane, we will be recognised. He has seen us. We will be arrested on the spot as the thieves who stole it or, even worse, arrested as enemy agents."

Henry's face sank. The idea of walking into that base to a hero's welcome had really grown on him but Lily was right. He knew if they were deemed enemies of the state they would be sent to prison for sure. Without a trial, with little hope of ever being released and with no hope of ever seeing each other again. The possibility was heartbreaking.

***

It was mid-afternoon by the time the couple had walked the long route to the nearest town. The roads had been completely empty. Not a single vehicle had passed by and not a single person seen. Yesterday's major event in Dallas was causing ripples around the world. Even the small suburb they had reached seemed eerily still. There was a lot of support for the West, even on this side of the Berlin Wall. A high proportion of the communities were desperate to be reunified or live under a Western government. Though they wouldn't dare mention it. Not even to their nearest friends in fear of being reported to the Stasi. Henry wondered if the people were mourning. He wondered if they would dare but also considered there may have been a suddenly imposed national curfew so the military had easy access to manoeuvre if needed.

They entered a small coffee shop, ordered a drink and a pastry and sat at a far table to try and assemble a plan. How they wished Stan was here to help. The bell above the door chimed. Lily noticed the man entering carried a large bag over his shoulder and left a small motorcycle outside.

"Sind sie ein kurier?" she asked the man.

The man tapped on his bag and nodded his head.

"Eine minute bitte," said Henry as he knew exactly what Lily was thinking.

He ran out of the coffee shop and was gone all of a few minutes. When he returned, he handed a well-wrapped and very secure package to the courier. Written on the front were the words, *FAO General Coltrane*, followed by a small note that read, *Sorry for causing you any problems.*

The courier saw the address on the package and thrust it back at Henry.

"Nein," said the courier.

Henry reached into his pocket and withdrew the roll of US dollars. He slowly placed them in the hand of the courier. One after another. With each note he placed, the courier's defiance eased. This was a big ask and a delivery that could result in a lot of questions. Something the courier did not fancy becoming part of their day. The courier thrust his hand full of notes back to Henry. Refusing to take on the job. Lily took the hand of the courier. She pointed to the name of the addressee on the package.

"Amerikanisch."

The courier looked at the coffee shop barista behind the counter who offered a look of support and encouragement.

"For the greater good," said Lily.

The courier looked at the other patrons in their tatty clothes and worn faces. The hardship they had endured, the hardship he endured and the hardship his family endured must not be the hardship his children endure. The courier nodded and took the package from Henry. Henry passed the courier the money he had offered but the man refused it.

"For the greater good," said the courier, and left at once.

Henry and Lily sat back at their table in the corner.

"What now?" said Lily.

Henry reached into his pocket and placed the remaining money in front of them.

"But we can't go back," said Lily, 'ever.'

Henry reached back into his pocket with a smirk and this time withdrew two blue US passports.

"He never sent them?" said Lily, as she grabbed at the documents, "but we still can't go back. They will arrest us on arrival."

Lily opened the passport to see Henry's photo attached.

"Oh, this is yours," said Lily.

She was about to hand it back when she suddenly paused. Bemused, she looked up at Henry. He just kept smiling at her.

"George Brooks?" asked Lily.

George handed the other passport to Lily who eagerly opened it.

"He made me younger like he promised," said Lily, "Emily Williams. I am not sure I like that surname."

George took Emily's hand in his.

"How about Emily Brooks?"

MARTIN AND EMILY

It was the early hours of the morning and everything was quiet bar the regulated beep indicating life. To anyone who ever spent time in this small room, it would feel for that period this was the whole world. There was nothing past the door as nothing beyond held a shred of value. It may have only been three feet away from another room containing birth, death or anything in between but that held no significance in this bubble. Emily sat in a corner chair, curled up under a blanket. Her head rested on her arm and her face displayed the anguish of her dreams. The rhythmical beeping was feeding into her subconscious, forming visions which, though abstract, would always result in the unthinkable solid monotone. A sound recognised by all, yet experienced by few. Which was a good thing. Nobody wanted to experience it in real life and it was best left to the compounds of television drama.

George lay unconscious in a bed in the centre of the room. Wired up to a heart monitor and various other medical equipment. This was a fight George would have had no trouble winning throughout his life but, now in his eighties, his body was not what it once was. His mind was as strong as ever and was willing his body to follow suit. Like encouraging an old dog, on its last legs, to go on a walk they had many times before. Their eyes show desire, but their frail form won't comply.

Emily was woken by a yelp. Martin had got there as quickly as he could but struggled to enter the room. He stood in the doorway absorbing the scene that greeted him and all he could do was crumble. The strong young man, full of ambition and ideals had reverted to a lost little boy on discovering his role model wasn't immortal after all. Emily approached Martin and took him in her arms. He collapsed on her at once. Thrusting his face into her shoulder in an attempt to shut out reality.

'Oh Gran, why?' cried Martin.

That was a much bigger question than Martin realised. It could open a whole can of worms and Emily was not in the right frame of mind. Why did it happen? Why were you both participating in a road race? Why can't you act your age and conform to society? Why can't you just be normal grandparents? Emily offered no answers but drew him in tighter. He was broken, as was she, but she had greater resolve and would use every ounce of it to help Martin. Nobody could predict the outcome of this hospital visit as much as they could predict the outcome of the next week or month or year but Martin had a real future ahead of him and the remainder of Emily's life was to be dedicated to making sure he would be okay once both she and George were no longer around.

Martin gently pulled away from the embrace. He wiped his eyes with his sleeves and tentatively walked to the side of George's bed. Believing any sudden movement or unnecessary noise could be detrimental to his grandfather's condition. He took one of George's fingers in his hand and lightly squeezed it. He let out a gasp.

'What is it?' asked a desperate Emily.

'Nothing,' sobbed Martin, 'like squeezing a stick.' Emily sat back down and pulled the blanket limply across her legs. Her head fell against the back of the chair. Martin stared at his grandfather and studied him. Was there anything to be seen around the eyes? Was that a smile on his face? Was he at least comfortable? Martin took the edge of the sheets in his hand and gently tugged at them. He would hate to think a ripple of dislodged bedding was digging into George's back, irritating him whilst unable to do anything. Suffering in silence.

"I wish you both could just act your age," whimpered Martin.

There was a knock on the door frame and in the entrance stood a boy and his mother.

"I'm sorry to disturb you but we heard about the accident on the radio. I know this must be a terrible time for you, but Tommy told me about the incident the other day. He shouldn't have strayed from our block but... well, we just wanted to thank George."

Emily gestured them in and Martin turned to hide his tears. He realised he had been wrong about everything and there was a grave possibility that his last conversation with his grandfather would have been him berating him. It was heartbreaking.

"Can he talk?" asked Tommy.

"Not at the moment," said Emily, "but he can hear."

Tommy shuffled towards George, continuously looking back at Emily and his mother for reassurance. He placed a bunch of grapes on the bedside cabinet and laid his hand on George's. He leaned over and gently kissed George on the forehead.

"Thank you, Mr."

"His name's George, Tommy," said his mother.

"Thank you, Mr George."

George let out a guttural sound and the heart monitor flatlined. The monotoned solid beep nobody wanted to hear sent the room into a panic. Tommy ran to his mother's arms.

"George," screamed Emily, "Martin?" Martin rushed to seek immediate assistance. The mother took Tommy from the room as a crash trolley rolled in closely followed by a doctor and his team. One nurse set a defibrillator as another prepared the patient. The doctor gripped the paddles impatiently as they all waited for the machine to reach its charge.

"Clear," instructed the doctor as he thrust the two paddles onto George's chest. He shocked his heart but there was no response. Martin held his gran, hoping to protect her from this being her last memory.

"Clear," called the doctor again with no response.

"Not like this, George," called out Emily.

"Increase the charge." The nurse followed the instruction and ramped up the defibrillator. The team all stepped back further than before. Martin and Emily held their breath.

"Clear." The paddles were placed back on George and a much higher charge was sent through his body. He jolted and almost levitated for a moment. Everybody in the room stared at the monitor. Pleading to science, God and even George. After, what felt like an eternity, a beat appeared on the screen and George's vitals stabilised. The doctor was paged and the crash trolley was needed elsewhere. The medical team rushed out.

"Oh, gran—"

"Don't. Please don't." Emily could see, even in their current situation Martin was going to once again ask why. This was not the time and, although he just wanted to understand why this had happened, he knew to listen to his gran.

"A drink would be good right now," said Emily.

Emily had the room to herself. Just her and George together, though so far apart. She stood beside her love and stroked his cheek. George's eyes opened wide and he stared straight at Emily.

"George? George?" As quick as his eyes opened, they closed again.

"Martin! Martin!" called Emily but he was not in earshot. She looked at George's face again, hoping to God that was not a sign of an impending end. She placed her hand back on his cheek.

"George," she whispered. His head lulled to her side and his eyeballs flittered behind his lids.

"George, can you hear me? It's time to wake up." George's eyes slowly opened and he, once again, stared straight at Emily. This time it felt different. It felt real. As though he was truly present in this moment. His mouth slightly opened and he tried to speak. The sound was inaudible. Emily squeezed his hand in encouragement and moved her face closer to his.

"I am here, George." He tried to speak again but couldn't get the words out.

"I will get the doctor." Emily kissed George on the forehead and made to leave. George tightened his grip on her hand.

"Lil." The name startled Emily; she had not heard it in so long. Though she often slipped up and called George, Henry before correcting herself, he had not once done the same. The sound of the name coming from George sent shivers down her spine. It took her to a place they had long been away from, though never forgotten. It took her to a time when anything seemed possible and the future was one exciting adventure yet to be determined. She had claimed she remembered Henry and Lily but this had just been to appease George. Now, she truly remembered. That one name coming from his lips, after nearly sixty years, had brought it all flooding back. She was Lily. Emily turned back to see George's eyes fully open.

"Lil." Emily moved back closer to George.

"Henry?" George warmly smiled at her. An actual smile. With all the strength he could muster, he raised his hand to her cheek.

"Thank you, Lil," whispered George, but Emily knew she was really speaking to Henry. Emily held his hand firmly against her face, removing it only to curl his fingers and place them against her lips.

"My Henry. My Hero." George's arm began to go limp and Emily gently placed it back down by his side. His eyes grew heavy once again.

"Henry?"

"My Lil." George's eyes closed entirely and the heart monitor flatlined. Martin returned to the now all too familiar monotoned sound of the unthinkable.

"I will get the doctor."

"No. it is time. He has finished the game."

***

It was a rather windy afternoon, nobody would deny that, but it was far from an approaching hurricane as Martin kept arguing. With his beloved grandfather no longer around, he had vowed to be there more often for his gran and had been visiting every weekend without fail. He cherished these moments. Even though they kept taking a turn for the extreme and removing him far from his comfort zone. Still, if this was how his gran wanted to spend her twilight years, then who was he to disagree?

This particular weekend, he found himself standing on the edge of a cliff preparing to jump. He had absolutely no desire to do this and could see no logical reason for it, but logic did not come into it. It was about making his gran happy and that seemed to be achieved by many illogical actions. He was curious as to why. Over the course of his life, he had, of course, grown to know his grandparents extremely well. He had never seen such an extreme side to either of them but he had noticed little oddities. Well, mainly one oddity which had led him to ask a question a few times that had never been answered. He would always tell himself it was just a senior moment, but he never fully believed it.

Emily completed her final safety checks, tightened her helmet and adjusted her goggles. She took hold of her hang glider and moved towards the edge of the cliff.

"You ready?" A very nervous Martin tightened his gloves, completed his safety checks for the fourth time and shuffled beside his gran. An officially placed sign warned people of the risk of death should they get too close to the edge.

"Don't look so scared, Martin."

"Shouldn't we have an instructor? Have my checks been done properly? Should I do them again? What if something goes wrong?"

"Life is for living." In Martin's mind, life could be lived at a much slower and more calculated pace. Every part of his being was screaming out 'What are you doing?' But he knew he was fulfilling a promise to be a good grandson and give Emily companionship. Still, one thought kept crossing his mind, what if one of them didn't make it back? No, they will be fine. Though he considered his gran's actions suggested she was reckless and possibly a little crazy, he believed she would never put him in any real danger and she seemed to know what she was doing. Well, he hoped she did. With the thoughts of a possibility of a splattering end coming their way, he had to try and ask that one question again in the vain hope he would finally get an answer.

"Gran, why did you sometimes call Gramps, Henry?" The question that had so often been ignored or brushed under the carpet was now met with a new reaction, a huge grin from Emily. Once again it offered no answers but at least confirmed Martin hadn't been imagining it. He just hoped she would one day let him in on the secret and, one day, she would.

Emily leapt off the cliff and fell earthbound. Martin rushed forward to look down as the hang glider zoomed past his face and his gran soared upwards into the graceful air.

"Come on Martin, I can see your petticoat from here." Martin waddled to the edge, gave himself a sign of the cross and scrunched his eyes tight. Cursing to himself, he leaned forward until he was at the point of no return. He gripped tight to the bar of the hang glider as he too began to career down to the hard ground before the wind caught in the sail cloth of the wings sending it soaring back up. Soon there were two hang gliders dancing together in the afternoon sky. One flown by an octogenarian adrenaline junkie with a huge secret and the other by a grandson desperate to know it.

THE END

Emily Brooks

Emily contacted me in late 2018. She said I had been recommended by a friend, though I can't fathom who this friend was, and Emily would never tell me. Such is her way. In the summer of 2019, she arranged our regular meetings at various coffee shops around Los Angeles, with no discernible pattern and very little notice.

I was only in Los Angeles for fourteen days and in this time, we shared seven afternoons together as she would tell me the tales contained within this book. Through these meetings, I felt I got to know Emily very well, but also not at all. She was always holding something back, was always extremely alert and constantly glance over my shoulder towards the exit. She would insist on facing that direction. The last time we met, she told me she would be in touch for our next meeting, I never heard from her again.

I have absolutely no way of contacting Emily and absolutely no idea where she may be. I am not even sure her real name is Emily Brooks or was ever Lily. But I believe there was much more to her life than what she ever told me, and this book is the tip of the iceberg. I would love to know what happened next and only hope, she finds a copy of this book, is happy with my work, and invites me for coffee again.

As a thriller writer, **James Thornton** likes placing characters in extreme situations and turning the screw. He enjoys writing historical fiction as real life offers new avenues to explore and adding his own characters allows him to keep asking the question, what if?

His writing has achieved quarter-final finishes in the Screen Craft Screenwriting Fellowship (2022) and Creative Screenwriting UNIQUE VOICES Screenplay Competition (2021) amongst others.

James is inspired by the novels of Len Deighton and John Le Carré, and as a cinephile, revels in the movies of Quentin Tarantino.

You can find James on LinkedIn
www.linkedin.com/in/jthornton1980/and Facebook
www.facebook.com/JamesThorntonWriter

Printed in Great Britain
by Amazon